BECOMING
A RACHAEL KNIGHT NOVEL
EVELYNE CROWE

PIXIE WARRIOR PUBLISHING

FOREWORD

Please be safe, my lovelies, and read all the pertinent content contained herein:

Graphic depictions: religious trauma, religious extremism, misogyny, sexism, classism, fatphobia, diet culture, no hate like christian love, estranged family, energy crisis, police interrogation and misconduct, murder, corpses, graphic depictions of injuries (including brands), blood, stalking, kidnapping, a pyre, ptsd, dissociation, flashbacks, hospital stay, trafficking, psychological abuse, emotional abuse, sexual harrassment.

Brief, off-page, non-graphic: suicide mentions, drugging, whipping mentions, torture, homophobia, hate group mentions, mentions of spousal abuse, whorephobia, violence against women, murder.

To my mother. Every kind word, every kind gesture, every moment of empathy in this book directly results from her influence in my life.

CONTENTS

THE ARRIVAL

Rachael stepped off the electric bus clutching her duffle bag and hurriedly moved to the side so other people could disembark. She had never been so far from home before. Travel of any distance had become very rare since the Conversion some twenty-five years or so before, and yet here she was three hundred miles away from where she was born. On top of that, she was born and raised in a religious compound that decried magic as evil. There everyone dressed the same, the population was small, and she very rarely left the safety of the fences that surrounded it. She took a deep breath and looked around, trying to get her bearings as people flowed around her. There were so many of them! The noise and bustle were overwhelming. The last time she had experienced anything like this chaos was at the bus station in Los Angeles, and there she had still been in too much shock to really pay attention.

She watched as strangers found their family ms or friends who greeted them. Rachael chewed on her lower lip nervously as she realized how truly alone she was here. There were absolutely no friends or relatives to greet her, no one with a shared history or understanding. She was a stranger in a strange land and not here by choice. Tears pricked her eyes, and she blinked rapidly, refusing to cry in the middle of the street. She could cry later in her room, but not here where people would stare and see and wonder.

Well, there was nothing for it. Rachael had to get busy or she would collapse into a depressive mess of self-pity, and that would never do. She knew there was a welcome center, and that was where she needed to go. As she walked toward what looked like downtown, she took in the sights, sounds, and smells. Yes, she thought, smells. Davis, California was still a center for agriculture in California and when the wind blew just right, you could smell manure from all sorts of large animals: horses, cows, and pigs being the largest in number. Her guess was that after the Conversion the numbers of animals farmed increased locally as people moved in and started smaller farms and feed lots became obsolete. You couldn't move large amounts of meat without trains. Overall, though, the smell wasn't overwhelming and wasn't constant and once she was well and truly among the people in town, not present.

Downtown itself was a neat and orderly place full of small shops and restaurants, each building topped with solar panels, some even with wind turbines. Rain barrels met each gutter pipe, and Rachael was simply agog. Her home was far behind Davis in this regard, refusing many such advancements, claiming it to be hippy nonsense. Frowning, she kept walking, looking into windows she noticed that many shops used mirrors to bring light further in to help save energy as well as cutting skylights into the ceilings. No one was naked, yelling profanities, or having sex in public as they had always warned her magic users did. She tried to ignore the fact that all the trees were different here and that the air was so much drier. She didn't want to think about the fact that out of the city it was just flat and treeless, mostly open space; so far from the tall buildings and sprawling suburbs that had surrounded her home.

She missed seeing palm trees and the tough live oaks with their loads of acorns and their needle-sharp leathery leaves. She missed the morning cloud cover the ocean tossed inland and the humidity it gave the air. She missed the security of the fence around the compound, knowing that she would be locked in securely at night and that all manner of evil things would be locked out. Everything here seemed so . . . so open. The oak trees had broad flat leaves, the pines had wider needles, the flood plain outside the city was flat and open, and there was no fence. People were just able to go about wherever they wanted.

Stop it, Rachael, she told herself. *You don't live there anymore. They kicked you out.* She had to adjust her thoughts and expectations. She had always been aware they were wrong about magic; they were bound to be wrong about a lot of other ideas. *Keep an open mind and try not to step in shit.*

She took a deep breath to calm herself down and kept walking, casting about for some sign that she was headed in the right direction. When she had called, a woman with a 'D' name (Daisy? Dee?) had said they were close to campus, past Downtown, on A street. She was on A street, so she should just have to keep walking, right? The buildings on this street were a mixture of old homes and businesses with a scattering of restaurants on one side and on the other what appeared to be University buildings, including one that looked oddly like they had encased it in sheet metal. Some buildings were neatly kept and had signs that read everything from, "Joseph Pedott Center for Jewish Life," and, "Davis Christian Fellowship," to "Tea" with a cute little cartoon design next to it. And finally, nestled between a quiet ministry and an apartment complex, was a tidy building with a tidy sign that said, "Welcome to Davis: New Citizen Registration Center."

A tiny tinkling bell rang when Rachael opened the door and a short, curvy, bright-eyed, blonde, white woman of middle years called a greeting from the back of the building. Rachael waved and looked around curiously. Not much to it really, a small waiting area with just a few empty chairs of hard plastic, several desks with computers on them, and a counter with a register. She heard a printer running somewhere. There were very few overhead lights, instead there were several skylights cut into the ceiling letting in natural light, and bright rugs dotted the floor. Plants hung from macrame hangers and stood in stands everywhere, and bright instrumental music played from a speaker in the corner. All of it combined to made a very welcoming atmosphere, and Rachael relaxed a notch.

"Hello and welcome!" the woman said again, closer this time as she had approached as Rachael inspected the place, and extended her hand. "I am Diana Archer, lead welcomer here. Please come set down that bag and let's get you a glass of water. You looked exhausted. Did you just arrive?"

Rachael shook Diana's hand by reflex, having had manners beaten into her from a young age and then bemusedly allowed herself to be bundled into a chair in front of a desk while a larger younger woman got her a glass of cold water. "I, uh, yes. Oh! Thank you," she took the glass of water and nodded to the woman, who then disappeared behind another desk with a smile. Rachael sipped it, realized she was very thirsty, and took a gulp. "Oh, thank you. This is wonderful. Yes, I arrived on the bus just 30 minutes ago. I am Rachael. Rachael Knight."

Diana nodded. "Of course. We've been expecting you since you called. We weren't sure when you would arrive, so we've been keeping someone on staff here twenty-four hours a day, just in case. Buses are sometimes inconsistent."

"You . . . twenty-four hours a day? For me?" Rachael gaped at Diana. "But you didn't have to do that!"

The older woman cocked her head to one side. "Well, of course we did, honey. Not a single one of us was going to have you sleeping on a park bench your first night here in a strange city. That would never do."

Rachael's mouth opened and then shut. She ducked her head and stared at her hands clenched in her lap, her eyes burning with those fucking tears. She took a deep breath, heard it shudder, and closed her eyes. She felt the tears fall. Damn it. Damn it, damn it, damn it.

"Here, love." Diana handed her a tissue and placed the box on the desk in front of her. She squeezed her shoulder briefly. "I know you don't know me, but I give good hugs if you want one. If not, I'm happy right here, so there's no need to rush. You just cry and let me know when you're ready."

Rachael grabbed the hand and squeezed it in thanks, but didn't take the offer of the hug, knowing that would prolong the crying. She let herself cry for a minute, just one minute, dabbing at her eyes and blowing her nose, and then took another deep breath. She did it again. Deep breath. Okay. She was okay.

"I am so sorry, Mrs. Archer," she apologized thickly, her nose stuffy from crying. "Thank you for waiting."

Diana frowned slightly and shook her head. "Nonsense. And please, call me Diana. Well, if you're sure you are okay, let's get you settled for tonight, hmm?"

In a surprisingly short time Rachael had a key to a furnished apartment in what used to be an old dorm for the University, a temporary residency card, and a part-time job at a diner in town.

"I have a WHAT?" she asked incredulously.

"It's standard for people who are in your . . . position," Diana said tactfully. "I have found that it gives you a way to meet people and learn a bit about the city, as well as make a bit of money so you can find a place of your own a bit faster. If you find a different job you prefer, you can always do that instead. This just gives you a leg up. The owner of the diner is a good friend of the family and he has agreed to help us."

So, there were people here like her. People who had been shoved out of their home and pushed into an unknown world with no money, house, or even real knowledge of how things worked. She had been so sure there wouldn't be. She wasn't sure if that was a relief or not. Her skin jangled suddenly, and she looked around behind her to find that a squirrel had come in the open window on the other side of the room.

"Sam!" Diana admonished. "I told you I was on call until nine tonight. Rachael is here, as you can very well see, and I was just going to escort her to her apartment."

Rachael looked back at Diana and then at the squirrel. Sam? Must be a shifter then, maybe her husband. Would he shift here? She leaned forward, curious to see. Would his clothes be there? How did that work? Living in a place where magic was forbidden, she had never actually seen a shifter up close, but she could feel them around the compound all the time.

"I apologize for my husband, Rachael," Diana said, but with a tolerant smile that said she really didn't mind all that much. "He has been keeping

me company. If it's ok with you, he will come with us to your apartment?"

"Oh, um, yes, sure that's fine." Rachael nodded. She looked back at the squirrel, who bounded off toward the back of the office. Diana crossed the room as well and opened a door that Rachael hadn't noticed before.

"Bathroom," Diana explained, seeing Rachael's inquisitive look. "There's a change of clothes in there for him. It's a long walk for a squirrel and even after over twenty years I still don't like him climbing on me." She shuddered. "It's the claws. Rodent claws are rodent claws. Ick."

Rachael giggled before she could stop herself and clapped her hand over her mouth. "Oh my gosh, I'm so sorry."

Diana laughed. "Why? It's funny."

The bathroom door opened, and a very tall man emerged. He was dark-skinned and very handsome with startling blue eyes in a very gentle face. He smiled at his wife with a look that could only be described as loving, and Diana returned it. Rachael felt her face blush slightly. She had never seen her parents look at each other like *that*.

"Rachael, this is my husband, Sam."

"Sam? Sam the squirrel?" The words popped out of her mouth unbidden, and she gaped at her own rudeness. This was it. They would send her packing.

But Sam only laughed. "Mother Nature has a weird sense of humor. It's a pleasure to finally meet you, Rachael." He held out his hand, and she shook it. She was shaking the hand of a magic-user. Her parents would have died of shock if she hadn't already been exiled. *Well,* she thought. *Here's to new beginnings.* She had never been one to toe the line anyway.

His eyes took in her own red-rimmed ones, and he squeezed her hand once before he let it go. "So, to Primero Grove then? Is this your bag? Please, let me?" He waited for her permission and at her nod, picked it up, took a sharp breath at how light it really was for all of her possessions to be within, and then gestured for his wife to lead the way.

Rachael wrapped her arms around herself as she followed Diana, listening to her small talk with half an ear, the world falling away as she remembered her flight from home.

Rachael huddled in the dark room, clutching the ruined pieces of her shirt to her. The guard had been trying to catch a peek, the bastard, but he'd been very still for the last ten minutes. He must have fallen asleep. She sighed softly, leaning against the rough concrete wall, the tile floor hard under her. No chairs. No bed. There was at least a toilet. Thank God for small mercies. The condemned weren't afforded luxuries. Not even a shirt to replace the one Pastor Charles had sliced down the front. Tomorrow she was going to die. "Psst." Rachael sat up and stared at the front door. Surely she was hearing things. "Pssssst." The sound came again, and Rachael scrambled to her feet, rushing over to the door. Her father stood on the other side of the small window and her heart started pounding. "Dad?" She asked, softly.

"Shhh. Hold on." The doorknob rattled and then the door opened and the night air rushed in. "Come on. Hurry." He closed the door,

locked it, and carefully replaced the key on the hook next to the door. Her guard was sleeping on the ground, his quiet snores comforting. Her dad, nothing more than a familiar shape in the darkness, beckoned her, and he took off into the night, heading toward the side exit of the compound. She rushed after him, her heart in her throat, her hand clutching her shirt together, as he hurried off. They didn't run, but moved quickly, staying close to the buildings and in the dark shadows. It was late, very late, and no one was stirring. Guard dogs patrolled the compound, but Rachael knew they mostly stayed by the front gate; this side one was locked and well-lit, patrolled every hour.

"Here," her dad whispered, thrusting the backpack at her. He unlocked the gate quickly, grabbed her arm, and shoved her through. "There's money enough in the bag for a bus ticket. Go."

"Leave?" Rachael stared at him. Just like that? No goodbye? No, I love you? Not even a hug?

"Do you want to die?" Here under the lights, Rachael could see it, the disgust. She was tainted now. She had magic and she couldn't stay, but he didn't want her dead. So, she had to go. That was all he would do for her. That and a bag of whatever he had given her. Money for a bus ticket; who knows if he had given her food or clothing.

"Okay," she said, quietly. She looked up and down the street. She had never been out of sight of the compound in twenty-five years and now all she had was a bag and a shirt that was torn in half.

"That way," her dad gestured impatiently. "And for God's sake, cover up. You're asking for trouble." She swallowed hard and her shoulders came up at his tone.

"Yes, sir." It would do no good to tell him no one had provided a change in clothing; excuses were excuses. He nodded briskly.

*"Don't come back. They'll kill you." He swung the gate closed,
locked it, and strolled away.*

He never looked back.

"Rachael?" Rachael jumped at the touch on her arm. "Sorry!"
Diana immediately dropped her hand and smiled apologetically.
"It's just that we're here. You seemed lost in space for a moment."
She raised a brow in question and invitation, but Rachael shook
her head.

"Just tired." Rachael looked around. 'Here' proved to be two
stucco buildings connected with a roof covering bike racks and
staircases. Diana led them to the left building and climbed the
staircase. "Back in the day, they had ID cards that opened these
but with electricity being what it is, we are back to using keys."
She took Rachael's key and opened the outside door, and they
entered a long hallway. "Your apartment is this one, right here."
It was only the second one away from the outside door, and she
saw Sam frown disapprovingly at that, but he said nothing. Diana
unlocked the door and they entered a small apartment.

"We stock the kitchen with basic kitchen stuff: plates and utensils for two, a pot and pan, and maybe a spatula. Dishwasher is
disconnected, electricity you know, but running water works. The
fridge DOES work because we try to discourage food spoilage, but
if it breaks, there are no replacements. It's old, so fingers crossed."
They passed the opening of the kitchen and entered the living
room, which faced the kitchen opened with a bar with two stools.

There was a small sofa and a comfy-looking chair in the living room and a sliding glass door led to a small deck which faced a courtyard.

"There's a small dining area by the front door," Diana said, turning. "It's all very open; I can't believe this used to be for college students. It's a proper apartment." The bathroom was just past the dining area and had everything a bathroom needed, even a bathtub.

"And this is the bedroom," Diana said, opening the door. "It's small, but it's yours."

For some reason, that made her heart contract. It's hers. The room was small, containing a small desk, a twin bed, and a dresser. There was a small closet as well, but there was also a window that looked out at the courtyard. It was more than she had at home, and it was all hers. She didn't have to share it. The whole apartment was hers. The luxury was staggering.

Sam set her bag just inside the door, but stayed respectfully outside of the room, shooting her a smile at her quiet thank you. Rachael was eager for them to be gone now that the tour was over and she stood awkwardly, unsure what to say. She had no food or beverages to offer, anyway.

Neither Diana nor Sam were incapable of reading body language, however, and they quickly bade her farewell. "The phone on the wall works, hon," Diana informed her as she walked toward the door. "The number is on the counter by it." She gave a low laugh. "I miss cell phones, but they are so horrendously expensive now. Don't forget, tomorrow is your first shift at the diner and, if you're willing, we'd love to have you for dinner." She looked so hopeful that Rachael didn't have the heart to say no, so she nodded.

"Yes, ok. Thank you, Mrs. Archer."

Sam squeezed Diana's shoulder, and they turned away. "Lock your door," he said, as he closed it. "I'll wait until I hear the bolt. *Both* locks, now."

Rachael walked to the door and looked through the peephole. Sure enough, they were waiting there for her to lock it. She turned both locks and heard them walk toward the door, the heavy outside door opened, then it slammed shut. And then it was quiet. She couldn't remember it ever being this quiet. After sharing a room with her sisters her entire life and the small shelter with her family, she was used to constant noise. The bus ride up was the same: noise from the engine, noise from the surrounding people. And now, for the first time in her life, she was completely alone. She turned and walked into her small living room, sat on the cheap, used yet still so precious sofa, wrapped her arms about herself, and cried.

THE TOUR

The next morning dawned bright, and Rachael awoke disoriented and early. Used as she was to a marine layer, it shocked her to discover that it was only 6:30 a.m., and she lay there staring at the blue cloudless sky angrily. *The sun isn't supposed to appear until 10:30 a.m. at the earliest,* she thought to herself. *It's just not natural.* Well, she wasn't going to get back to sleep, so she decided to get up. She had little in the way of clothing or toiletries, so getting dressed and ready took no time at all. She really was going to have to do something about that, but until she had money to purchase something, that was just going to have to wait.

A glance in her refrigerator—a luxury she had never seen before. Pastor David was rumored to have one in his house, but she had never seen it—found milk and there was she found cereal in a cupboard. It was fancy sugared cereal too, which she had only had once before when her father had bought it as a treat. Everything here felt like the height of decadence, but Diana and Sam had acted as though it were all secondhand.

She sat down and took a bite of the sugary cereal, closing her eyes in bliss. It was almost too sweet, but there was no way on Earth Rachael was going to refuse this opportunity. The fruity flavor filled her nose and she found herself humming a happy tune and bouncing in her seat as she ate. It was the first time since she left home that she felt anything resembling happiness.

An hour or two later, Rachael was at a loss. She had no idea what to do with herself. No possessions to unpack. No books to read. No art on the walls. She just had herself and time to kill. The phone rang, and she jumped, the sound loud and shrill in the quiet apartment.

Picking up the receiver, she looked at the keypad and pressed the "answer" button, hoping that was the correct thing to do. Reading about a thing and doing them were two different things entirely. "Hello?" she asked timidly.

"Good morning!" Diana's bright voice sang through the handset, and Rachael smiled. "I hope you slept well?"

"Yes, ma'am," Rachael said. And she *had* after she had cried herself out; travel and emotional exhaustion had seen to that.

"Wonderful," Diana replied. "Now, I know your shift doesn't start until this afternoon, so I've arranged for a tour of the downtown area for you. That way you can find your way home after work with no trouble. And since you just had the one bag, they'll see about getting you some supplies. There's a small sundries store there."

Rachael felt her face flush. "Oh, Mrs. Archer, really. You don't have to do this. I was going to save up and—"

"Nonsense," Diana interrupted. "There's a fund set aside for this." She paused. "The town puts into it every month. It's part of our taxes. Refugees aren't as common as they used to be, but they are welcome. We created this program for you, Rachael."

Refugee. That seemed a better word than any she could think of, she supposed. What else was she, anyway? Chased away from her home because of what she was and fleeing to a sanctuary. Pilgrim? She snorted. Hardly. Refugee it was. "Ok, then. I guess that will be fine then. Thank you, Mrs. Archer."

"Okay, Drake will meet you in front of the Black Bear Diner at 11:00 a.m. You can meet with Mr. Barlett and get set up for your first shift this afternoon, and then maybe have lunch before you head off for shopping." Diana was all business as she filled in Rachael's day for her, but Rachael found she didn't mind. It was nice having it settled.

"Thank you, Mrs. Archer," Rachael said, meaning it. "For everything."

"Oh, of course, dear. Is there anything else you need?"

"No, ma'am."

"Please, call me Diana. You are making me feel about one hundred years old," Diana laughed. "Okay, eleven o'clock, Black Bear Diner." The line went dead with a click, and Rachael placed the handset back into the base. She picked up the paper next to it and saw that along with her own phone number, Diana had left her personal number as well as the business line for the center. She took a deep breath and went into the bathroom, feeling both comforted and uneasy, unused to such kindness. Charity was given only after you tried first, right? You had to prove you were worthy.

The mirror showed a young woman, tanned skin worn from working outside, auburn curly hair tucked into a bun to be out of the way. She was of average height, around 5'4', and very curvy, something her mother always lamented. Well, she wouldn't have to worry about her opinion anymore, Rachael thought, fighting back the tears which made her green eyes shine. In fact, Rachael stuck out her chin and stared defiantly at her reflection.

"I'm fat." She said. Her chest constricted and something that felt like panic flashed through her, followed quickly by relief. She wasn't 'curvy.' She was fat. And now that she was here, maybe she could finally just be fat and stop pretending otherwise. The tears that were shining in her eyes overflowed and made wet tracks down her cheeks. She had to stop crying, honestly, or it would put the customers at the diner off their food.

At 11:00 a.m., Rachael stood outside the Black Bear Diner on 2nd street. There were decorative black bears carved out of wood posed on either side of the entrance, one behind a bike and one holding a welcome sign. The front doors themselves were under a brown and green slanted arch where a rustic sign dangled from chains and the stuccoed columns bore lanterns. She stared at the stylized image of a bear riding a bicycle that was displayed prominently on the side of the building and grinned. Davis really did have a theme: cows and bikes.

She opened the door and was hit in the face with the scents of syrup and fried food, the sound of clanking cutlery, and the low murmur of people conversing as they ate their meals. The warmth and smells and rustic ambiance were very welcoming despite the heat of the day and she felt herself relax a bit as she scanned the room for someone who looked like Mr. Barlett.

"Can I help you? Just one today?" A bright voice spoke next to her, and she jumped, turning to see the hostess smiling politely at her, holding a menu. She was tall and slim with blonde hair, brown eyes, and lightly tanned white skin. Rachael noticed her ears were pointed and jutted out from under her neatly brushed and styled hair. Each ear was decorated with several piercings.

"Oh! No, thank you, I'm not here to eat. Is Mr. Barlett around? I am Rachael. I'm starting today, and I was supposed to be meeting with him?"

The bright smile disappeared immediately, and a look of interest replaced it. "Oh yeah, he mentioned you'd be coming. His office is back there, through the kitchen. Just go straight back." She pointed to a gray swinging door that servers continually kept going in and out of, swishing open and shut, offering glimpses of the kitchen beyond.

"Thank you." Rachael's stomach knotted, but she walked on. The compound had a tiny restaurant, but nothing like this. Also, it was run by volunteers, so they did not have a set menu, they just served what they made that day. Payment usually comprised doing dishes or other work around the restaurant. This . . . this was something else entirely. She took a deep breath and squared her shoulders and strode forward as if preparing to enter a cave to face a dragon.

Twenty minutes later, she exited the bustle and noise of the kitchen holding her apron and name tag and wearing a smile. Mr. Barlett was a sweet man middle-aged man who had put her at ease immediately. Balding, slightly overweight, and on the shorter side, Mr. Barlett reminded her of the head cattle caretaker back at the compound. The one man there who had never yelled at her or told her how to behave, he had been patient, kind and soft-spoken. Mr. Barlett was the same. He had helped her fill out all of her employee paperwork, including tax information, and welcomed her to the team. And all without making her feel stupid for not knowing how to do it already. Now all she had to do was survive her first shift.

There was a tall man standing with the hostess when she arrived back at the front, casually leaning on the podium, making small talk. His skin was a light brown, his hair done in short twists, but his bright blue eyes immediately caught her gaze; they stood out from his face, even focused as they were on the hostess, the combination not one she had commonly seen. *This must be Diana and Sam's son,* she thought. He was tall, but not extremely so, and lean. His face was expressive and his affect was warm, welcoming, and sociable. Sam and Diana had a very handsome son. The hostess certainly thought so; she was giggling in a way that made Rachael arch an eyebrow at her back.

The man caught the look and flashed her a grin, which she couldn't help but return. "Hello, there." He stood up straight and spied her bundled apron and glanced back at the direction she had come. "Rachael?" he guessed.

She nodded. "Drake?"

The hostess had stopped giggling abruptly at Rachael's appearance, and Drake turned back to her. "Thank you so much for this delightful diversion while I waited for Rachael here, Michelle. Is there a table for 2 available?"

Michelle gaped at him for a moment. "*She's* your lunch date?" She asked incredulously.

Rachael frowned at her. Well, really, what the hell? How rude.

She turned to Drake, dismissing Michelle completely. "Thank you for waiting. I hope it wasn't long." Before she finished, she felt as if someone had poured a bucket of ice water over her head: the feeling of someone very close to her embracing magic. She twisted her head back to stare at Michelle, who was glaring at her, her once very normal brown eyes now glowing gold. A shiver went down her spine at being so close to magic being used so openly. It took all of her willpower not to step back.

"Michelle, what are you—" Drake started, but Rachael raised her hand up, asking silently for him to wait. She may be new to the city and to magic, to so many new things here, but she wasn't new to people or women. It was common for men and women to be separated for work back home because it was believed some jobs are for men and some for women. With no men present, conflicts were settled by the women, and as she had gotten older, she had learned how to establish boundaries herself. She had to work with this woman. If she didn't take a stand now, Michelle might think Rachael was someone she could push over. Drake nodded, waving her on. Rachael had to fight a smile at that, but was grateful that he subsided. She knew that if he hadn't, she would have caved almost instantly.

"Don't," Rachael said calmly. "I don't think your job is worth it, for one. And honestly, you were the one who was rude first, for two. And three, it won't work." It was true, most magics didn't seem to work on her or reflected back on their users. She wasn't really sure what happened, but it never worked right when someone tried magic on her, not that it had happened a lot, what with where she was from. Ok, so it had happened a grand total of twice, but Michelle didn't know that.

Michelle stared at her a moment more, golden eyes flashing, and then her eyes returned to their normal brown and the cold water feeling faded from Rachael's skin. "Right this way," she said sullenly, grabbing two menus, spinning on her heel, and practically jogged into the recesses of the restaurant. She led them to a booth near a window, tossed the menus down, and fled the scene, stomping back to the hostess station.

Drake watched her go for a moment before turning back to Rachael. "After you," he said, gesturing to the booth awaiting them.

Rachael picked a side and slid in. "Thank you."

Drake slide in the other side, all lithe grace, his eyes carefully studying her. "You sensed her magic before I even noticed her eyes."

Rachael opened her mouth and then closed it. She wasn't used to talking about it. It was a secret, had been a secret since she knew she had the ability as a child. So, she just nodded. He scanned her face and whatever he saw there made him just nod back and pick up his menu. "I like the hamburgers, but my mom always gets the fried chicken Cobb salad. Says it's the best one she's ever had."

She smiled at him gratefully and picked up the menu. They studied in silence and gave their orders to the server. Drake watched as Rachael looked at each condiment on the table as if it were gold, but made no comment. He had helped many refugees from non-magic compounds before, and many had acted the same. Shunning outside aid, they had few items most people considered staples. Some things were truly rare now, like cell phones or other electronics that required batteries or mining of rare materials. But ketchup and sugar? Those could be brought by electric vehicles or even made in house by a restaurant or home garden. Still, there was something about Rachael that made him want to wrap her in swaddling, an air of fragility as if a sharp tap would make her crack. Yet she had handled Michelle just fine. He realized she had said something to him and shook his head. "I'm sorry. What was that?"

"Thank you for taking the time out of your day for this. I'm sure you had better things to do."

He shook his head. "Better things than eating lunch with a pretty woman? Nonsense." A flush rose up her neck, and he stared at it in fascination. He had never seen someone blush such a deep red before.

She waved away his compliment, deciding that ignoring the blush and his stare were the safest route. "I know you are doing it as a favor for your mom. I really do appreciate it, though." The server brought their drinks, water for her, and a soft drink for him. She gratefully stopped talking, unsure what to say now, instead putting all her energy into placing a straw into her water as if it were the most intellectually complicated task in the world. She was unused to compliments and thoroughly unused to compliments from people she found attractive. She found herself flustered and annoyed at herself for being flustered.

She heard Drake snort, but when he spoke, it was, thankfully, on a different topic. "I know you are from a non-magic compound. You do not have to tell me about it, but do you have any questions about magic?"

She sat up straight, suddenly very interested, and he smiled at her interest, encouraging her with a nod. Thinking, she tapped her fingers on the tabletop. "Give me a moment. That is a weighted question."

He nodded and leaned back, happy to wait. She lowered her gaze and thought. Twenty years ago, the Earth had finally gotten tired of the abuse heaped upon it and had struck back, releasing magic back into the world. As if that wasn't enough, earthquakes had swallowed oil drills and mines around the world, effectively ending human reliance on fossil fuels for electricity. Her family belonged to a very strict Christian sect that had segregated itself when the Conversion had happened They had shunned all magic as being of the devil and refused any help from the outside or from anything connected with magic. They knew some people turned into animals, hence their conviction magic was evil, but as the years passed and rumors intruded that other magics had also been unlocked that fateful day, they had locked down even further. She had cared for her five younger siblings while her parents toiled in fields to raise enough food for the compound and fibers to make clothing. They traded for some items, but if magic touched it, it was forbidden; that included people.

She remembered the first time she felt someone use it. There had been a horrible accident. She had been too young to remember exactly what had happened, but the end result of it had been a young man, perhaps only a teenager, lying in pain in the dirt clutching his bleeding arm. There had been so much blood, she remembered that, because she had been fascinated in a horrified way. Her mother had grabbed her hand and tried to turn her away, extolling her to not look; there had been yelling and running feet, and the distinct skin prickling feeling that she now associated with magic. She had shivered, not knowing what had caused it and when she looked up, she saw that the healer had started wrapping the boy's arm, but she had seen the skin closing before the bandage had covered it. Young though she was, she knew magic was *bad*, and she had looked around to see if anyone had noticed.

The boy she had been healing had. He had a sick look on his face.

"Witch!" he had yelled, scrambling away from her. The crowd had frozen and then converged. Rachael had been carried off, and she had never seen the healer again. It had been enough, though, for her to say nothing about feeling the magic to anyone ever. Until last week.

"Rachael?" She blinked and looked up to see Drake frowning at her in concern. "Are you ok?"

"Oh!" Shaking her head free of the memories, she nodded. "Yes, sorry. Um, well, let's start with the basics, I guess. I really don't know much." She cocked her head and looked at him. "You are a shifter." It wasn't a question, and he sat up.

"How the blazes did you know that?!" he asked, shocked. "No one can tell, for sure, just by looking."

She shrugged. "I can. So, you are and your dad is, but your mom isn't. Does it run in families?"

He narrowed his eyes at her, but he answered her question, leaning back once more. "Yes, the ability to shift does. Magic does, in general. Now," he added, raising a finger. "That doesn't mean the shape is passed down, just the ability. Dad is a squirrel, but I am a raven," he grinned at her surprised laugh, "and my sister, Ember, is a bobcat. It appears to be a dominant gene rather than recessive as well."

"Okay, the magic is passed on. So, a pair of shifters will have babies who are shifters." Drake nodded. "Michelle . . . she has a different magic."

Drake nodded but refrained from speaking as their food had arrived. Rachael stared at her cheeseburger and fries in awe, hardly daring to believe it was all for her. The first bite made her moan in delight, and she closed her eyes in bliss.

Drake chuckled as he dug into his own food, enjoying her enjoyment, but then continued their conversation. "Michelle is part of a magic group people have started calling 'Fae Magic.' This group can do things like glamor, charm, and heal. There are good and bad sides to all of those magics. Michelle can charm. She could have convinced you to dance naked on a table if she had a mind to."

"Unlikely," Rachael said, certainly. "She would have tried. If a shifter marries a person with fae magic, the children can have either?"

Drake nodded, chewing the large bite he had just taken, and then washed it down with a swig of soda. "Yes. Very, very rarely, they can have both."

Rachael twirled a fry in her ketchup, pondering. "Are children ever born with magic to parents who don't have any?" She kept her eyes on her fry, drawing patterns on her plate, feeling Drake's gaze on the top of her head.

"Yes, all the time. New magic is constantly appearing, or at least it was for a long time after the Conversion. It's slowed down the last five to ten years or so, but yes, it's absolutely happened."

She wasn't a mistake, then.

"A mistake?" Shit, she must have said that out loud. She looked up to see him looking at her in a confused and horrified way, could actually see his brain connecting dots as he realized that one, she thought of herself as a mistake, and two, she mostly likely thought that because someone had told her she was.

"Uh," uncertain what to say, she just shook her head and shrugged. "Kids who were born with magic to non-magic parents were evil, mistakes, bad. It's what I was taught, what we were all taught."

His horror faded, his dark skin flushing darker with anger, and she sat back, swallowing. He noticed and closed his eyes, taking a breath. "I am not angry at you." His voice was deeper, but calm. When he opened his eyes again, the flush had faded a bit, but his eyes were black: the black of a raven she realized. He was still angry, but in control. She relaxed. "You. Are. Not. A. Mistake." He said, enunciating each word. "Here, when a child like that is born, they are celebrated. They are seen as a gift." Rachael watched in fascination as his eyes brightened back to their human blue. "You are a gift."

She just gaped at him; she did not know what to say to that, did not know what to do with the feelings those words caused, and she was still uncomfortable with how horrified he had been after her slip up.

Drake sat back and said nothing for a moment, just watched her. He nodded. "Ok," he said, dropping the subject. "You need dessert. Let's get pie."

And then, as she took her first bite of chocolate cream pie, he said, his voice kind and warm, "Congratulations on your gift, Rachael. It brightens the world and strengthens us. May you use it wisely and with purpose."

She froze, fork halfway to her mouth. "What?"

Drake smiled. "Those are the words we say to a child when they manifest magic. There is usually a celebration to go with it as well, but when a child does their first bit of magic, a parent or guardian will usually say something like that to them. It's kind of a ritual. Since you never had it, I thought maybe you were owed."

She ate her bite of pie to cover the flood of emotion that evoked. It was so different here. That bit about using magic wisely? Pastor

Charles wouldn't like that at all. It meant that magic users were careful and aware, not just mindless evil devils.

Here she could actually use her magic, practice it, figure out what it actually did. She knew she could detect other people's magic, like Drake being a shifter, and she knew Michelle could use magic and as well as when Michelle had used her magic. Now that she had felt it, would she be able to identify a charmer, just by the feel of their magic? Was that all she could do? It seemed like such a passive, useless skill.

She would have to practice, even though the thought made her stomach tighten in habitual fear.

Her first work shift had ended. She walked home, footsore but proud, and with tips— actual money tips— in her pocket. Mr. Barlett had started her out refilling ketchup bottles and salt shakers, which suited her just fine as it had also allowed her to people watch. The diversity of the population fascinated her. Clothing, hairstyles, tattoos, makeup—the freedom of self-expression she witnessed was shocking to her senses while also exhilarating because she knew that now she, too, could wear anything she wanted, whenever she wanted, however she wanted. It was almost giddying.

Chuckling, she thought back to shopping with Drake earlier that day. He had taken one look at the clothes she had selected to try on, shaken his head, selected a pair of jeans and a long-sleeved high necked top, and taken the rest back. "Don't move. You are not in Kansas anymore and from what I can see," his eyes had swept up and down her body, hidden in a baggy oversized shirt handed down from her dad and raggedy jeans, "you cannot hide how nice your figure is." He left her stuttering. In the end, he hadn't picked out super revealing clothing, but the clothing was in her actual size eighteen, which made all the difference.

"I cannot go outside in this," she protested, looking over her shoulder at her butt in a pair of shorts. "It's obscene." She had never shown this much skin in her life, and it had taken all of her courage to leave the fitting room, chanting "it's only legs, it's only legs, it's only legs."

"Nonsense. It's conservative on most counts. In the summer, most women wear super short shorts. At least, I think they do?" Drake shrugged, giving her a lopsided grin.

She narrowed her eyes at him. "I think you might be biased," she commented dryly. "These seem awfully short. Why on Earth are you here and not your mom?"

"She's busy. I think you look great." She turned around and looked herself up and down in the mirror and sighed, finally meeting his eyes in the reflection. He was smiling and his eyes had never left her to wander around in boredom. *I'll be damned,* she thought. *He does think I look great.* "Well, okay, just this pair though. I don't know if I will ever bring myself to wear them, but okay."

Besides clothing, he had purchased toiletries, groceries, and cleaning products with the funds provided by his mother. The amount on the register when it had all been rung up made her gasp, but he merely took out a stack of bills and paid it.

By the time they had finished everything, she had to rush back to the restaurant for her shift, so she had lent him her key. "I'll bring it back to you after I drop off the stuff," he had promised, hoisting all the bags and marching off. Rachael was very unused to allowing help; it made her very uncomfortable, but she didn't have time to worry about it because she was almost late and Mr. Barlett was waiting.

Opening her door now, she took two steps in and then stopped, shock. Expecting a pile of bags on the counters and floors, instead, everything had been put away. In addition, he had thrown in some extras. There was a soft looking throw blanket neatly folded on the couch, and some flowers in a vase on the bar separating the kitchen from the living room. A small two-seater dining room table had appeared in the dining area, and it held a bowl of the apples they had purchased set on a neat table cloth they had not. A pillar candle sat in the middle of the coffee table and next to it was a note. *"Welcome home, Rachael. Congratulations on your gift. It brightens the world and strengthens us. May you use it wisely and with purpose. Sincerely, The Archer Family."*

"Oh, oh, my." Rachael's legs slowly gave out, and she sank onto the sofa and cried there, for the second night in a row, but this time, this time with hope and not loss. Maybe, just maybe, everything would be okay.

PRACTICE

Her days settled into a routine, and she grew more and more comfortable with her new home. Slowly, her natural sense of humor and dry wit, stifled at home, emerged and even flourished. The clothing purchased that day with Drake which had made her feel self-conscious at first had only gotten her compliments, and her confidence grew. Working with people in the restaurant also helped her people skills and ability to make small talk. Not everyone was kind or pleasant, but most people were, and she found the freedom to be herself to be the most amazing thing.

There had been security of a sort living in a strict community in that she had the surety of knowing exactly how to behave and how to expect others to behave. The downside was that everyone was expected to be exactly the same and, in order to keep it this way, no one was really allowed access to much outside their little world. Rachael had lived in Los Angeles, one of the largest cities in the world, and she had never passed outside one mile of her tiny compound. She had never been to a grocery store, a coffee shop, or anywhere else that everyone here took for granted. So, while Davis itself was a relatively small town, for her it seemed gigantic and bustling and full of the strange and bizarre.

Rachael's first trip to the grocery store had led her into such paralysis of choice that she had stared at the cereal options and left with none of them. It was simply too overwhelming. Back at home, she had berated herself mercilessly for being a ninny, especially in the morning when she had no cereal.

"Honestly," she muttered to herself, as she made a peanut butter and jelly sandwich. "This is not a breakfast food. I could be eating any kind of cereal I want and instead I am eating a sandwich!" She took a bite with enough rage that she tore way too much off, but she just jammed it into her mouth. "Arrghh!" she waved the offending food around in frustration.

She went back that afternoon after her shift at the Black Bear and marched back to the cereal aisle, only to pull up sharply when she spotted Drake standing there pondering his options. He was wearing jeans and a t-shirt, and some kind of trendy tennis shoe that she couldn't identify yet. Rachael found her eyes scanning him from head to toe, lingering a bit too long on his arms—had they gotten bigger?—and forced them back to his face. Maybe he hadn't noticed her. She could back up and sneak around to the other aisle and he would never know. She just could not bear to have him know she couldn't buy a simple breakfast food. She took a step back.

"Rachael?"

Damn it to hell. She put on a smile. "Drake!"

"*Whoa, that was a bit too bright there,*" she thought, "*tone it down, Rachael.*"

He smiled back, turning to face her and giving her his full atten-tion. "It's good to see you. How are you doing?" His eyes never left her face, and his tone was soft and curious. Rachael could almost believe that he wasn't just being polite, and was actually curious about her.

"Oh, I'm fine. Just doing some shopping." Good grief, had she just said that? She was in a grocery store. Of *course* she was shopping!

He cocked his head and narrowed his eyes. "I see that," Drake said, slowly. "You don't have a basket or cart, just getting a few things?"

Shit, fuck, damn—Rachael never used profanity out loud; it had been expressly forbidden, and she had learned not to say it, but her brain was quite proficient—she had forgotten one of those cart things. "Oh, yes, just one or two items."

"Uh uh." He didn't say anything else, just looked at her with an eyebrow cocked in question.

She crossed her arms and didn't say a word. He grinned, his eyes sparkling. "Rachael Knight, you came in here marching like a conqueror. Did the cereal offend you?"

Rachael straightened, her mouth fighting not to grin back. "Cereal can be quite dangerous, Drake. You have to be prepared."

He made a snorting sound, but then his face softened. "Come on, I'll give you a tour."

Without another word, Drake took her down the aisle and explained the different types of cereals and which ones were his favorite—Fruit Loops. Rachael picked out a small box of those to try and he let her place them in his cart, which was almost empty.

"I had just started. Mom would have a tizzy; you're always supposed to start shopping in the Fruit and Vegetable section and work your way through."

"Why?"

Drake laughed. "I don't know, but that's how she taught me to do it."

They went back to the produce section, Drake got a new cart, and they spent the next two hours walking the store. Rachael found it much less stressful having someone there with her, and Drake was good company.

"Cookie dough? Pie crusts? *Cinnamon rolls?!*" Rachael dove at the refrigeration case, practically pressing her nose to the glass.

Drake laughed loudly. "We don't always have them; you got lucky today. Shipments are rare and you never know what kind of cookies you'll get. Pie crust are especially rare. Look at the cost!"

Rachael looked and gasped. It was nearly a quarter of her rent and she immediately dropped any hope of buying ready-made pie crusts, but she just could not get over that they existed in the first place. "But *look* at them!"

Drake shook his head and smiled fondly at her, letting her look as long as she wanted. "Here, let's wipe that drool off your chin," he swiped a finger up her chin teasingly.

She batted his hand away. "You hush. This store is amazing."

They continued, chatting, until finally reaching the registers. Drake unloaded first, showing her how he placed all the cold things together, the produce together, and then the household and cleaning supplies together. Rachael then placed her supplies on the station. The employee rang her up with amazing speed and dexterity, typing in codes at the speed of light and tossing items down to another employee, who shoved them into cloth bags that Rachael was also purchasing.

Finally, Rachael paid and felt a sense of accomplishment at buying her own food with her own money.

Outside, she hefted her bags and got ready to walk back home.

"Do you want a ride?" Drake asked. "Our family has a solar car and I'm happy to give you a lift back."

"Oh," she looked down at the bags she had. She had purchased much more than she had thought she would, and a ride was probably a good idea. "Yes, please. Thank you."

A car, Rachael thought, was much smaller and more intimate than a bus. Drake seemed to fill the entirety of the four-seater sedan and their arms kept brushing on the middle arm rest. She was also fascinated by watching how his hands competently handled the steering wheel and gear box, and listening to the sound they made as they slide over the synthetic material.

"Almost there," he said, and Rachael blinked, surprised. She had been so immersed in watching him drive that she had lost all sense of time.

"I really appreciate you taking the time to help me out in there," Rachael said. "I didn't realize how overwhelming it would be."

He shook his head, dismissing her thanks. "Lots of refugees get overwhelmed. It's very common."

Her stomach sank. Of course, it was his job. She was such an idiot. "Next time, I'll call the main office and make an official request for help. You didn't have to do this on your personal time." Her voice sounded hollow even to her own ears.

Drake stopped the car, and Rachael realized they were in the parking lot of Primero Grove. He turned to her, eyebrows furrowed. "What?" He asked, as if he couldn't understand what she had just said. She couldn't meet his eyes; she didn't want to see pity. How did she open the damn door?

"Rachael, wait." Drake's voice was calm, but insistent. Rachael froze, but didn't look at him. "Do you think I did this because it is a service of my mom's business? That I am getting paid for it?"

Rachael's shoulders were up around her ears now. "Well, isn't it? Helping people like me adjust to life here?"

"Please look at me, or at least in my direction." Rachael turned, her eyes looking at his chest. "I did it because you needed help and I enjoy spending time with you. I am not getting paid for this."

Rachael's brain seemed to have stopped working. She had heard what he said, but the words weren't making sense. "I don't understand." Her eyes moved up to his nose.

His mouth twitched slightly, like he wanted to smile, but he controlled himself. "If you had called my mom she would have absolutely helped you; however, you didn't. Today is my day off and I get to spend it however I want. I wanted to spend it watching you freak out over ready-made pie crusts and teaching you about the difference between sparkling water and still. I am not an employee today." He paused and then said, "My mom would have given you a grocery list of weekly items most commonly bought -and favorite brands-, a recipe booklet, and had you out of there in forty-five minutes. I don't know if you noticed, but I failed miserably at doing all of those things."

Rachael's green eyes moved up and met his blue ones. "Hi," he said, allowing the grin to happen this time. She took a deep breath and her shoulders dropped.

"Oh." Embarrassment warred with relief and she wanted to bolt, but also needed to get her groceries and really thank him. "Thank you. I really had a good time."

The grin broadened into a brilliant smile that shone out of his face. His beauty took her breath away. "I did too. Come on, let's get your food before stuff melts."

As she unloaded her groceries, she pondered how his magic felt compared to other magic. Sam's – Drake's dad's – magic had jangled against her, jarring even shielding like she always did. Michelle's felt like cold water. There had been some other magic in the restaurant that had felt like ants crawling all over her skin; it had been very unpleasant - she was jumpy until the customer had left.

But Drake . . . Drake's magic was soothing. She barely noticed it unless she actively tried to feel it; and when she did, it was like wrapping a warm blanket around herself. It contrasted greatly with his physical presence, tall and imposing as he was, but fit his personality well. What did he look like when he shifted? Ravens were not common in Southern California, but they had a lot of crows. Were ravens bigger? She had always had a fondness for crows Her parents had always shooed them off and the general consensus was they were a nuisance, but she had watched them. Rachael, with her magic, had always felt a kinship with the outcasts. She never made a lot of close friends nor was she part of the popular group. People called her responsible and capable and smart and then they picked someone else for any kind of award or recognition. Her family relied on her and her sisters trusted her, but no one really *knew* her.

Somehow, Rachael thought the crows might be the same way. Misunderstood and dismissed, but secretly gifted. She had watched them, and she had always had the feeling they were watching her back.

Sighing, she shook her head. She'd probably never see him in his raven form. While she had seen some shifters in their animal halves, she hadn't spent any time at all with shifters long term. This afternoon and the few hours she had spent with Drake were it. She had no idea what the protocol was for shifting or when they did it or why. There was a big grizzly shifter that slept on one of the University fields she passed on the way to work sometimes. Rachael let out a chuckle. It must be nice, just lying in the sun on the grass.

Davis had become a haven for the magical. After the Convergence, magical people had been shunned by many out of fear. Rachael was too young to have lived through it, but Diana and Sam had been alive then. They had started the refugee program here, bringing up those who fled danger and persecution as well as creating a place refugees could live in peace. This city was unlike any other Rachael knew about. Laws were in place to protect them and ensure equal education, employment and living situations. And while there was such a high number of magical people, there were also a high number of non-magical people. Most cities, she thought anyway, had a minority of magical people to non-magical people. The harmony only proved to Rachael that it was absolutely possible for the two types to co-exist. It would have been unheard of for a shifter to just take a nap on the grass in a park in Los Angeles in their animal form. Not without some sort of protection anyway. At least, as far as she knew. But she was beginning to understand that she had been spoon fed a lot of lies. For all she knew, equality was the status quo. As she finished putting away her groceries, she decided to research magical history and ask Diana to help her understand the refugee program.

The phone rang, making her jump. No one called her with any regularity and the sound was loud in her apartment.

"Hello?"

'Rachael!" Drake's voice rumbled through the receiver, and Rachael's heart leapt. Uh oh. She needed to calm down.

"Hi, Drake!" That was not calm. That was the opposite of calm.

"It has occurred to me that perhaps you haven't been on a proper tour of the city yet."

"Um, not really." It was true, Rachael had stuck pretty close to home and work, afraid of how large and busy everything was.

"Well, I thought maybe you would like to go for a walk around the University and Downtown with me tomorrow? The Farmer's Market will be open and that's always fun. Plus, I can show you all the Egghead statues; those are famous."

Egghead statues? Rachael frowned in confusion, but gave a mental shrug. "Sure, that sounds great. I have the day off tomorrow."

"Excellent. I'll meet you bright and early at 4th and C street." He sounded very excited, actually. Rachael found herself grinning.

"Uh, just one question," Rachael said quickly, before he hung up.

"Yeah?"

"Is there a place I can buy a used bike?" Davis wasn't large, but Primero Grove wasn't exactly central to Downtown and it was quite the walk to get anywhere. A bike with a large basket would be ideal.

"Oh, you bet, several. We'll look around tomorrow. I should have thought of it."

"Great, thank you," Rachael hesitated, unsure how to end the call.

"Until tomorrow," he said.

"Goodbye," she replied, somewhat breathlessly. She pressed

"end" and set the receiver back in the cradle.

Was this a date? No, surely not. This was friends hanging out. Right?

"Wait, you don't know how to ride a bike?" Drake looked stymied for a moment as he held a bike for her to sit on.

Rachael shrugged helplessly. "We weren't allowed to ride anywhere and we could walk wherever we needed to go. Bikes were instruments of freedom. Like cars or make-up or profanity. So, I never learned." She eyed the bike like it was an explosive. "It can't be hard to learn, right?"

"Well, no." Drake looked down at the bike, back at her, and then shook his head. "We'll deal with it later. For now, all you need to do is sit on it and make sure it's the right size."

"OK, I can do that." She walked over and slung her leg over the bike, sliding onto the seat. Drake kept one hand on the handlebars and one hand on the seat until she was able to put both toes down on either side. He was so close she could feel his body heat and smell the scent of the soap he used. Her heartbeat sped up, and she had to fight the urge to press her face into his chest and inhale.

Stepping back, he tucked his hands into his pockets and cleared his throat. "How does that feel? You should be able to barely touch the ground."

Rachael flexed her hands and tested the handlebar brakes. Her toes hit the ground in her tennis shoes, and the seat was fairly comfortable, although she could tell it was made for a smaller butt than hers. She had dressed today to be comfortable since she knew they would be walking a lot; shorts that were long enough to prevent any kind of chafing and a green t-shirt. Her auburn hair was up in a simple ponytail, leaving her neck bare. It was hot in Davis during the summer and she could just not handle the idea of walking around in pants or with her hair down. She was getting used to wearing the shorts, but she still felt like it was showing too much skin. Hopefully, today helped with that, too.

"I think this is good then," she said, turning to look at Drake with a smile. "I mean, you would know better than I."

His eyes studied her on the bike, sliding down her legs to her feet and then back up again. She felt a blush redden her cheeks even though she knew he was doing it just to see if they needed to lower the seat. "I do think you're right," he said. "You look just about perfect." His eyes had met hers on the last sentence and suddenly she felt warm for reasons other than the weather.

"I'll teach you how to ride it later," he decided, approaching to hold the bike steady so she could dismount. "We don't want to miss the farmer's market. Besides, I don't have one for me to ride."

She slid off the seat, away from Drake, and they stood facing each other with the bike between them. "Thank you so much for finding one for me. How much do I owe you for it?"

He shook his head. "It was my sister's. She never uses it anymore, and she said you were welcome to it. It's a gift."

They had to stop doing things for her, she thought, fidgeting. She couldn't pay them back and it made her uncomfortable that they were being so kind. In her experience, people often brought up kind acts as a way to get other people to do things for them. Surely they were going to call in all of these favors at some point.

"Oh, well, thank her for me. But please, let me give you something for it? I feel terrible just taking it from you."

"Nonsense," Drake said. "You aren't just taking it from me. I am getting to spend all morning with you. That's plenty in way of payment."

After locking up her bike in the rack, he drove her downtown to start the tour of Davis.

Rachael cocked her head and looked at the white statue in front of her. "It really is an egghead."

Drake laughed. "The description is accurate, for sure."

She walked around it, grinning. The bald, egg-shaped head was face-down on an open book, nose in the spine, ears protruding and was rather comical. "These are scattered all over campus?"

He nodded back. "Not all over, but yes, there are several scattered around. This one is my favorite, but I also like Stargazer."

"I would love to see all of them," Rachael said, truthfully. This one was near the library. Was Stargazer near a star-themed place?

Drake grinned. "Okay. But not today."

Rachael's face fell, and Drake shook his head with a chuckle. "You are turning red in this Davis sun, Red." He reached out, tapped her nose, and tugged a strand of her auburn hair that had worked loose from her ponytail. "I am afraid you have a sunburn."

She gasped and her hands flew to her face. "Oh, nuts!" she exclaimed. "Is it bad?"

"Nuts?!" Drake laughed. "No, I don't think so, but hats and

sunscreen, Rachael." He chided gently.

She scowled. "I know that. I can't believe I forgot."

"Come on, the car isn't far." He gestured for her to walk with him, and as she passed, he put his hand on her back. "We should get you some water, too"

Oh, god, did he just feel how sweaty she was? She wasn't used to this infernal heat. The last twenty minutes had been torture for her and she just wanted to sit in the shade and drink a gallon of water. Maybe sleep for a while. Definitely not move. "I'm fine," she said. She just needed to get home, and they were on their way. She could last a little longer.

She lasted until the middle of the quad, which was only about two minutes. Her legs simply stopped working. She sank down under a tree, blinking up at Drake bemusedly. "I just need a minute. Really."

"Shit. I'll be right back. There's a student union right there. Don't move." Drake sounded panicked. Why was he anxious? Was he ok? Move? How could she move? What was moving?

Then Drake was gone. She lay back on the cool grass and looked up at the large tree. It was so pretty and sparkly, the way the sun shone through the branches. Relaxing some more, she sighed, easing up on her mental shields as well.

"Ok, I'm back." Drake's voice floated to her, and his magic rolled over her skin, making her shiver. "Whoa, are you glowing?! That's fucking amazing."

"Your eyes, too. Rachael . . ." She knew what he was seeing. With her magic released, her eyes, skin, and hair all glowed— skin white and luminous, eyes green like an emerald star, and hair auburn waves like fire. Hiding her magic had been a constant physical battle her entire life because not hiding it meant shining like a star.

"Come on, Brightness, time to hydrate," he put a hand under her back and lifted her, sliding a leg behind her so she was leaning against him. She opened her mouth for the water bottle he held to it and greedily gulped the cool liquid, bringing up her hand to take it from him. "Take it easy," he said, pulling it back after she had downed about half of it. "Here, let me do this." He dampened a handful of napkins and began blotting the sweat from her face and neck.

She moaned in ecstasy, letting her head fall back on his thigh behind her and his hand froze for a moment before resuming. He cleared his throat and re-doused the napkins before slipping them into her hands. "Here, you can maybe do this now." he said gruffly.

She opened her eyes, looking up at his face, realizing suddenly how close she was to him. His pupils nearly obscured his eyes, turning his piercing blue eyes nearly black as he looked at her, and he was breathing quickly. Her heat-flushed skin blushed more, and she tensed, afraid he would do something. Afraid that he wouldn't. She had never been this close to such a large confident man before, and her head, if she turned it, was nearly at his crotch level. She should move. She never wanted to move. What the hell was wrong with her? Her stomach ached in a pleasant way, and she really, really hated that he stopped wiping her down.

Her one hasty sexual experience with a young, inexperienced boy behind the schoolhouse had not prepared her for this. That had been fumbling and fear and guilt and ten minutes of gasping, only to have him finish before she had even gotten started. Rachael had been left with an ache between her legs, splinters in her ass, and a great deal of wondering what the big deal was. It certainly had not been worth the sneaking around and the fear of being caught.

This feeling though, this was insistent and hot and needy and scary in its intensity. She would let Drake take her behind that schoolhouse and do anything he wanted, and damn the consequences. She had a feeling he would be much more competent than Jimmy Jr. had been.

"Rachael," he said, his voice deeper than usual. "You can't look at me like that right now. You are suffering from heat stroke and I can't do a damn thing about it."

"Like what?" she asked, lowering her eyebrows, but never looking away from his face.

He shook his head. "Even more reason we need to get you home. Come on." And, to her regret, he was a perfect gentleman who got her home and made sure she was hydrated and healthy before he left. He didn't once cup her face and kiss her, or press her against a wall, or otherwise take advantage of her.

Damn it.

MEET THE ARCHERS

She had never realized how afraid she had always been until she stopped being afraid. Once Rachael realized that, she also knew that she could never ever return home, even if they welcomed her with open arms. That realization had come to her about six weeks after she had arrived in Davis. She had finally been shopping on her own, had gotten used to the fancy kitchen appliances to cook her own food, and she had decided one morning to make biscuits and sausage gravy.

Humming to herself, she reached across the used cast iron pan to grab the pepper, unwittingly resting the underside of her bare arm on the scorching hot handle. "Mother fucker!" she cried out, jerking back, cradling her arm and hissing in pain. And then she froze, fear washing through her for a split second, waiting for someone to take her to task for her language.

"Mother fucker." She said it again, deliberately. Her arm throbbed and the milk on the stove was scalding, but she didn't care. "MOTHER FUCKER!" And then she said it on repeat, dancing around her kitchen while the smell of scalding milk filled the air.

She pulled the skillet off the stove and set it to the side to cool before cleaning it. The biscuits would still be ok; she'd have them with butter and homemade jam. The freedom to say whatever she wanted still rolled within her like a thunderstorm, and she wished she had a radio so she could dance. She could listen to whatever music she wanted, dance however she wanted, and at whatever volume she wanted and no one was here to tell her otherwise. For the first time, Rachael actually felt like an adult, even though she was twenty-five.

After eating some biscuits slathered with homemade raspberry jam, she walked to work with a spring in her step and makeup on her face. She had yet to wear any of the make up Drake had helped her purchase; she could never bring herself to wear any. Laughing to herself, she remembered her chagrin when he had asked if she needed any.

"Make-up?" Rachael had asked, shocked, staring at the display of colorful palettes, lipsticks, and what she assumed was foundation. She had no idea what any of this was actually for.

Drake cleared his throat and Rachael could tell he was trying to answer delicately; she realized this was another moment where she was out of step with the norms. "It's totally acceptable to wear it or not wear it, as is your preference." He cocked his head and asked, "maybe you could buy some and try it? See if you like it?"

That seemed reasonable. So she had pondered colors and allowed herself to purchase a tiny amount of make-up, which had sat in her bathroom unused. Rachael shook her head as she reflected on her reticence. She didn't care if other people wore it, had in fact admired some of their skills in applying it. Yet every time she saw her own make-up, still in its wrappers her stomach tightened, and she went about her day unadorned.

Today she wore it. Not a lot; she did not know how to apply it most of it, but there was some eyeshadow, mascara, and lipstick on her face were there had been none before. Her clothing was more formfitting, the neckline actually showing some neck and even a bit of chest, and there was a spring in her step.

Since it was a morning of firsts, Rachael also relaxed the hold she constantly had on her magic. Her skin began to shimmer, like a prism in the light, her whole body glowing just a little. She sighed, rolling her shoulders, enjoying the release of tension, of just being. To her right, sunning itself was the grizzly bear shifter in bear form, but she could *feel* him now. Over head she felt a shifter sparrow dart past. The woman walking toward her had glamor magic, she thought. Rachael couldn't be sure, but she thought that's what it was. Oh, this was *fun*. She wanted to do this all day.

At the Black Bear, she went to the employee work room and put her purse in her locker, humming to herself. "Rachael! Here, these are your share of last night's tips. I didn't want to leave them just lying around." Mr. Barlett handed her an envelope with her name on it but froze as she turned. "Oh!" He peered at her. "You . . . are you *glowing*?"

Rachael blinked and looked at her hands. "Oh, um, yes?" She gave him a half-smile and a shrug.

"Ok," he continued to peer at her. "You look . . . good. Happy." He said finally, handing her the envelope with a smile. "The glowing eyes are different, but happy is good."

Rachael smiled back, accepting the envelope. "Thank you, Mr. Barlett. I'll be right out."

She spent her shift practicing her magic on her customers. It was harder here, where everyone was in human shapes. She could always tell when someone had magic, but she couldn't always tell what type of magic they had. What was very obvious was that her tips were much larger today.

"It's the outfit and make-up," another server said, when Rachael had commented on it on her break. "It shouldn't matter, but it does." She peered at her in a similar manner to Mr. Barlett. "Also, you're glowing?"

Toward the end of her six hours, Drake came in with a tall black woman. Her black hair was shaved close on one side and styled into locs on the other, the locs dyed red at the bottom. The ear opposite the locs was pierced from the lobe to the top, each hole filled with studs and dangly earrings, and she had a nose ring. Colorful tattoos disappeared under her sleeves on both arms and under her collar. She was the most fascinating woman Rachael had ever seen, and she really didn't like that she was having lunch with Drake. All of Rachael's new additions to her clothing seemed so minor now. She ran her hand over her hair, pulled back in a simple ponytail, tendrils falling out limply after her long shift. Her lipstick was long gone, and her mascara had not been waterproof and had smudged from the heat in the kitchen. The very idea of approaching this confident woman was daunting.

Well, they were in her section; there was no help for it, once more into the breach. "Well, hi there!" Good grief, why did she say it like that?

Drake smiled at her. "Hi, Rachael. I was hoping you would be working." Rachael's stomach did a little flip at that, but she told herself that he was just being kind. While they had hung out a few times in the last month, it was mostly to show her around town and help her get used to Davis. They may have had that one moment, but she *had* been suffering heatstroke. Maybe she had imagined it.

"Well, here I am," she said brightly, in her "customer service voice," as the other servers called it. "What can I do for you?"

Drake blinked at her, startled, and the woman kicked him under the table. "Introduce me, you ass." she said as Rachael stared at her for a second and then giggled. She *giggled*? Why?!

Drake reached under the table and rubbed his shin. "Ow! Damn it, those steel-toed boots hurt!"

"No, they don't. You are a shifter. I would have to run you over with a steamroller to hurt you. Now stop whining and introduce me." The woman rolled her blue eyes at him and smiled at Rachael.

"Rachael," Rachael, who had been watching this exchange with great interest, turned back to Drake. "This is my sister, Ember." Ember? For goodness' sake, even her name was amazing.

Drake guffawed and Ember smiled broadly, and Rachael realized she had said that last thought out loud. "Er . . ."

"No, you said it and now I shall own it." Ember said, tossing her head proudly.

Drake groaned and covered his face with his hands. "There'll be no living with her now. None."

"Well, um, nice to meet you?" Rachael wanted nothing more than to melt into the floor and disappear, but even with magic, it didn't look like that was happening anytime soon. Mr. Barlett rounded the corner, and she prayed he would pull her into the back for something. How had she not realized she was his sister? Now that she looked, there was absolutely a resemblance. Certainly it hadn't been jealousy clouding her judgement? Not so soon?

"Rachael!" He beamed at her. "I tell you what, why don't you put in their orders and put in yours and then you can sit and eat with them. Your shift is over, right?" It was all Rachael could do not to snarl at him, the traitor.

"That sounds perfect," Ember said and Drake nodded, his blue eyes bright, and his lips fighting a smile.

Stuck, Rachael took the orders and managed not to stomp back to the kitchen. She took off her apron and went back to their table, feet dragging. As the booth came into sight, she realized she had to decide who to sit next to and she almost stopped walking. *Okay, Rachael, you can do this.*

In the end, it was decided for her. Ember had grabbed her arm and pulled her down next to her. "Here, sit next to me." Once sitting, Ember had released her immediately, but remained turned toward her, her face open and interested. Rachael gaped a bit and looked back at Drake. He smiled at her from his seat, leaning back with his arm slung across the back of the bench.

"So, Drake has told me you've only been here for six weeks or so?" Ember's eyes were a darker shade of blue, Rachael realized. At her nod, Ember continued. "How are you settling in?"

"I . . . -" she looked around. "Um, okay, I guess. I haven't really done much besides work. Drake has taken me sight-seeing a bit, but that's about it."

"Hmph," she made some sound, something in-between a grunt and a growl. "Parks and giant head sculptures?" she asked, casting him a dark look. He sat up and looked offended.

Rachael tried not to laugh. "Um, yes, actually."

"Typical. Look, how about I take you out tonight, show you around for real, introduce you to some people? You know, help you make some friends?" She shot another look at Drake; he would be dead where he sat if looks could kill.

"Oh, I don't know, I've never . . ." she hadn't ever gone partying or clubbing or even to a bar. What would she wear? And *people?* More than one person?

Ember cocked her head to one side. "Okay, how about this, I'll come over, help you dress and it'll just be you and me. Next time I'll introduce you to my friends."

She brightened. "Oh, yes, that sounds wonderful. Thank you!"

Drake scowled at Ember. "She never expressed any interest in it before!"

Ember stuck her tongue out at him. "You probably never asked. Honestly," she said to Rachael. "I just don't know what to do with him."

Rachael ducked her head to hide her smile, but said, "He's right. I really wasn't interested before."

Drake placed a hand over his heart and sighed dramatically. "I am always misunderstood. She just assumes the worst."

"That's because you are the worst," Ember responded, rolling her eyes.

Rachael giggled again and looked back and forth between the two of them. "Drake and Ember. Were your parents hoping for a pair of dragons?"

Drake snorted, and Ember laughed. "I think Dad was overcompensating for being a squirrel. Mom never worried about it, and he never complained, but it doesn't sound very masculine, does it?"

"Hey! You can do really cool things as a squirrel! Remember when he crawled into the school and managed to connect the wires to the fire alarm? No one could reach them; the opening was too small, and they didn't want to tear open the wall."

Rachael cocked her head. "Well, from what I've seen, your mom has never given your dad any doubt about his masculinity. I saw her making out with him in the office just a couple of weeks ago."

Both siblings groaned. "No restraint, either of them," moaned Drake with a shudder. "Clients could walk in at any time."

"Well, yeah," Ember said, "One did!" She pointed at Rachael. "They should act their age, honestly, not like a couple of horny teenagers!"

Rachael tapped her chin. "I don't know, Sam is awfully good looking. I don't think it would take much convincing to make out with him in an office building if I were married to him. "

On cue both siblings threw sugar packets at her. "You take that back," Ember said, "ugh."

Rachael laughed, ducking. Drake leaned back and studied her. "I like the green eyeshadow."

Oh, he noticed. Her chest expanded, and she felt her cheeks redden. "Thank you. I thought I'd try it today. The mascara melted off." Why had she said *that*? Now he would be staring at her melty mascara eyelashes.

"You need to find some waterproof stuff. I'll bring some tonight. I think I have a new tube. Black should be ok for you," Ember studied Rachael's eyes.

Their food arrived, and Rachael rolled up her sleeves before unwrapping her utensils, only to freeze at Drake's growl.

"What happened?" he asked, grabbing her wrist and turning her arm over.

"What are you talking about?" Rachael asked indignantly. "Let go!"

Ember suddenly growled, too, and Rachael rolled her eyes, losing all sense of self-preservation in her frustration. "What is going on? Would you stop growling at me? And how do you growl, anyway?" she asked Drake, pointing with her other hand. "You are a raven!" That distracted Ember enough to make her huff a surprised laugh, but Drake was too focused on her arm to be deterred.

"Your arm," Drake said, running a finger around her forearm, circling where she had burned her arm on the cast-iron skillet. "What happened?"

"Oh, that," Rachael laughed. "I accidentally burned myself this morning making breakfast. It's fine, really. Can I have my arm back now, please?"

Drake let go reluctantly. "Did you disinfect it? It should be cleaned and wrapped loosely in gauze-. . ."

He stopped at Ember's kick with a wince, but Rachael smiled at him. "Yes, I did clean it, thank you." She didn't miss Ember's significant look at Drake or his uncomfortable shrug, but other than asking what they were worried about, which she wasn't sure she wanted to know, she would remain in the dark.

Rachael started eating, looking at her food because if she kept looking at him, she was going to think about the feel of his hand on her arm and the light touch of his finger on her skin. *He doesn't want you that way, Rachael, knock it off*. It didn't work, but she kept telling herself that, anyway. A rapping on the glass window made her look up and there, waving and laughing, were Sam and Diana. They indicated they were coming in and then disappeared around the corner.

In the end, it was decided that instead of going out, Rachael was to come to the Archer house for dinner, despite her objections.

"Nonsense, dear," Diana said, waving her words away like smoke. "It is obvious you are *not* just a client. Neither of my children has ever taken such an interest in any of my clients before. They certainly have never taken any of them to lunch or on park tours. Dinner. My house. Tonight. seven o'clock. Don't worry about how to dress. It's a ranch. Casual is how it is. And no claiming exhaustion this time; you're not getting out of it." And so it was settled. The blonde woman really was impossible to argue with. It wasn't that she was unkind; it was the opposite. Her kindness disarmed everyone, and people just found themselves agreeing with her.

"But how will I . . ?"

"I'll come get you," Drake said. "I'll be in town until then anyway." Ember, who had opened her mouth a fraction of a second later, closed it and studied her brother, but didn't say anything.

"Oh, well, oh, okay." she said helplessly.

"Excellent! See you then, dear."

While she had gone walking with Drake a couple of times, she had never been to the Archer home, and she was full of anxiety. She took a shower to wash the grease out of her hair—the kitchen at the restaurant just oozed grease—and changed into fresh clothes, keeping to her new look of fitted clothing and slightly lower neckline. Still pants though—the shorts were just too much for a dinner with Drake's family—and the skirts she owned just were not long enough. She left her hair down and decided that more makeup was called for.

This time, she used the pinker lipstick and, since he had liked the green eyeshadow, stuck with that. Mascara. She really needed to learn how to use the rest of this stuff. Looking at herself in the mirror, Rachael shrugged. This was as good as it was gonna get.

The Archer ranch was really a ranch, Rachael realized as Drake drove up the dirt road toward the farmhouse. Pastures extended out dotted with cattle, and she saw stables behind the house. "What do you raise here?" she asked, craning her neck.

"Some cows, but they eat a lot. Goats and sheep are easier and give milk and fleece as well. We sheer our own sheep and sell both raw and spun wool. Mom has started experimenting with natural dyes now and is often very colorful." He wiggled his fingers at her and she laughed.

"How does she have time for the business in Davis with all of this here?" ask Rachael curiously. "This seems like a ton of work."

"Oh, it's plenty," Drake said, "But that refugee work is mom's passion. After the Conversion, she and Dad came up here. They travelled about as far as you did, somehow survived through all the feral rabid new shifters, the lawlessness, fires, looting, and once they arrived, she realized people were going to need help." He shook his head. "Religious cults started executing shifters and magic users and cutting themselves off, and then orphaned magical children whose parents died during the Conversion or were kicked out of their homes needed a place to go, so she formed a fund. Went around and badgered everyone in town for a donation." They slowed to a stop in front of a light blue farm house, windows thrown open to the day, oak trees surrounding it, somewhere a guitar was strumming. Drake turned off the car and turned to Rachael. "They made Davis a haven. Dad backed Mom up, glowering behind her at city council meetings, where she ran and won and then put in laws against discriminating against magic users. Dad never wanted the limelight, but he did want a place his kids could grow up safe. By the time Ember was born, the word was out and people were flooding here from all over. It's not the only city like this, but it was one of the first."

"You're proud of them," Rachael said, nodding. She wondered what it was like to feel that pride and love for a parent. At the moment, she just felt rage and loss for her own.

Drake nodded. "Damn right. And glad, because without them, you wouldn't be here to meet them. Come on." Blithely unaware of how his words touched her, he exited the vehicle and jogged around to open the door for her.

What was it he sees in me? Wondered Rachael as she followed him up the porch steps. *"I'm no hero, no crusader. Just a quiet scared woman learning how to be free."*

The screen door slammed opened and a giant dog burst out. "Oh shit," Drake, said. "He's really friendly—"

Rachael didn't have time to listen because the giant black dog was barreling down at her, drool flying, full speed. There had been guard dogs at home, but she had never had a pet dog before. The guard dogs had patrolled the compound and lived in kennels. They were not nice dogs. This one wasn't barking though, so she braced her legs. It wasn't enough. "OOF!" She landed on her ass, a giant Rottweiler licking her face. "Hey!" she laughed, trying to avoid the wet slobber, but the dog actually pinned her down with one large paw. "Get off!"

"Get off of her, you ass!" Drake grabbed the dog and hauled him off, lifting him as if he were nothing, shifter strength shining through. "Fuck, are you okay?" He passed the dog to Sam, who had run out at the commotion, and moved to Rachael. "Ah, he got you good, didn't he?" Drake laughed.

Rachael was wiping her face. "Yeah, he did. Geeze. What is that thing, anyway?" She took Drake's extended hand, and he pulled her easily to her feet.

"That is Pixie, mom's dog."

Rachael stared at him. "Pixie. You named the largest dog I have ever seen, Pixie."

Diana emerged, wiping her hands on a towel. "You stop making fun of my baby, or you won't get any dessert. He's just adorable." The last part was said to the animal in question, with kissy noises. Rachael's eyebrows shot up into her hairline.

Drake laughed but cut it off at his mother's stern look. "No, ma'am. I wouldn't dream of making fun of Pixie. He's just the sweetest. Absolutely the cutest puppy ever." He said this with the straightest of faces.

Rachael's incredulous look transferred to him and now Sam was having a hard time keeping a straight face. "Come on, Rachael, before she kills the lot of us. Leave your shoes by the door, please."

She followed him, mouthing the word "puppy" to herself, causing Drake to laugh once more, kicking off her shoes as she entered the house. Inside was warm and bright, decorated with neutral tones on the walls and in the big pieces of furniture, but with bright accents all over. Large pillows and dog beds dotted the floors, colorful handwoven hangings hung in every room she passed, and the wooden floors were scrubbed and well swept. Hooked rugs and rag rugs were thrown around, a large one in the main living area, for human feet. The air was full of voices laughing, joking, and the smells of cooking. It was possibly the happiest building she had ever walked into. The whole building oozed family and home.

"Welcome, dear," Diana looped her arm through hers and escorted her back to the kitchen. "Ember is out patrolling the pastures; she'll be back soon. The rolls are just finishing up, the steaks are almost done. Would you like a glass of wine or tea?"

Wine. She could have wine if she wanted. "Wine, please."

Sam handed her a glass of ruby red wine and poured one for himself and Drake. None of the glasses matched. Rachael didn't care. It was lovely. A noise signaled the arrival of Ember, and Drake opened a back door. A sleek bobcat padded in, gold eyes reflecting the lights of the kitchen. Rachael's breath caught slightly; some part of her brain could not adjust to there being a bobcat in the house. The hair on the back of her neck stood up. Her magic swelled in response and her skin started to glow faintly. Ember sat and looked at her, and then, with extreme nonchalance, licked a paw and cleaned one tufted ear.

"You're beautiful," Rachael whispered to her. And she was, golden fur and sleek muscle and bobbed-tail, all adding up to a gorgeous animal a little larger than a house cat. Then Drake leaned in over her from behind and dropped a feather on her head.

She exploded, running, chasing the feather like an overgrown house cat. "DRAKE!" Diana said sternly over the scratching of claws as Ember ran out of the room. There was a crash in the other room, and Drake winced. "Sorry, mom."

Ember reappeared several minutes later dressed in comfy lounge clothes. She greeted Rachael warmly and handed Drake his feather, a little the worse for wear. At that signal, food was dished up, people sat, and dinner was begun. Rachael spent most of it watching the family talk and laugh, an odd feeling of envy in the pit of her stomach. Dinners with her family had been tense affairs, with prayer and terse questions and stern reprimands. It had never been this bright, happy and open exchange of ideas and jokes.

"Rachael?"

She realized Drake had asked her a question, and she cleared her throat. "Sorry. What was that?"

"Did you want to come with me to check on the barn? I need to lock up the animals and make sure their feed and water is done for the night."

"Oh, yes, please!"

It had been her favorite thing at the compound, bedding down the animals for the night. They had kept two goats for milk and it was her job to do the evening duties. With so many siblings, it was often the only time she had to herself and she would take her time in the quiet warmth. Drake grinned at her and jerked his head toward the back. "This way."

Sam and Ember started clearing the dishes as she and Drake walked toward the back. The sun had just set, twilight still lingered a bit. Drake led the way with his shifter eyesight, and Pixie trotted beside her. At the barn, he lay down outside the door, ears perked, listening. "He really is a good dog," she said, bending down and scratching his ears.

Drake chuckled as he opened one side of the barn door. "Oh yes. He'll let us know if he hears something out of the ordinary."

Inside, he turned on one lightbulb for illumination – for her benefit, Rachael doubted he needed it – and led her to a stall on the right. Inside, a herd of goats jostled and baahed at them, each vying for food with the energy of the starving. Laughing, Rachael took the proffered bucket and waded into the fray, pouring pellets into a trough, talking nonsense and chiding troublemakers. She absently pulled her shirt out of the mouth of one and a shoelace out of the mouth of another and then took the now empty bucket back to where Drake stood, grinning at her. "You're a natural."

"Oh, this I can do. Feeding and milking is old hat for me." She exited and closed the gate, latching it securely. Wandering down the aisle, she greeted a questing horse, who blew at her, lipping her hand and her hair, making her laugh.

"Careful with that one!" Drake was suddenly there, an arm around her waist, pulling her back. She was pressed against him, hearing his heart pound, and she gripped his forearm with her hands. "That's dad's stallion. Damn bastard bites everyone, given a chance, and will throw or kick you, preferably off a cliff. He's a mean one. I don't know why dad hasn't gelded him, but he just says that he wasn't meant to be a gelding and so he stays intact.'

Rachael knew he was talking, but all she could do was feel him there behind her. His magic was like soothing velvet against her jangling nerves, and she just wanted to bury herself against him and hide there. She could smell him from this close, clean sweat, goat, soap, and some other unidentifiable scent that must just be Drake. If she were bolder, she would turn and kiss him. His lips would be soft and he would slide his tongue . . .

She jerked her mind back to the present. Horse. There was a dangerous horse or something, right? She became aware that the horse wasn't acting dangerous at all, was in fact just looking at them. "Drake?" He was still holding her, but his arm had loosened, so she turned and stepped back. He tightened his grip, though, so she didn't get far. Now she was looking up at him in the dim light, posed as if they were about to dance.

"What were you thinking just then, Rachael?" Drake's voice was soft, no hint of mocking, his eyes, so bright during the day, here in the dark, like a moon, shining with their own light. His other hand came up and tucked her hair behind her ear, and shivers ran down her back. She turned her cheek into his hand slightly and he cupped her face, rubbing her cheek with his thumb. "Whatever it was, don't stop thinking about it." He leaned in and pressed his face into her neck, not kissing, but inhaling. Rachael's skin broke out in goosebumps and she pressed her thighs together, locking her knees to keep from swaying closer to him. "I would very much like to kiss you," he said, searching her eyes.

Her heart pounded. Oh, god, yes, she wanted him to kiss her. The side of his mouth lifted slightly, but he waited. He was going to make her say yes or no, wasn't he? Her eyes dropped to his mouth. "Please, Drake," she said, so softly she could barely hear herself. "Yes."

He moved slowly, giving her time to change her mind, but his lips brushed hers, softly, so softly, his hand still on her face. Her hands slid up to rest on his chest and she pressed herself to him, kissing him back and he pulled her in, so that their bodies were touching.

She gasped at feeling all of him, lifting up on her toes, and his tongue took advantage, slipping into her mouth. She moaned, her hands now on his neck. He groaned in response, his hands also busy. One was on her ass, lifting and pressing her against him, the other on her neck, holding her face for his lips, which were getting more and more hungry the longer they kissed.

Pixie gave a sharp bark at the barn door and Rachael gasped and pulled back. Drake let her go and smiled ruefully. "Someone is coming to look for us, I imagine."

Indeed, Ember met them in the yard and eyed them suspiciously, but merely walked with them back to the house. Drake regaled them with the story about how Rachael had met Sam's stallion and lived to tell the tale. Soon, it was time to go, and Rachael climbed into Drake's car to return to her apartment, sad to leave, but happy to have some time to think.

Drake made no further demands on her, merely said goodnight and kissed her hand, but he made sure she got inside and waited for her to lock her door before leaving. Rachael lay in bed later, her fingers tracing her lips and then drifting down to cup a breast. The other hand found the wetness between her legs as she remembered that kiss, the feeling of his hard hands, and how good it felt to be pressed against his body. The thrill of knowing his groan was because of her. And when the orgasm caused her back to bow, and her hips to thrust, it was his name that came gasping from her mouth.

She was in trouble. How could one kiss make her feel like this? How could one kiss make her feel more passion than an entire sexual encounter?

Also, falling for the first man who showed her any interest couldn't possibly be healthy. She sighed and rolled over. She was going to sleep. Tomorrow was soon enough to think about all this.

ZAKARIA

"Hey, go easy with that!" The sharp masculine voice rang through the corridor outside her apartment, infiltrating her quiet and cozy home. Frowning, Rachael peered through the peephole to see if she could spot who was speaking. Sam walked by carrying a couple of boxes, then Diana with a suitcase . . . there, who was *that*. Must be a new arrival? And he had all this stuff? Who the hell was this?

She stared at the door warring with herself. She really had no desire to meet him—he seemed like an ass, barking orders and making complaints—but it would be best to get off on the right foot and the neighborly thing to do would be help him get settled. She plastered a smile on her face and opened the door.

"Oh, hello, dear!" Diana greeted her warmly, pausing to give her a hug. "Don't you look lovely this morning. Here, I've brought you a neighbor. Zakaria, this is your neighbor, Rachael."

Zakaria was extremely attractive. He had blond hair with a bit of a wave that fell perfectly around his face, crystalline clear blue eyes, like sapphires, sparkling at her from a tanned face. *Where the heck did he come from?* Rachel thought. *What did he do, seduce the pastor's daughter?*

"It's nice to meet you, Zakaria," Rachael said, sticking out her hand. He shook it but didn't smile. He studied her seriously.

"Pleasure." He pulled his hand back and wiped it on his pants, discreetly, but everyone saw.

Rachael saw Diana's eyes narrow and Sam, who was approaching from down the hallway, oozed menace. She cleared her throat and turned to Diana. "Does he have the entire package, too? Job, apartment, the works?"

She shook her head, but Zakaria responded before she could. "I have sufficient funds. I do not require menial employment."

"*Well,*" huffed Diana.

"That is everything," Sam all but growled, placing a hand on Diana's arm—to restrain, Rachael thought, not soothe. "We'll leave you to get settled. Rachael, did you need anything before we go?" *Did you want to come with us?* The question was plain as day and she smiled at him, the dear man.

"No, thank you. I have some chores to get done." And a lock on the door. She'd be fine. After the outside door had closed, she turned back to Zakaria. "Okay then. Welcome to the building." She turned to make her escape only to hear him say, "oh, wait." Groaning inwardly, she turned around.

"I was hoping you would escort me to a place we could have coffee? I have nothing set up yet and I'm afraid I would get lost."

She had never wanted to say no more in her life, but years of being told to "be nice and smile," and, "he is your neighbor you *have* to have a good relationship with him!" took control of her mouth and "yes, of course" slipped out before she knew what was happening.

After grabbing her purse, she led him down the street, toward downtown. "A bike is a good investment," she offered, as they walked. "Everyone owns one and there are several good shops in town. It will help your mobility a lot."

"Bikes? Not cars?"

She cut her eyes at him, shocked. And then she was shocked that she was shocked. When she first arrived, she too was surprised at how few cars there were, but she learned that her cult clung to cars far longer than most people had. Those people who lived far outside the city had a car to transport them there, but they ran on solar power and they didn't go very far or very fast. Buses were used the same way for public transport to larger cities, but by and large, most people got around with a bike. Shipping used solar trucks, the entire top covered in panels. The world had gotten a lot smaller since magic was released and fossil fuels were removed from reach. While her family and everyone who lived around them didn't actually *own* a car, they still saw cars as the best way to move around. Their whole outlook was so backward.

He made a noise after she explained this to him, something between dismissal and disbelief. Fine, he'd learn. This foray, for example, would take them most of the morning walking.

"How is it you came to be here?" he asked her after they had finally arrived at the cafe and ordered their coffee. Their table sat next to the front, close to the door, and she was enjoying the breeze after the exertion.

"I'm sorry?" she stared at him. "That's a bit personal."

"Is it?" He asked, startled. "We are both exiles in a strange land. I was merely hoping for a familiar story." He looked down at the table.

Exiles. Not refugees. He wanted to go back. He missed it. "You miss it. I remember first arriving. It was such a startling change."

She laughed softly. "I remember feeling way too exposed. I thought for sure something was going to get me at any second."

"No wall." he said nodding sagely. He looked around. "How can they just walk around like it's safe out here?"

She leaned forward. "But it is safe."

He looked back at her, unsure. "How can it be? There's so much magic out here. They could do anything with it if they wanted!"

Rachael nodded. "True, they could. But anyone at home could have killed me at any time if they wanted to. I could have tripped walking down the stairs. A guard dog could have attacked me." she shrugged. "There are always dangers."

He shook his head. "It's not the same." Their coffee arrived. He watched her add cream and sugar. "You like it very sweet," he commented.

Her stomach tightened, but she kept stirring her coffee. "Yes, and you don't." *There, you ass, I can state facts, too.*

"It's probably very easy to fall into bad habits out here."

She sipped her coffee, trying to pretend his words didn't affect her even though they wormed into her brain and made her appetite disappear. Her mother used to say the same things to her growing up, hoping it would force her to slim down. Nothing worked, of course, and she ate the same as everyone else, worked the same as everyone else. Her weight just was higher. It didn't fit the ideal and so must be fixed. She had gotten so used to the Archers never commenting on it and she had clothing that fit; it had just been so *pleasant.*

"It's easy to be kind as well," she said. "Wise even."

He stared at her, taken aback. She would never have said that before. Women weren't really accustomed to talking back. Not in public certainly.

"You mentioned that you had everything you needed. How is it you had time to gather all of your stuff?" she asked curiously.

"What do you mean? I just packed up?" he made it a question.

She shook her head. "I was chased out. If I had stayed to pack, I would be dead."

He froze and stared at her hard. "You have magic," he spat the word as if it were dirt in his mouth.

"You don't? Why were you exiled?" What was his story?

He shrugged. "It was a misunderstanding. One I am sure soon will be rectified."

"Oh," she sipped her coffee. "Was it the leader's daughter? Or his wife?" Honestly, what was the matter with her? Two months ago she would have been too afraid to even look at him the wrong way and here she was deliberately needling him. There was a tap on the window and she looked over.

"Drake!" She waved at him and he moved toward the entrance.

Zakaria glowered. "You know that man?"

"Of course. He is Diana and Sam's son."

"The two employees from this morning?"

Rachael ground her teeth and managed not to say anything insulting. "Yes."

Drake finished ordering and came over to their table, sliding a chair over and straddling it. Rachael let her eyes linger on his arms resting on the back of the chair for a moment before making the introductions.

"Zakaria, nice to meet you." Drake extended his hand and Zakaria took it as if it were a snake, the smile on his face mostly a grimace. "How are you settling in? Need anything?"

"I am doing quite fine, thank you. Rachael has extended her company for coffee, which was all I required this morning."

She sat up at the implication of his words. Did he really mean all he needed was her company, the little rat?

Drake never stopped smiling, but his body stilled, like a predator spotting another predator. "I see." He sipped his coffee and turned to Rachael, his smile softening. "I'm glad I ran into you. You left this in my car last night." Reaching into his pocket, he pulled out a hair-tie that she had kept on her wrist last night in case she needed to put her hair up, which she had in the barn while feeding the goats. But the impression he was giving Zakaria was not so innocent, and he knew it. She narrowed her eyes at him.

"Thank you," she said shortly, taking the hair-tie and sliding it onto her wrist. "Well, I really must be going. I have some things to do before I start work this afternoon."

Zakaria and Drake stood when she did, gentlemen both, at least in manners. "Here," Drake handed her a package of baked goods. "Mom said she interrupted you before breakfast."

The scent of warm cinnamon and sugar rose from the wrappings, and her mouth watered. "Oh, thank you! These smell amazing!"

Zakaria shook his head. "You do her no favors by giving her sweets."

"*Excuse* me?" Rachael asked him incredulously. Drake was silent, but his face was stony anger.

Zakaria gestured at her, from her feet to her head. "I just worry about your health, that's all. It's not healthy to carry too much extra weight. Since you already do, I assumed you would be limiting your food intake. I can give you exercise tips, too, if you'd like."

Nothing in his tone was biting or mean; he spoke as if he was just stating the truth and he did indeed wish to help her.

The words punched her like tiny fists. Those were the words, exactly, that her mother had told her so often, that her father had repeated, that well-meaning elders would say in hopes of helping her. Her chest tightened and though she knew, *knew*, that they were untrue, to hear them spoken aloud, *here* and in front of Drake

. . .

"You fucking bastard!" Drake was standing in front of her, between her and Zakaria, blocking her view of him. "Rachael, it's not . . ."

"It's fine." She cut him off. "I have to go." She did, before she lost it right here in front of strangers. In front of Drake. Before he saw how much she let Zakaria get to her. She fled, hearing raised voices behind her, but unable to stop. She ran from her past and she ran from her potential future. She left them there, fighting, like a coward.

Unfortunately, it was a very long walk back home and since she didn't want to risk running back into Zakaria, she took an even longer route. Tears had left salty streaks down her face and her chest felt heavy and leaden, while her head felt stuffed with cotton. It had all been just too much all of a sudden, just all too much. Now that she was away from it, the emotion spent, she could look back and think rationally about it.

"Rachael!" Startled, she dropped the rein she usually kept on her magic, letting it flood out all at once, and whipped around. She could tell her skin was luminescent, but she couldn't see that her hair was glowing like a ruby and her eyes like green fire. Even in the bright sunlight, she stood out. Ember shied back slightly, claws and teeth extending from her hands and mouth, a growl from her throat.

"Ember!" Rachael gasped and stepped toward her, but Ember shook her head.

"Stop, it's too much." She backed up. "Can you turn it down?"

Rachael took a deep breath and tried to calm down, forcing her magic down a notch, another breath, another notch. Ember walked closer and her claws retracted. 'Wow, I've never felt anything like that and you looked . . . ' she shook her head. "You were glowing. Did you know you glowed?"

Rachael huffed a laughed feeling some tension ease within her. Ember's blue eyes held no fear, but Rachael was wracked with guilt. What had she done? What could she do? She had no idea, and her friend had almost paid the price for it. "Yes, but I've never done it quite that brightly before. I am so sorry. I didn't realize I was so jumpy."

"Drake called the office, I was holding down the fort while Mom was checking on some dyes at home. He drove to your apartment, and you weren't there. He's worried."

"He called from my apartment?" Rachael's brows drew together.

"Of course not. What do you take him for? He went to a pay phone." Ember studied her. "That asshole did a number on you, didn't he." It wasn't a question.

Rachael rubbed her forehead. He really had, she realized, more than she had known. Everything about Zakaria, his manner, his words, his attitude, brought her right back to her past, still so fresh she was only two steps away from it. It felt all too easy to fall back into.

"Come on, I'll take you home. I don't think you should be alone. While we walk, why don't you tell me what you and my brother were doing in the barn last night?"

Shit.

Ember chuckled. "Relax, that look on your face is answer enough." They walked for a bit in silence. Rachael took a deep breath, feeling calmer, steadier. Ember's magic wasn't as soothing as Drake's, but it was still like putting soft velvet on her skin. "Are you going to be okay with that asshole living down the hall from you?"

Rachael tucked a stray hair behind her ear. "I think so. I don't have to see him if I don't want to." She didn't mention that she had this almost indescribable curiosity about him. Why was he here? Why was he exiled? He just didn't *act* like he was never going back to his old home.

Primero Grove appeared ahead of them and Ember bumped into her gently. "If you need anything, *anything*, you just call us, okay?"

Rachael nodded. "I will, I promise." And she would. Maybe.

Zakaria was locking his door when they entered into the building. His eyes scraped over Ember, taking in her ripped jeans, dyed locs, and tattoos, and then flicked over to Rachael, dismissing Ember completely. Ember cocked an eyebrow at that, not used to that reaction; usually people paid her too much attention.

"There you are. I was concerned. You ran away and didn't tell anyone where you were going." Was he *chiding* her?

Rachael's magic started spilling out everywhere again, and she pulled it back, desperately trying to keep a rein on her temper. Ember was growling, picking up on her anger, but Rachael was watching Zakaria. He wasn't upset or angry or emoting anything at all except slight concern. Like she was acting so inappropriately that he didn't know how to address it.

"Ember, please go home. I just want to go have a cup of tea." Rachael turned to her friend, placing a hand on her arm, trying to soothe the tension she felt there.

"This man is a menace." Ember's eyes finally turned down to Rachael's and went from bobcat gold back to their normal dark blue. "Remember what I said. Anything at all."

"I'll remember." Ember left without a backward glance, and Rachael finally saw a flare of anger on Zakaria's face; he was obviously not used to being ignored either.

"What are you doing?" she demanded, hands crossed in front of her. "You are not responsible for me. Why would I let you know where I was going?"

Surprise covered his face, no that was shock. *Got ya,* she thought. He walked toward her, frowning severely. It really was a shame that such a handsome man was so ugly.

"Are you sleeping with her?" He asked. Again, he acted concerned for her, with a bit of anger underneath.

Rachael stared at him for a full minute before she burst out laughing. "You know, two months ago that would have shocked me to my toes, but now it's just sad that you think that would upset me. She's beautiful and I would be honored if she wanted to date me." She looked him up and down as he had Ember. "I think you might be jealous. But of Drake or Ember?"

And with that parting shot, she entered her apartment and left a red faced Zakaria standing in the hall. Before she could close the door; however, he put his hand on it, preventing her from doing so. He put his face inches from hers. "Drake isn't who you think he is, Rachael. He's using you. His whole family is using you. You know you can't trust magic! They are just using you for the money it gets them, nothing more. You are nothing to them."

Rachael lifted her leg and brought it down on his instep. He hissed and stepped back. "You are a liar and bring nothing but trouble. Go. Away." And she shut the door and locked it.

What she couldn't do was unhear the words and as much as she didn't really believe it, his words wormed into her brain, insidious and poisonous, breeding doubt where there had been none before. Hadn't she wondered if Drake was really interested in her or if he were only hanging out with her because it was his family business? And she was having such a hard time controlling her own magic right now; it would make sense if other magic users also suffered from a lack of control. Maybe Zakaria really was concerned about her.

Wrapping her arms around herself, Rachael stood immobile, trapped in self-doubt. How could she ever figure out what was real and what wasn't?

THE ROAD TO HELL

S he really didn't have time for this drama. Rachael had *just* started celebrating her freedom. She wasn't going to start bouncing around between Zakaria and Drake wondering who was telling the truth and who wasn't.

"Zakaria is an ass," she said to her reflection. "He is creating trouble for some reason." And while she did believe that to be true, it was also true that if she didn't harbor any feelings for Drake, Zakaria wouldn't have tried to use them against her. So, she decided to just take a break from everyone for a bit.

"Nothing permanent," she said, as she swept the floor. She realized she was talking to herself and that it was a weird thing to do, but it helped her think. And who was going to tell her to knock it off? The broom? "I'll just take a week or two for myself and not see anyone. Yeah, no drama, just work on myself. Practice my makeup, work on my magic, make money. No. Drama." She emphasized those last words by banging the dustpan into the garbage pail.

Making some tea, she went to sit on her patio for a bit, only to find Zakaria out in the courtyard, shirtless, doing some sort of martial art. He held a staff and was slowly going through formations and after a set would let out his breath is a "huh" sound. She sat in the single chair, sipping her tea, refusing to be chased off. It really was a shame; his body was perfect. Sweat glistened off his abs, indicating he had been at this for a while already, and after about ten minutes, he stopped, only to drop and start doing push-ups.

"Oh really," Rachael rolled her eyes. Did he have to do that *here*? Still, the view wasn't terrible. She wondered if Drake did push-ups, but she also knew that Shifters had naturally stronger and more fit bodies. "*Hmmm, Drake doing push-ups though, now* that *I would really like to see,*" she thought, lost in her own imagination for a bit. She blinked and realized she was still staring at Zakaria, who was now staring at *her*. A knowing smile spread across his face as he picked up a towel to wipe the sweat from his body, and Rachael gasped.

"No, damnit!" she said loudly, her face blushing. "Mother fucker, I was not looking at you!"

But it was too late; he believed the worst. He gathered his equipment and walked around the building, obviously done for the morning, and Rachael wanted nothing more than to disappear into nothingness. The idea of Zakaria thinking she found him at all appealing . . . her stomach roiled. Avoiding him was now at the top of her list. She would avoid him until the day she died.

Good intentions never worked for her, she decided, watching Zakaria enter the restaurant during the lunch rush. She had managed to escape her apartment without running into him and the first part of her shift had gone very smoothly, but now here he was, right there, and she couldn't avoid him. Maybe they would seat him at the counter or in another section.

And they didn't because that would have been way too easy. Rachael groaned inwardly and then marched over to him. Better to get this over with. "Welcome. Have you visited here before? We have a number of specials today, if you want me to list them for you."

Zakaria leaned back. He was wearing khaki pants and a blue polo shirt, his blond hair brushed away from his face. "Hello, Rachael. No, I'll just have a hamburger and fries." He handed her his menu, his eyes never breaking contact with hers. "I wish you could join me."

"Sorry, it's the middle of my shift. Burger and fries, got it." And she made her escape. Ew, a date with Zakaria, never in a million years. She could just imagine him raising an eyebrow at what she ordered, and then shaking his head in disappointment when it wasn't a salad with no dressing.

"Who is that dreamboat you just waited on?" Michelle eyed him from the hostess station as Rachael dropped off the menu. "He is eye-fucking the shit out of you."

"He's *what?!*" Rachael's skin crawled at the very idea and tried to look at Zakaria without him seeing her looking. Michelle wasn't kidding. His eyes hadn't strayed one inch, and they were glued to her in a way that made her very uncomfortable. "Oh gross. Oh, gross gross gross." She shuddered. This had to stop; she had to nip this whole mess in the bud now.

"You don't want him," Michelle's eyes started glowing and Rachael's skin erupted in goosebumps as the ice water feeling. "Can I try?"

Rachael eyed Michelle, who was younger than she, even if she was apparently more sexually experienced. "Michelle, I am not your keeper, or even really your friend, but please, hear me when I say that man is not a good man. Be very careful."

Michelle hesitated for a second, but then she smiled. "But the bad guys can be so *fun*."

"Michelle!" Rachael hissed, but she was gone, sashaying away to Zakaria's table. Ohhh, this was a bad idea, Rachael knew it. She didn't know why or how, but it was going to be bad. She watched Zakaria finally pull his gaze away from her and turn to Michelle, his lazy posture focusing on the hostess the way it had just been focused on Rachael. Fickle creature, wasn't he? They chatted for a minute and Michelle offered her hand, which Zakaria took, held up to his mouth for a moment, and then Michelle walked back, her face glowing victoriously.

"Oh my *gawd* that man is sex on a stick!" she squealed to Rachael, fanning herself with a hand back at the hostess station. Zakaria was watching, a small smile on his face. Rachael pointedly didn't look at him. She had to go grab an order, but she tried one more time.

"Please, Michelle, *please*, be careful."

"Don't be so boring, Rachael. Now shoo, go do your job."

Rachael walked back to pick up Zakaria's order feeling the oddest sense of foreboding. There was no reason for it, she knew that, but she also knew that she did not want Michelle anywhere near him. Zakaria had shown no indication that he was violent or dangerous. He was just an asshole. Swinging by the condiments, she picked up the ketchup for the fries, and then headed toward his table, unaware that she was stalking more than necessary.

"Here you go," she said gracelessly, plunking his food on the table with a thud, causing several fries to slide onto the table.

"Is this the kind of service this establishment expects of its staff?" Zakaria picked up a fry and took a bite, while looking at her with a cocked eyebrow, no doubt expecting her to go into raptures.

"It's the best you are going to get. Is there anything else you need." She did not phrase it as a question, making it clear she didn't want to get him anything at all.

"A date," he said with a smile.

Rachael closed her eyes and counted to ten. The audacity of the man, to ask her this at her job, after flirting with Michelle not ten minutes ago, as if she even wanted to say yes. He was just . . . "Okay, then, so nothing else." She spun and walked away, acutely aware that he was watching her go. Honestly, if he found her habits so unappealing, why was he even interested?

Her shift ended at 10:00 p.m., but with her closing duties, she didn't leave the restaurant until closer to 10:30p.m. Michelle's shift had ended several hours before hers, and Rachael had worried about her for hours. Her date with Zakaria was supposed to have started already. She said goodbye to Mr. Barlett, who had asked if she needed an escort home, the sweet man, and the cooks, who also asked if she needed someone to walk her home. She had her bike and a bright headlamp which should be nice and charged from sitting in the sun all afternoon. As she unlocked it, though, she wished she had taken one of her co-workers up on their offer. Someone was watching her; she'd bet money on it. The hair on the back of her neck tried to stand up, and she tried not to act like she was suspicious. If only there was some way to feel out magic without glowing like the sun; it was a rather big tell.

She rode quickly, keeping up a brisk pace that wouldn't tire her out but would get her home fast. And, as an added bonus, if whoever was watching her was on foot, hopefully they couldn't keep up with her. The night air was chilly, but she didn't slow. A shifter owl drifted overhead, letting out a screech that was hardly the "hoo" one thinks of owls making. She felt a shifter off to her left, on the college campus, but it was too far for her to see, probably behind a building. Something else, not a shifter but magical, flew in the night sky, a dark shape against the stars, and, not for the first time, Rachael wondered what the world had been like before the Conversion. What had it been like without all these wonders existing together? In some cities there were warring factions, shifters against fae magic users, against who knows what else. She was still learning what existed and felt woefully ignorant. Maybe it was an evil thing that was going to swoop down and carry her off.

With that happy thought, she pedaled faster, thoroughly spooked. *"This is ridiculous,"* she thought to herself. *"You haven't been this scared at night in weeks. Knock it off!"*

She turned into Primeo Grove's courtyard and found her building quickly, locking up her bike as fast as she could. As she climbed the stairs and opened the door, she heard voices behind her and turned, only to see Zakaria and Michelle approaching.

"Hey girl!" Michelle said, waving. She was wearing a short skirt and a crop top that fell off one shoulder, revealing a red bra underneath. Her black combat boots only enhanced the bareness of her long legs. "Zakaria said he lived next to you! You have been holding out." She made a pouty face at her.

"It didn't come up," Rachael said feebly. Zakaria had his arm around Michelle's waist and her lipstick was on his neck and mouth, making it very obvious that this was not their first physical connection of the night. Michelle's hand rested brazenly on Zakaria's ass, sitting inside his back pocket. Rachael opened the door and moved inside. "Well, goodnight."

Zakaria's chuckle chased her inside; she heard him say something to Michelle who giggled in response. Rachael rolled her eyes. Let them make fun of her; let them think it was jealousy. The reality was she wanted to be near a phone in case . . . she wasn't sure what. She also didn't miss the hypocrisy in Zakaria feeling free to date whomever he wanted, but she couldn't, according to him. All of it was a roiling bundle of apprehension and rage inside of her that had her bouncing from room to room, cleaning and picking up in a whirl.

You have gotten paranoid, she thought to herself. *Zakaria has given no sign he'd hurt anyone.* Still, a phone nearby—and she'd stay awake until she was reasonably sure Michelle was safe. She threw trash into the can and tried to think back and figure out *why* she suspected Zakaria so much. He was openly an asshole, but that didn't make him physically abusive or dangerous. She just got this weird feeling around him.

The outside door opened, and she heard moaning and stumbling steps as Zakaria and Michelle made their way to his apartment down the hall. The walls were thin and she could hear almost everything from her spot and she began wishing she had gone to the couch; she could have done without this knowledge in her head.

Just past her dining room their steps stopped and there was a thud on the wall followed by Michelle moaning louder. *Oh my god, He's got her pressed up on the wall,* thought Rachael, frantically trying to find a place to go where she could escape this onslaught of noise. She turned on the kitchen faucet and covered her ears, which helped somewhat, and after several minutes, there was a disappointed noise from Michelle and then they were moving back toward Zakaria's apartment. Rachael shut off the water and sank onto the couch. Oh, holy God, that was close. She did not want to know what Zakaria sounded like *in flagrant,* as her mother used to call it. Just the idea made her shudder. Picking up a book, she settled down to wait, hoping the distraction worked. If she knew Zakaria, he wouldn't ask Michelle to stay.

Bang!

Rachael sat up with a jerk, realizing with shame that she had fallen asleep on the couch.

"ASSHOLE!" Michelle yelled, banging on Zakaria's door again.

Rachael got up and went to her door, opening it to see Michelle, clad in nothing but her underwear, standing in the hallway. "Michelle?" she said her name gently, trying not to startle her. "Do you want to come in?"

Michelle spun, clutching her clothes to her chest, tears streaming down her face. "I . . . oh, yes," she sniffed hugely. "I guess I should." She walked over to her door; Rachael let her in.

"Are you . . . ok?" Rachael wasn't sure how to ask the question she wanted to without risking Michelle's embarrassment or anger. "Did he hurt you?"

Michelle laughed bitterly. "I'm fine. He didn't do anything I didn't ask him to." Still, her eyes were slightly wild and haunted under her tears, and Rachael felt there was more to the story, but she didn't press.

"Ok. Shower?"

"Oh yes, please."

Rachael showed her to the bathroom and, once the water turned on, she went to the phone.

"Hello?" Rachael's stomach did a flip at the sound of Drake's sleep roughened voice.

"Hi, Drake, it's Rachael."

"Rachael? What is it? Do you need help?" His voice sharpened and took on a growling purr that made her hair stand up in warning, but also somehow made her feel safe.

"No, no, I'm fine," she assured him. "I'm sorry for calling so late. Is Ember there? I need her help."

There was a long pause, but then Drake said, "yes, a moment." The phone made a clunking noise as he sat it down and then she waited while he went to get his sister. Guilt ate at her, but she didn't have time to explain before Michelle got out of the shower. Ember would have to do that later.

"Rachael?" Ember's voice came over the line, concern filling it.

"Ember, can you bring the car as soon as you can? There's someone who needs a ride. Zakaria . . . " she sighed. "I don't think he hurt her, but she's shaky and I don't want her walking home alone."

"I'll be right there." She didn't say goodbye, just hung up. Rachael knew she was just putting on shoes over whatever she was wearing and hopping in the car. Hopefully, the battery would last. She didn't know how solar worked at night.

The shower turned off. Rachael went and put the kettle on for some tea, pulling out the chamomile. If there was ever a need for a calming tea, now was it.

Michelle came out of the bathroom, hair damp, but looking more together. "Thanks. That helped a lot."

"No problem. Here, I have some tea brewing. Do you take honey?"

Michelle gave her a funny look. "You don't have to do this, you know."

Rachael frowned at her. "Do what?"

Michelle gestured between them. "*This*. You don't have to pretend to be nice to me."

"Michelle," Rachael turned at the whistle of the kettle, grabbing two mugs and the honey. "I am not pretending anything. Sit down and have some tea. You don't have to talk if you don't want to, but I am not letting you walk home at," she checked the clock, "two-thirty in the morning by yourself. I have someone coming here with a car to give you a ride home. Since you are stuck here anyway, you might as well have a drink." She slid over the mug of hot sweetened tea and gave Michelle a look that would do her mother proud.

Michelle gaped at her for a minute and then smiled a little. "Okay." She warmed her hands on the mug, staring into it as if it would tell her the future. They drank in silence for a few minutes, Rachael content to let Michelle just sit if she wanted. "You were right," Michelle said finally, her breath hitching a little.

Rachael sighed into her own tea. "I didn't want to be, Michelle. Are you ok?"

Michelle shrugged. "It's weird. I don't . . . I'm not *hurt*. Like, I have had sex rougher than that and enjoyed it. But something about him . . . he made me feel *dirty*. " She sniffed. "As if he wasn't doing it too!" she said louder, glaring at Rachael, daring her to argue.

Rachel nodded. "I understand." She got up, and carefully not touching Michelle, looked at her in her eyes. "You did nothing wrong. He's an asshole."

Michelle's lip trembled, and she sighed. "It's hard. He was very convincing." They both turned at a knock on the door. "Your friend?"

Rachael nodded. "Yes, are you ready? You can stay here tonight if you need to. I can tell Ember to go home."

Michelle nodded. "Thank you, no. I just want my own bed."

Rachael smiled. "Okay. Goodnight, Michelle." She went to the door and let Ember in and made introductions. Ember instantly took Michelle under her very protective wing; there was something wounded about her that made Rachael want to wrap her up and keep her safe and with Ember being a shifter, her protective instincts were raised one hundred percent.

Confident that Ember would see her safely home, Rachael shut and locked the door, weariness wearing her down. She fell into bed, barely pausing to change into pajamas, and fell into fitful sleep full of dreams of unseen stalking monsters.

She had the next two days off and Rachael luxuriated in not having to rush about. She cleaned her apartment and ran some basic errands, but by mid-morning found herself with more free-time than she knew what to do with. She should have known; however, that Ember wouldn't just let the whole thing go.

"I brought lunch," Ember held up a paper bag which was emanating the most mouth watering smell and Rachael merely shook her head in defeat and gestured to the dining room table.

"Sit down. I'll grab some napkins and such."

"What the fuck happened last night?" Ember asked between bites of fish tacos, scowling. "That girl was . . . traumatized is putting it nicely. There wasn't a bruise on her that I could see, but . . ."

Rachael nodded soberly. "I know, I don't know exactly what happened, Michelle wouldn't say, but Zakaria . . ."

Ember sat up straight as an arrow and narrowed her eyes. "She slept with Zakaria. He did that to her?"

Rachael gulped, swallowing half-chewed burrito, and started coughing. "I didn't do it, so stop glaring at me!" Rachael coughed some more, swallowing to make sure her airway was clear. That was the most terrifying look she had seen and she almost, *almost*, felt pity for Zakaria. "And yes. Michelle arranged a date with him yesterday and I saw them go into his apartment last night. She was fine when she went in, but when she came out. . . Ember, you didn't even see her right after." Whatever Ember saw in Rachael's face made her eyes glow gold.

"He is proving more trouble than he is worth," she said, grabbing another taco. "I will talk to Mom. He cannot stay here if he is causing this type of trouble."

Rachael nodded, relieved. She didn't like living so close to him. As if summoned, they heard his door open and shut and they both stilled, listening to his steps travel past. He was whistling, to all intents and purposes like a man who enjoyed himself immensely the night before. Both women stared at each other, anger filling the air; Rachael was surprised it didn't crackle.

In an effort to calm down, Ember said, "I told Drake the truth, that you needed a woman for a ride for a sensitive matter. He wasn't too happy that you asked me instead of him."

Rachael's mouth thinned, but she wasn't sorry. "I couldn't put Michelle in a car with a man. I just couldn't."

Ember nodded. "Of course not, and Drake understood when I got home and told him what was what." She gave Rachael a small smile. "He has an ego, but not a giant one. He can see reason."

Rachael laughed but sobered quickly. "I also. . . Ember I can't-" She stalled, unsure of what she wanted to say. She frowned at her burrito, trying to find the words. Finally, she said, "I am just learning who I am as a person, really. I lived with people who were just like Zakaria my whole life—judgmental, controlling, mean, and totally willing to crush me to suit their beliefs." She felt tears pricking her eyes, and she took a deep breath. Ember reached out to her, but froze when Rachael pulled back. If she was touched, she wouldn't be able to say this. "I spent my life living as someone else. I spoke a certain way and dressed a certain way and believed a certain way. Now that I am *-free-*"she stressed the word, "I want to *be* free for a bit. It scares me, a little, to think that I might love your brother. He's the first man I've really gotten to know."

Ember's face cleared. "I get it. I totally get it. You need to date. Meet people, mingle. Have one-night stands," she waggled her eyebrows at Rachael suggestively and Rachael laughed.

"Oh my god, I don't know about *that*, but yes, date, mingle, those things for sure. But I also don't want to hurt Drake," she sighed miserably.

"I will handle Drake," Ember declared. "And I will take you out tonight. Girls" night out to meet and maybe make out with, since a one-night stand is off the table, a man." She paused and then added, "or maybe woman?"

Rachael gaped for a second. "Um, I don't think so?" she said hesitantly.

"That is not a no," Ember laughed. "An open mind is a fun mind. Excellent, I will pick you up at seven for dinner, drinks after. No, I will be here at six to help you get ready," she said, changing her plans mid-way, looking Rachael up and down. "We will find your style and work it tonight."

Rachael blushed and agreed. "Six then. Thank you, Ember."

A girls' night! As Ember left and Rachael finished cleaning up lunch, she felt the excitement and anticipation build. Oh, this would be fun! And maybe, just maybe, she could put away the fear and doubt she had.

GIRLS NIGHT OUT

"You don't think this is too revealing?" Rachael stared at herself in the bathroom mirror, or more accurately, at the expanse of white cleavage that spilled from the top of her blouse.

Ember shook her head. "You are just busty, the blouse isn't cut too low, your nipples are well hidden, but it looks scandalous because your chest is so large. You got 'em, flaunt 'em."

Rachael gave a breathy laugh, too nervous to really rock that energy. The shirt was emerald green and cropped shorter than was her wont, stopping just above her waist, with a deep v-neck that really did draw attention to her cleavage. Her black jean shorts were tight and *short*, stopping below her ass, but only just. She wasn't sure how she was supposed to sit or bend over. Under the shorts she wore black tights woven with a pattern of climbing vines interspersed with deep red roses. On her feet were strappy gold sandals, flaunting red painted toes, courtesy of Ember. Rachael found herself constantly tugging down her shirt, trying to cover her stomach and hips, only to become annoyed at herself and smooth it back into shape.

"Hold still, we're going to fix your lipstick." Ember had shown her several tips and tricks with the make-up that Rachael was sure she would forget as soon as she left the apartment, but they made her face look amazing. Her eyes looked bigger and her mouth was just sinful. What could Ember possibly need to fix?! Ember did something with a pencil and her lips now looked thicker than before.

"It's magic, right?" Rachael asked, staring at her reflection.

Ember laughed. "No, just shading. I think you're ready. The lipstick won't come off, even when you eat, but you will have to use that make-up remover to get it off. Let's go! I'm starving."

Ember was wearing a red button-down shirt that was one size too small and opened several buttons. It was tucked into a pair of blue jeans that Rachael swore must have been sewn on her, they were so tight; she didn't know how she could sit in them. Her make up was dazzling, her eyeshadow shades of red and her mouth glossy. Her brown skin sparkled with glitter, thanks to some sort of lotion she used, and her tattoos merely added to her beauty. Even done up and given approval, Rachael was sure no one would pay her any mind standing next to Ember.

Woodstock's Pizza had been in Davis for as long as people could remember. College students had been coming there for pizza and beer for decades now and the smell of hops and melted cheese and pepperoni filled the air, accompanied by the raucous laughter of its patrons. It was everything one wanted in an old-fashioned pizza joint—pizza pans on the wall to indicate size, wooden booths, green tables, sticky green tile floors, and pizza that was absolutely to die for.

Ember went to order and Rachael snagged a booth, sliding in just as the previous party was leaving. She hastily gathered every-thing for the server or busser, whoever got there first, and placed it at the end of the table. Settling in, she eyed the crowd. Most were definitely college kids—younger than her, and grouped together, but obviously on the prowl. Groups of friends clustered around, laughing and joking; every once in a while, one person would break off to go speak with someone else who had grabbed their interest. These couples would speak for a minute, and then break off, heading back to their home groups. Scanning, she saw some older people, some her age, some a little older. They stood out from the college crowd by their stillness. They stood and chatted, but their eyes moved, looking for others who might catch them.

"Pizza is coming! Here, I got some beer," Ember slid in across from her, handing her a giant mug of beer, expertly poured. Rachael wrinkled her nose. Beer wasn't her favorite, but when in Rome . . . She slid over her half of the pizza money in exchange for the beer.

"Thank you," she said loudly, over the music playing. There was a jukebox in the corner and she was curious what songs were in it. Sheltered as she had been, she was still learning what music she had missed and found that she loved listening to everything.

"Who were you looking at?" Ember asked, eyebrows raised.

Rachael shook her head helplessly. "No one. But I think you need to teach me more about the type of magical beings there are because that person over there has *fangs* and the whole drinking blood thing doesn't do it for me."

Ember laughed. "I don't think we have vampires, but don't hold me to it. Some people have been born with fae-like body types—long and tall and beautiful, but also fanged. They can have magic and sometimes are impossible to kill except by beheading or extreme injury. And I do mean extreme. Violet eyes are also common with fae-born. I heard they are also extremely talented in the bedroom, any gender, and I highly recommend you find one and if you do, tell me if that rumor is true."

"Ember, honestly!" Rachael laughed. "I am not out here just to get laid!" Although, it had been a long time since that schoolhouse disappointment, and Drake's kiss had ignited something she didn't even know had gone out.

"Now, that fellow over there," Ember nodded her head discretely to a very large man, tall, long hair and bearded. "He bred true to the Norse blood. He could cut his hair and trim his beard, but it would be just like that again in a few days. Tall, burly, hairy, and very, very strong with a tendency toward blood lust and berserker rage." Ember eyed him. "I would climb him like a tree," she mused, running a finger around the rim of her beer mug.

"Er," Rachael, made a noise indicating reluctant agreement, although for her blood lust and berserker rage were not high on the list for desired sexual partners. But then, she was far more fragile than a Shifter.

"So, there are Fae and Vikings," she recapped. "And I saw something with wings flying around last night."

Ember turned back towards her, eyes very interested. "Flying?! As in had wings and it went flap flap? And it was a person?"

Rachael shrugged. "I couldn't make out if it was a person or an actual entirely mystical being, but it was absolutely going flap flap."

"Huh, I'll keep an eye out. I have no idea." She turned back to the tall, bearded man, who was now returning her look with interest. "Excuse me for a minute?" And she slid out of the booth, going to make her move.

Chuckling to herself, she watched bubbles in her beer, only to startle when someone sat in the booth across from her. "Drake!

What . . ?"

"I know, girls night out," he said, holding up his hands defensively. "But you owe me a conversation." He looked at her, not angry, but definitely not calm either.

She sighed. He was right, she did. "I . . . Drake, how many girlfriends have you had?"

He sat back, startled. "I don't know, several?" He frowned. "Is it important to you? The number?"

"No, but I have had one and that one a secret because if my parents had known I would have been . . ." she shuddered. "Well, it would have been bad." Drake reached for her and she let him take her hand. "I want to live a little. I want to be free for just a while." She smiled at him. "I know where you live and I assure you, I won't forget. But . . ."

"I understand." He squeezed her hand and nodded. "I do. It's difficult for me, but I have no claim on you. As you said, you are free. I hope you find what you are looking for, Rachael." His jaw was tight, but he smiled at her, his hand gentle. "I can't watch you do it though. So, for now, good night." And he kissed her hand, maintaining eye contact as his lips touched her skin.

"Oh!" Honestly, that had no right to be so sexy—it was just a chaste kiss on the hand—but the look in his eyes as he did it made it something more. Was it warmer in here all of a sudden? "Thank you, Drake," she said, realizing her voice was huskier, but unable to do anything about it.

He gave her a grin and slid out of the booth, weaving in and out of the crowd with ease, and she sat there wondering if she really needed to do this dating thing. She looked for Ember and found her making her way back from the Norse guy, a big grin on her face. Seems it went well for her.

"Okay! Pizza is on its way! Just saw it zooming over here . . ." sure enough, a large pepperoni pizza was set on the table before them with plates and napkins before she could finish. "Yum!"

Shifter bodies needed more energy and while Rachael could eat several slices, Ember ate most of the pizza herself, humming happily after every bite. Rachael sat there grinning, enjoying her friend's happiness, sipping on her beer, and doing more people watching. Several people were watching her back, and she tossed her hair with a grin, pulling off a pepperoni. Nothing like some appreciation for a self-confidence a boost.

"Having fun?" Ember grinned back at her. "Almost done here, next stop? It's ALL fun." Ember winked, and Rachael had no idea what that could possibly mean.

The Wunderbar was as close to a club that Davis offered and was across the street from Woodstock's. "Club" was probably way too inaccurate; it was a bar, but it was also darker and louder and where most of the hookups for the young and looking population of Davis took place. To Rachael, who had never been in a bar, it felt like walking into a den of sin. That might have made her feel guilty once, but tonight, with Ember there, she just felt *normal,* if a little naughty.

"Okay, Rachael, shots!" Ember set down two shot glasses full of clear liquid. "One shot now, and then some water. First lesson of drinking," she said, pushing one shot glass over to Rachael. "Don't do it too fast. Actually, scratch that, that's the second lesson. First lesson is never take a drink from a stranger or someone you don't trust absolutely."

Rachael lifted the shot glass, and they toasted each other. "Bottom's up," she said. She upended the glass into her mouth and tried to swallow the entirety of the burning liquid and ended up coughing.

Ember laughed. "The first one is always like that. Okay! Come on!" and she towed Rachael to the dance floor, which was crowded with people.

"I don't know how to dance!" Rachael said, panicked, staring at the gyrating and laughing people around her.

"No one does!" Ember yelled back, humor dancing in her eyes. "Just move your hips to the music and raise up your hands. That's it!"

The alcohol started to seep into her veins, and she loosened up. A woman, fae-born by the look of her, started dancing with her, placing her hands on Rachael's hips. Ember was at her back dancing with a short, voluptuous very feminine black woman who wore her hair in large twists. It was hard to tell where Ember ended and the other woman began.

"Your hair is gorgeous," the fae-woman said in Rachael's ear, her breath sending shivers down her body, her lips almost close enough to touch her. Ember's question from the night before rang through her mind, *"or woman?"*

"What's your name, lovely?" Fae-woman asked, her hands sliding around to her ass, her fingers skimming the short hem of her shorts. "I'm Scarlett."

Rachael stared, spellbound into violet eyes that glowed from a face made of ebony skin. Tight braids ran down her shoulders, beads clacking as they danced. "I'm Rachael."

"Find me later, Rachael, if you're interested." Scarlett leaned into her, pulling her with the music. "I am *very* interested."

Before she could respond, the song ended, and the woman turned to a new partner, and a man took her place. Tall, white, with a beard, he didn't hesitate before placing his hands on her hips and pulling her close. They were close in height, he being only a few inches taller than her, and their eyes were nearly level. She put her hands on his shoulders, enjoying their breadth, and he grinned at her before suddenly spinning her so that she was pressed against his chest, her ass on his very erect penis. She gasped at his audacity, but was drunk enough to continue dancing, one hand rising up to cup his neck as she ground back against him.

He groaned into her neck and she felt herself getting wet. This was so outside of her experience, so forbidden! Spinning her again, he looked into her face and then they were kissing. It was hot and frantic and surrounded by the bass of music, and Rachael let herself be lost for just a moment. Then the song changed to a slower beat, and she pulled back. He looked at her, his eyes dark with lust, and she shook her head, panic rising. She didn't even know his name!

A rueful smile passed over his lips as he turned to find another partner and Rachael went to find Ember. She was obviously drunker than she thought she was. Kissing strangers on a dance floor?!

"Whew, girl! Who was that?" Ember grinned at her, impressed.

"I don't know." Rachel stared at Ember, appalled at herself. "I didn't even ask his name!"

"Hon, you are a quick study." Instead of chastising her, as Rachael had half expected, Ember merely craned her neck and followed Rachael's admirer as he moved through the dance floor. "I am thoroughly jealous. That was some fucking kiss! This whole club should be on fire!"

It really had been. Rachel's lips felt swollen and her whole body was achy and needy. She turned to find mystery man, but instead saw a pair of piercing blue eyes staring back at her from across the room. Drake, at a table with several other men, his face like granite. Her body swayed toward him, as if pulled by some invisible force.

"Come on, let's get some water," Ember's voice cut through her reverie and she startled, breaking eye contact with Drake. Ember had missed the entire exchange, it having lasted mere seconds, but Rachael would never forget the intensity of those blue eyes.

Soon they were sipping water from bottles purchased at the bar. Ember had secured the phone number of the woman she had been dancing with and who was watching them from a position at the bar where she was with a group of friends.

Rachael nudged Ember. "Holy shit, she's amazing."

Ember laughed but seemed very proud of herself. "Have you decided to get Mystery Man's number? I won't go anywhere until you're settled, one way or another."

"No, I'm just-" she cut off as an arm was slung around her shoulders.

"Well, well, look who's here?" Zakaria looked down at her, smirking, blue eyes dark.

Rachael's skin tried to crawl off her body. How dare he touch her? "Get off of me, Zakaria," she lifted his wrist and twisted out from under his arm, moving to stand next to Ember in the same move.

"Ah, I see. Are you together then? That explains a lot," Zakaria shook his head .

"Stop. Talking. Asshole." Ember spat at him. Her blue eyes had turned golden and shone brightly in the dim lighting.

"Tsk tsk. Temper, temper." He turned to Rachael, leaning forward. She leaned back in response, uncaring if he noticed. She didn't want to be anywhere near him. "Magic makes people, unstable; you know this. I am sure it's . . .thrilling in private," Rachael gasped at his audacity, but then, decided she was tired of dancing to his tune.

Rachael smiled slowly and inched closer slightly. "Go away," she said, flicking her fingers as if he were an insect. "You are boring me." His face reddened. Rachael noticed he really didn't like it when she talked back to him. Was it her, or women in general?

He stood up straight, looking down his nose at her. "When you get into trouble, don't come crawling to me then!"

Ember and Rachael burst out laughing as he walked away. They could see him tense; he didn't like that at all.

"Mom is kicking him out at the end of the week. Something about it's not legal to just make someone homeless." Ember's eyes were still golden as they followed him moving toward a girl who couldn't be more than twenty-one. "Personally, I'd like to cut his dick off and make him eat it."

Rachael saw no problem with this course of action at all. The girl tittered at something Zakaria said, and Rachael's jaw clenched. "I am going to-" but before she could finish the thought, Drake was there, his arm around the girl's waist, smiling at her and whispering in her ear. The girl was a horrible actor and was visibly confused, but she turned and said goodbye to Zakaria, who was glaring daggers at Drake. Drake saluted him and took the girl off, handing her to her friends, and saying something to them. The girl turned her body into Drake's, whispering up at him, the invitation very clear.

Rachael cleared her throat, unexpected jealousy rising.

"Shit," she said, in chagrin.

Ember nudged her. "Stop staring. Unless you've decided to take *him* home."

Rachael tore her eyes away, but not before Drake looked up and met her eyes, a questioning eyebrow rising at her look.

"SHIT."

"Girl, we have got to find someone to distract you." Ember shook her head sadly. "You are acting absolutely twitterpated."

"*Twitterpated*?" Rachael collapsed into giggles. "Twitterpated. Oh, my God." She stumbled. While they had been distracted, someone had come up behind her, and he slung an arm around her waist.

"Careful there. Up you go."

Rachael looked up into a pair of laughing brown eyes. "Thank you," she said, breathlessly, still fighting the occasional giggle.

"For what?" He smiled at her, apparently serious, and she snorted.

She shook her head at him. "You know what! It was probably just an excuse to get within touching distance."

"You wound me! Straight in the heart!"

"Oh. My. God." She laughed. "You did not just say that."

"But I did! It hurts me that you doubt me." He tucked her hair behind her ear. She looked at him, so close to her; she leaned in, face tipped up, his lips brushed hers. His hand slid down her arms with the lightest touch and she pulled back, opening her mouth to ask if he wanted a drink.

"Rachael." Drake was there suddenly, and she frowned at him. She heard Ember calling her name loudly behind her, but it was like she was underwater or behind very thick glass. It was very far away and unimportant.

"What are you doing here? I thought I told you I needed some space?" Rachael couldn't believe what she was seeing. He had promised. How dare he interfere! He had no right!

"No, Rachael, this isn't that. This guy isn't what he seems. He's not . . ."

Rachael turned to look at the guy. His blue eyes were kind. *Wait,* she thought, *I thought his eyes were brown?* "What the hell?" She asked loudly, jumping back.

Zakaria smirked at her.

Bile rose in her throat. She had *kissed* him. Her legs backpedalled so fast she almost fell. Ember caught her; Drake was there between them, and his eyes were black. Their faces were fraught with confusion and anger. Up until now, there had been no sign that Zakaria had any kind of magic skill. Rachael couldn't get enough air.

Zakaria alone seemed completely nonchalant. "Magic, it really is a bitch. You see how it can fool you? And don't you have it, Rachael? Aren't you gifted in someway?"

She was, she thought frantically. *Why hadn't she been able to sense the glamor he'd used?* The panic was clawing at her now and all she wanted was to run. So close. She had been so close to going home with him.

"Breathe, Rachael," Ember's voice was low, for her ears only. "In and out, slowly. You're hyperventilating. If you don't calm down, you will pass out."

And all the while Zakaria stood there smirking. He was right, magic wasn't trustworthy. She couldn't trust herself anymore than she could trust him. She hadn't even sensed a simple glamor when she was *touching* him.

"Take me home, now." She turned, and Ember shared a look with Drake, but followed. "Rachael . . ."

"No. Now." They didn't speak on the ride home. Rachael was shaking and Ember could sense that she wasn't ready to talk yet. At Primero Grove, Ember went to walk her to her apartment, but Rachael stopped her. "No. I just . . . No. Go home, Ember. Thank you for taking me out tonight." Her words were wooden, all emotions locked away.

"Rachael, please, let me stay with you tonight. I don't think you should be alone."

"I'm fine." And Rachael left her there, locked her door and then racing to the bathroom where she stared at her reflection. What had she been thinking? Starting the shower, she scrubbed herself in the scalding water, finally letting the tears flow, great gulping sobs, as she washed the feeling of his hands off her body.

"*Oh, God,*" she thought to herself that night in bed. "*What am I going to do? Who am I here?*"

THE BREAKING

The next morning Rachael woke feeling heavy. Her brain didn't want to work right, and everything seemed far away or muffled, like she was watching it from the other side of a piece of glass. Her body felt sore even though she knew nothing had happened to her physically, but maybe the dancing had been more than she thought.

Pouring herself a bowl of cereal, she stared at it, watching it float there, listening to it make tiny crackles in the milk, until it had gone quite mushy without ever eating a bite. Sighing, she cleaned it up, but she didn't remake it. She wasn't hungry and there was no point in wasting food. The fog showed no signs of lifting, and nothing held her attention for very long. She couldn't focus on anything—reading, or exercise, or even the radio. Finally, she called it a lost cause and just went to work. She had a mid-morning shift, and they were always busy at breakfast; they wouldn't mind if she came in a little early. Better to be busy than bouncing around like a bee in a bottle.

The restaurant was packed, and Rachael was welcomed enthusiastically. She went through her work automatically; this was familiar and required no real effort. Even the responses to the customers required little thinking. Mr. Barlett frowned at her a little and asked if she was okay, but she assured him she was. He just grumbled at her and disappeared into his office muttering about a phone call.

And then, an hour into her shift, Zakaria walked in. Her breath whooshed out of her lungs and she fled into the kitchens. *I can do this,* she said to herself. *He's not in my section. I just have to do my job and ignore him. I can* DO *this.* So, out she went, taking orders and dropping off others, all the while feeling his eyes on her the entire time. Cracks started forming around the edges of the glass she was watching the world behind, and little noises were beginning to startle her. Another server asked her something, and she snapped at them, making her feel guilty.

She took a break and stood in the bathroom, trying to breathe, to relax. She didn't know what the matter with her was, but this couldn't continue. She needed to pull it together. Washing her hands, she splashed cold water on her face, and then opened the door only to practically walk directly into Drake Archer.

"God damn it, Drake, what the fuck are you doing here?" Her stress was clear in her language, and she just couldn't take any more surprises. And how DARE he show up at her JOB?! "Are you stalking me now? How did you know I was here?"

"I was worried about you? I am not stalking you," Drake backed up, hands up, like she was an injured animal, and it just enraged her more. Before he could say anything else, she planted both hands on his chest and shoved.

"Go. Away!" And she pushed past him, only to career into a server carrying a full tray of food. It went crashing to the ground, plates breaking in a clatter and Rachael's mind shattered, skipping, the breaking of ceramic suddenly sounding like applause, the laughter and cheers from the patrons in the restaurant became jeers and booing. Suddenly, she was no longer in Davis, but four hundred miles away and several months earlier.

"Look upon the face of the devil and tremble!" Father David hauled her up on the dais, holding her arm tightly, shaking her. The crowd below cried out, as if on cue. "Evil has hidden amongst us, sly as a serpent, waiting to bite the unwary!" He shook her again for good measure, his fingers biting her skin and making her cry out in pain. "See how she shies away from me, a Holy man? See how she fears me?"

"Stop hurting me," thought Rachael, "and maybe I'll stop trying to get away. Besides, who isn't scared at their own execution?"

"What has she done?" Rachael sought out the voice and found her father standing there, arms crossed, face impassive.

"She has magic!" Hollered Father David, so the entire crowd could hear. Rachael closed her eyes at the pronouncement; there was no going back now. The crowd murmured, and some hissed at her. Others made a sign against evil. One mother picked up her child and backed away, as if magic were catching.

"Impossible! I would have known!" Her father stood for her against the tide, and Rachael felt a thread of hope grow in her chest. Maybe . . . maybe he could do this . . .

"She fooled even you!" Father David shoved Rachael down to her knees, and she screamed involuntarily as she fell, landing with a thud, her knees aching. "I have seen it for myself, with my own eyes!" He grabbed her hair, yanking her head back, causing tears to pop

into her eyes. He leaned down and whispered in her ear. "Shine for them, witch!"

But somehow, after twenty-five years of obedience, today was the day she decided to disobey. Today was where she drew the line in the sand. And with twenty-five years of practice at hiding her magic, she was very, very good at it. "No."

Father David snarled and hauled her up again, grabbing her wrists in a crushing grip that caused her bones to grind together. He raised them over her head and slipped them through a rope that was hung from a pole in the middle of the stage—the whipping post. Someone else tightened it, so that she was pulled taut and Father David came to stand in front of her, grabbing her chin and forcing her face up to look at his face.

"I will not be brought low by a fucking magic user," he said, his eyes full of rage. He smiled slowly. "Before I am done, you will beg me for the whip. Tell me, when has your father last seen your breasts?" His eyes dipped down and he stared at her breasts, pressed hard against her shirt due to her current position.

Rachael gasped at the wrongness of his words and tried to back up at the look in his eyes, but couldn't move. His eyes slowly climbed back to her face, and he grinned at what he saw there. "Oh yes, I am going to tear that shirt off and bare you to the world. Can't whip you with your shirt on, can I?"

"You can, actually," Rachael replied.

He just shook his head, grabbed her shirt and tore it in two. It hung there, leaving her covered, but barely, and he moved behind her giving her a glimpse of the crowd. They were staring, silent, and her father, oh God, her father was right there in front.

Father David whispered behind her. "They love it, you know. They love these whippings. So many go home and fuck afterward, turned on by the nakedness and the blood." He pressed against her, leaving her in no doubt where he stood on the matter.

"Well, fuck," thought Rachael. She could remain stubborn and push it, get whipped and humiliated, or drop her shields and endure the consequences. It was really no question. If it was drop her shields or sexual assault by Father David . . .

Her shields fell all at once, and her skin, hair, and eyes immediately began to glow. The crowd cried out as one and took a step back, but Rachael only had eyes for her father. He looked at her for one moment, but then he turned and walked away.

He walked away.

"See! Women are the original secret keepers, the original sinners! They will bring all men low!"

"Oh, shove it, you pervert," Rachael said. It was over now; she had nothing to lose, nothing to protect. No reason to remain submissive and respectful. Every second of pretense and illusion, each moment of trying to fit in and belong was now pointless. She might as well die her true self.

"Hear her lack of respect!" The crowd booed and stamped its feet. Something sailed by her head. The rope holding her was lowered and her hands freed, only to be captured once again by Father David. "Here she stands, guilty of possessing magic! What is the penalty of such a crime!"

"Death!" The crowd roared as one, blood lust rising.

"DEATH!" Echoed Father David. Rachael looked out at the people who had an hour ago claimed to be her friends. Their faces now held disgust, hatred, and betrayal. There was no forgiveness or love or acceptance; wasn't that also preached from this pulpit once a week?

Sadness and rage warred with each other for dominance; fear didn't even stand a chance amidst the mix of emotions. "Rachael Lillian Knight, I sentence you to death by fire, to be carried out tomorrow at sundown."

Fire. Burning. He walked away.

Someone took her hands and tied them, but she wasn't paying attention. They took her to the shed they used to house people who broke the laws of the compound; she followed blindly, dimly aware as she approached the windowless building that someone was calling her name.

"Rachael! Rachael!

"Rachael!" Drake was in front of her, carefully not touching her, but also close enough to grab her if he needed to.

Rachael blinked and gasped, coming back to the present with a shuddering breath. She looked around, realizing it was eerily quiet, and then saw that a lot of people were looking at her, and that Drake and been calling her name for some time. "Oh God." Embarrassment flooded her, and she backed away, bringing her hands up.

"Rachael," Drake said softly. "It's okay. Really, let me take you-"

"NO!" She couldn't. She didn't. She wasn't. Her brain couldn't form thoughts yet except no. No. NO. She gave Drake a wild look, not realizing tears were rolling down her face or that her arms were wrapped around herself, and then ran.

"Rachael!" She heard him calling her, but she couldn't stop. Her body just ran. She had to get away. There were too many people, too many feelings, too many everything. She had no destination in mind, no plan or goal; she just ran. The hot outside air slapped her face, and she shoved by people as she ran; angry voices raised behind her, a concerned woman called after her. She kept running, buildings flying past, through the campus, down the quad, around lecture halls, until her lungs ached and her legs slowed and stopped.

"Where am I," she wondered, bent over and trying to breathe. Wherever it was, it was quiet, no cars or bikes here, just scattered people walking down pathways. Finally, she stood up and looked around, spotting a sign up ahead. Groaning, she dragged her legs forward—they didn't want to move at first—and walked over to it.

"Davis Arboretum," she read. The sign explained several native plants in the area. She took a deep breath. This was perfect.

She started strolling down the pathway, enjoying the quiet, looking at the plants on either side, and smiling at the occasional lizard she startled at its sunbathing. There was a river nearby, and its quiet rush was soothing. After the constant buzz of her brain all morning, this quiet peace was so wonderful. She wasn't ready to think about what had happened back at the Black Bear Diner so she didn't, instead focusing on just existing here. She couldn't really stop crying yet, and her brain kept bringing up snippets of the flashback she'd had, so she just kept walking. Eventually, she came to a grove of redwood trees, and she stopped in awe. The giant trees rose up around her, larger than any tree she had ever seen, the lowest branches starting higher than the top of some trees. The wind blew through them with a haunting sound that was oddly peaceful, and she felt a bit of the tension she had been carrying ebb away. She walked over to one, stared at the reddish brown bark, and touched it, as if doubting it was real. But it was there. The giant existed, and she bent her head right back and stared straight up toward the top, amazed that a living thing could grow so tall.

The needles that had fallen from their branches carpeted the ground, except for the pathways, which must be maintained. She walked through the small grove and found a bench, settling herself on it, taking a deep breath.

"Rachael?" A voice called softly from behind her and she closed her eyes. Diana had found her, somehow. "Rachael, I know you're here. Please, just let me know you're okay."

Guilt flooded her, and Rachael sighed. "I'm over here."

Soft footsteps moved in her direction and Diana appeared around the corner, blonde hair in a hasty ponytail and wearing an apron covered in old dye stains. Her white hands were also colorful, a deep blue stain dotting the skin. She had interrupted her dying work to come here. "There you are," she said, relief filling her voice. "Oh dear girl, I'm so glad to see you." Her eyes raked over Rachael, taking in her flushed, sweaty face and crying eyes, but didn't comment on her appearance.

"How did you even know what was going on?" Rachael asked. A flutter of heavy wings above drew her attention, and both women looked up at the large raven that had landed on one of the branches. Rachael shook her head, understanding. "Oh, of course. Hi, Drake," she called up, waving.

"Please don't be angry with him," Diana asked, standing next to Rachael now. "Can I sit with you?" And then she waited.

Rachael nodded, and Diana sat.

"I feel like a fool. I'm so embarrassed." Rachael said, tears once again forming. Diana looked up and made a shooing motion and Drake took off, giving them privacy.

"Oh, love," Diana said softly, reaching up slowly to gently brush Rachael's hair off of her face. "I know."

And suddenly Rachael flung herself into Diana's arms, sobbing. Diana held her and murmured gentle soothing words to her, rocking her gently, just letting her cry. And when she stopped crying, just let her stay there as long as she needed and didn't press her or ask her questions. Her arms were so comforting, her soft body radiating a calm aura that Rachael soaked in like parched Earth.

"Thank you," she said, the words muffled.

"Do you want to talk about it?" Diana asked, not loosening her grip until Rachael pulled away, wiping her cheeks. "Don't wipe your nose on your sleeve, dear, here." And Diana pulled out a tissue from her apron, making Rachael smile. It was such a mom-like thing to do.

"I just . . . I don't know what happened, really. Everything got to be too much all at once." She blew her nose and sighed.

Diana nodded. "Drake said you had a panic attack. And he told me what happened at the bar last night with Zakaria."

Rachael felt her face turn red. "Oh God, he *told* you?"

"There is nothing to be embarrassed about. None of that was your fault." Diana said firmly. "Do you understand me? It was not your fault."

Rachael nodded. "I know. It wasn't what he *did* that made me freak out. It was . . . it was *everything* that he said and did over the last few days." She tried to find the words to explain, but Diana surprised her.

"Let me ask you a question," Diana requested. Rachael nodded. "You've been raised your whole life that magic is evil. You have hidden this wonderful gift you have inside of you for as long as you've known about it. On top of that, you were raised in a conservative culture that told you your body was precious and something to be guarded or you were dirty. Am I wrong so far?"

Rachael shook her head silently.

Diana nodded, holding Rachael's hand and stroking the back of it with her thumb. "Your magic is a part of you. It makes you, you. It's not good or evil, it just *is*. It seems to me Zakaria triggered your brain into thinking that you were evil, the asshole. And on purpose, for some reason. And *that* is truly evil."

Rachael sat there, stunned. "How do you know all this?"

She reached out and wrapped an arm around Rachael, pulling her in for a hug. "I have worked with a lot of people, I have seen a lot of things, and I am a mother. I also watch and listen a lot because my kids are grown and don't tell me everything anymore."

Rachael laughed.

Diana rested her head on Rachael's. "Your body is yours to give to whoever you choose and your magic is yours to use as you will. Be proud of both. Forgive yourself for having them. You are beautiful and kind. You moved four hundred miles away from everything you know to a community unlike anything you know. It's only been a few months. Give yourself some grace."

"Why are all of you so kind to me?" Rachael whispered.

Diana chuckled. "You draw people to you. Twenty-six years ago, this program of mine drew in so many more people. That building you live in? It was full. Entire families were fleeing persecution and violence. We were not the only safety net, of course, but we had our fair share of magical refugees come through here. Some carried their internal biases so deeply they could not adjust and returned to their homes. Some moved on to cities where more people like them lived, conservative but not *too* conservative. But you? Somehow, you *see* people. You see their humanity and you're willing to learn. That is a rare skill and one I value."

Rachael was uncomfortable with the praise, knowing she was unworthy of it, but nodded. She couldn't stand losing the Archer family. Diana was more a mother to her than her own had been, somehow, and even as fast as it had happened, she knew a relationship with Drake was inevitable.

Drake. Rachael groaned, sitting up and burying her face in her hands. "Oh, God, Drake. What am I going to say to him?"

Diana shook her head. "The truth. He's just worried about you, that's all."

A bobcat emerged from the trees, and both women greeted it.

"Your escort home is here, I see," Diana said, rising. "Now, I expect you at my house for dinner this weekend. No excuses. If you're working, then breakfast. I will not take no for an answer."

"Yes, ma'am," Rachael said, smiling and standing, to give her one more hug. "And thank you."

"Forgive yourself, Rachael. I can't even remember what it is you were supposed to have done." And with that parting shot straight to the heart, Diana left, walking down the path toward a parking lot.

She started walking slowly towards home and the bobcat rose and stretched and then trotted behind her. Drake took off from a tree down the way, flying back toward the Ranch. Her apartment wasn't far, really, cutting across campus, and she was home sooner than she expected.

Opening the outside doorway, she saw that Zakaria had propped his door open, an obvious play to hear her when she came in. Sure enough, he came out and leaned lazily against his doorjamb as she unlocked her own door. Ember hissed at him.

"Down, kitty," he said, tsking. "It's not polite to hiss at people."

"It's not polite to stalk people, glamor yourself, or sexually assault people either, and yet, there you stand," Rachael said calmly, opening her door.

Zakaria stood upright, all appearances of laziness gone. "You threw yourself at me. There was no assault. You wanted it."

Rachael dropped her shields, her shimmering skin and hair filling the hallway. Zakaria narrowed his eyes. "Stay away from me and stay away from my friends."

"Usually there is an 'or else' added to threats. You aren't doing it right." Zakaria said, smirking.

Rachael smiled, slowly looking him up and down, and then she laughed. "I think I'm doing it just right, Zakaria." And with that, she and Ember entered her apartment and she locked her door.

HEALING

E mber slept on her couch that night. They talked about how weird and creepy it was the Zakaria had hidden his magic and that Rachael couldn't feel it at all.

"That was part of why I spiraled so badly, I think," Rachael said. "I already have problems trusting magic and then this happens. I can't even trust my *own*." She shook her head. "It didn't help that you and Drake could see through the glamor so easily and I couldn't."

"Oh, no, that's just how a lot of glamor works," Ember assured her. "Unless you are directly impacted by the magic itself, you don't see it. He was directly targeting *you* last night. Everyone else could see exactly who he was. Zakaria could have applied the glamor to his body and fooled everyone, but he didn't. Different rules apply."

Rachael stared at her. "What an asshole!"

The next morning, Ember refused to leave until Rachael agreed to talk to Drake.

"It's just so damn embarrassing," Rachael sighed.

"I don't care. You scared the shit out of him, and he deserves an explanation. I deserve one too, but I can see you're doing better, so I can wait." Ember was wearing a borrowed robe and eating pancakes, scowling at her between bites.

"I'm sorry. I never should have gone to work, but I have never felt like that before and I thought keeping busy was the best way to handle it. I was exceptionally wrong." Rachael turned off the stove and poured syrup on her own plate of pancakes.

"Felt like what?"

Rachael stared at the syrup flowing down the fluffy cakes and sighed. "Like breaking. Fragile." She looked up and shrugged. "Everything Zakaria said to me, everything he did, broke something in me. It was like . . ." She shook her head. "I don't even know how to explain it."

Ember swallowed. "Hmph. Let me go claw him up a little. He's too pretty, anyway."

Rachael laughed. "That's true, but then they'd arrest you, and where would you be?"

"In jail, but happy," Ember replied immediately.

Rachael laughed again, but sobered at the knock on the door. "Shit, he's here already. That was fast."

"I told you he was worried." Ember kept eating, not concerned in the least.

Rachael went to answer the door, opening it at the same time that Zakaria opened his. "Zakaria, go inside."

Zakaria looked between Drake and Rachael. "A little early for a booty call, isn't it?" His voice was dripping with derision and his eyes scraped over Rachael from head to toe.

"Shut the fuck up, you ass." Drake said, his voice calm, but he shoved Zakaria back into his apartment and slammed his door shut. He strode back over to Rachael. "I really hate that guy." He said to her.

Rachael, realizing her jaw had dropped, snapped it shut, and nodded. "Same. Come on in." She moved back and let him into the apartment.

Ember nodded hello, rinsed her plate, and then got ready to leave. "You both have things to figure out. Rachael, I expect a phone call and a detailed explanation, you hear?"

"Yes, ma'am." She hugged Ember, hard. "Thank you for staying with me. I'll call you later."

"Drake, be nice, and eat some pancakes. They're good." And with that, she went into the bedroom and shifted into her bobcat. Drake opened the door, went and opened the outside door, and then came back.

They both stood there for a minute awkwardly. "Um, pancakes?" Rachael asked, holding up a platter.

Drake raised an eyebrow but nodded. They sat at the bar, eating silently, but after a few minutes Drake reached over and put his hand on her knee, gently rubbing her leg in a soothing fashion, as if to remind her that he was her friend. Rachael put her hand over his and gripped it, tight.

He helped her do the dishes, the silence now not quite so scary and tense, and then they moved to the couch, facing each other, so close their knees almost touched.

"Drake, I am so sorry," Rachael said, sighing.

Drake sat up. "What? What the fuck for?"

Rachael frowned at him. "What do you mean, what for? I . . . I yelled at you, shoved you, told you to leave me alone. In public no less! I was awful to you!"

Drake took both her hands in his and turned her so that she was directly facing him, and she was forced to look at him square in his face. "Are you under the impression that I am angry at you?"

Rachael blinked. This was not how this conversation was supposed to go. "Yes?"

Drake shook his head. "No, I am not angry at you." He squeezed her hands. "Rachael, you had one of the worst panic attacks I have ever seen, and I think you had a flashback in the middle of the Black Bear. I have been worried *sick* about you, not angry."

Now, why did that make her want to cry? She had been prepared for his anger and here he was telling her he was *worried*? "Oh." Her voice was small.

She didn't know what he saw in her face, but he made a noise and pulled her into him, hugging her to his chest, and stroking a hand down her hair. "Nothing you did yesterday requires an apology, Rachael. You were hurting." She brought her hands up and clung to him as if he were tying her to the Earth. "I wish you had let me take care of you, but even that you don't have to apologize for. You needed to handle it your way, and you did." His hand never stopped stroking, and his voice was so soothing. And his magic, dear lord, his magic was so calming. Her shields lowered and she let it move over her skin. His breath hitched a bit as her magic hit him, but he didn't stop holding her, or soothing her.

"Thank you for listening to me," she said, her voice muffled from speaking into his chest. "Although, how did you know I was there? I wasn't supposed to be working."

"Mr. Barlett called me. He was worried about you, too."

Now she really felt like an asshole. "Oh God, and I called you a stalker."

Drake chuckled, his chest vibrating. "You did, but it's okay."

She sat up a little, looking up at him, his face inches from hers.

"It's not, but thank you for saying it is."

Drake ran his thumb across her jaw, his eyes taking in her glowing skin and eyes. "Your magic is beautiful, Rachael. It just lights you up, like your personality is finally able to break through."

Rachael fought the urge to shrug off the compliment, uncomfortable. Insults were easy; compliments were not.

He huffed out a soft laugh and tucked some hair behind her ear. "It's true. Say,'thank you.'"

Rachael snorted, but smiled. "Thank you."

Drake slipped a hand behind her head, his fingers threading through her hair, holding her there while he looked at her. "I have been thinking about you for days. Wondering if you were okay. I hated seeing that asshat's hands on you." He took a deep breath. "And that was after watching you kiss that idiot on the dance floor."

Rachael shook her head or tried to. His hand kept her from moving much. "How do you know he's an idiot?"

"Because he let you go," Drake replied seriously. "I've been wanting to kiss you since, just to erase the feel of his lips on yours." His thumb coasted over her lips, his eyes focused on her face.

Asking permission, Rachael realized. He was asking permission, and she needed to kiss him, too. It was more than just lust; she needed to reaffirm their connection, too. To prove to herself that she hadn't broken them irrevocably. She adjusted herself into a more comfortable position, leaning on one hip, her far leg slung over his closest leg. "Okay," she breathed.

It was the opposite of the kiss in the barn; it was a reclaiming. He had watched someone else kiss her, their hands on her, and had seen her enjoy it. And then he had watched as she fell for Zakaria's surprise glamor, only to fall apart from the assault. Drake, Rachael realized, was doing his best to erase both of those men from her mind. He captured her mouth with his, his hand cupping her jaw, holding her in place, his mouth hot on hers. She made a small noise, opening her mouth and his tongue swept in. Molten heat exploded in her body, and she moaned into his mouth, returning his kiss and his fervor, her hands climbing into his hair, gripping it.

"I can't get close enough to you," she panted, straining against his side.

He groaned this time, sending shivers down her body, and his hand went to her hips and he jerked her onto his lap, never breaking the kiss. Her thin leggings were no match for the seam of his jeans which rose up over his hard erection and she couldn't help rolling herself over it, feeling like a teenager as they writhed together on her sofa. Drake pulled down on her hips, grinding upwards, and she cried out, breaking the kiss as she threw her head back. "Holy shit," she moaned, and Drake gave a soft laugh that turned into a moan as she rocked her hips again.

Looking back down, his eyes were fastened on her face, his fingers kneaded her ass; she couldn't stop moving against him. "I want to touch you, Rachael."

She panted, trying to understand what he was saying. Wasn't he already touching her?

He smiled. "I also feel like I need to ask, just so I know how to proceed here." He reached up and kissed her jaw, behind her ear, nipped her earlobe which sent a zing to her pussy and made her gasp. "Are you a virgin, Rachael?" he asked softly, nuzzling her neck, softening the question, giving her privacy if she needed it.

"Oh God, I'm a terrible kisser," she said, pulling back, instantly self-conscious.

He took her chin in his fingers so that she looked at him. "No," he said definitely. "But all I want to do is lay you down on this couch, rip off those silly leggings and fuck you until you are coming around my cock so hard they hear you screaming in San Francisco."

She just stared at him for a moment, imagining that, and then closed her eyes. "Okay." she said, rubbing against him again, feeling wetness seeping into her underwear.

"Jesus, Rachael," he groaned, dropping his head on her chest, laughing. "I don't want to hurt you."

So sweet, she thought, wrapping her arms around his neck. "No, I'm not a virgin."

"Thank God for small favors," he said, kissing her neck and back up to her mouth, where he kissed her, more gently this time.

"It's been a very long time though. And he wasn't . . . well, I didn't . . . " She ground to a halt, unused to talking about this.

Drake pulled back and said again, "I want to touch you."

Instead of answering, Rachael took off her shirt and then her bra, quickly, before she lost her nerve. Drake stared at her, hands lightly touching her thick thighs, her wide hips, and her large butt. "So fucking beautiful."

She started to shake her head. "I'm not. I'm too fat-" Remnants of Zakaria's words and years of her mother's attempts at making her smaller filled her brain and made the words fall out of her mouth before she could stop herself. She took a deep breath, reminding herself that just a few days ago she was making out with a stranger in a club where other people wanted her, too.

"Fabulous. Beautiful. Sexy. Hot as fuck." He was staring at her body like a starving man, and it was balm to her soul. He lifted a hand, but stopped, only then looking at her, waiting still for her permission. She took it and placed it on her breast, and both of them gasped, both finally feeling what they wanted.

He gently fondled her breast, plucking the nipple, and she moaned, her hips jerking. His other hand came up to do the same with the other breast, and he groaned. "God, they are fucking perfect." He leaned forward and wrapped his arms around her, lifting her, making her squeal in surprise, laying her down on the couch, and he knelt beside her.

"Drake," she whispered, missing the heat of his body.

"I'm right here, brightness. I've got you." And he lowered his mouth to suck on a nipple. She cried out, arching up.

"So, you didn't come during sex before? Do you make yourself come, Rachael?" he asked her, hands never stopping massaging her breasts, his mouth coasting down to kiss her belly.

"Yes," she groaned, arching into his hands.

Drake grinned. "Naughty," he teased, licking a nipple, and then nipping the side of one breast. "Show me how you touch your breasts when you touch yourself, Rachael. What do you like?"

Rachael looked at him, trying to decide if he was serious, but he had stopped touching her now, only stroking her stomach. "Drake, please." She whined, missing his hands on her.

He picked up her hand and placed it on her breast, but left his there, so that they were touching her together. "Together, then," he said, kissing her. "Show me, Rachael, how to please you."

She groaned and then squeezed her breasts. They had never been very sensitive and needed a lot stimuli; gentleness wasn't what she needed. At her nipples she pinched hard, groaning as the pleasure/pain shot to her pussy and Drake inhaled sharply. "You are full of surprises, brightness," he said into her mouth, before kissing her deeply. Trailing kisses down her neck, he bit her shoulder sharply, making her cry out in shock at the prick of pain, but the zing went straight to her pussy and her hips lifted in need. She felt him smile into her skin. At her breasts he sucked one nipple into his mouth, hard, and she cried out, her hands moving to his head, pressing her breast deeper into his mouth. His teeth closed around it and bit carefully. She writhed on the couch, until he let go and she cried out in protest. The other breast got the same treatment and by then she was practically incoherent with lust, her eyes glazed.

"Drake, I need . . . please!" She was convinced if he didn't touch her she was going to die.

He sat up and slid her pants down her legs, nostrils flaring at the scent of her arousal. "Damn, baby, you smell so good and you are so wet for me." He kissed the inside of her thigh and then her knee as he removed her pants. "I just want to lick you until you come all over my face."

She felt herself turn red at the thought, but her body liked that idea a lot. Still, she felt alone up here with him down by her legs and she flung her arm out, seeking, and he went back, so that she could grab him, using him as an anchor.

"I am going to touch your pussy, Rachael," he said, giving her an out if she needed it. She absolutely did not need it.

"You fucking better, Drake. Don't stop now!" The profanity once again slipping out of her mouth in her need.

Taken by surprise, he laughed. "Needy are we?" he asked, trailing a hand up her thigh. "Greedy." He kissed her breast again, reddened from his previous attention, and she panted, moving her hips to try to get his hand where she wanted it. "I like that you want me, Rachael." And he took her hand and placed it on his erection. "Feel how much I like it."

She groaned at the feel of him under his jeans and she wrapped her hand around him as much as she could.

He never broke eye contact as he unzipped his jeans and pushed them down his legs slightly. He groaned a little, happy to have his cock free from the constraining prison of his pants, and he wrapped a hand around it. Her eyes dropped to it and her whole body froze. "It's bigger than the last one," she said, staring. "Drake, I have never really touched a . . . cock before."

"Fuck I like it when you say that word," he groaned.. "You are going to touch this one. Just to play with today. I'm going to make you come, Rachael." He took her hand and wrapped it around his cock. She squeezed it, and started jerking it slowly, while he took the opportunity to cup her pussy. "God, you're so fucking wet," he told her, just running his fingers through her lips, enjoying the feel of her.

"Drake, stop teasing." The look she gave him should have incinerated him on the spot and he gave her an unrepentant grin before he slide one finger inside of her. "Oh fuck," she groaned, her head falling back.

"Don't stop now," he said, thrusting his hips, reminding her of what she was up to. She resumed stroking him, and he thrust his finger in and out slowly, and then put in a second finger. "So damn tight, Rachael," he moaned, and her hand clenched at his words. He groaned, thrusting his hips at her. She loved that he was reacting to her touch, and she tried to focus on what she was doing, but his fingers were too distracting.

She pushed her hips up, making small sounds, and he crooked his fingers slightly, sliding them in and out, looking for something. Suddenly, he hit a spot, and she jerked, her eyes flying open. "OH!"

"There it is," he said with a satisfied smile.

"There *what* is? Oh, god, Drake, that feels . . ." her hand clenched on his dick and he inhaled sharply. "Oh, sorry, I can't . . ." He rubbed his thumb over her clit now, and went back to playing with her nipples and her hand completely fell away from him, her eyes wide. He grinned.

"You are so sexy, Rachael." She was, her magic making her glow white and ruby and emerald, her body flushed and writhing with the pleasure that he was giving her; the sounds that she was making going straight to his already rock-hard cock. "You're so close. Are you ready to come for me?"

She moaned, panting. He bent down and replaced his fingers on her breast with his mouth and then took that hand to her clit.

Rachael was going to die. Could you die from too much pleasure? His fingers were hitting a spot inside her that was driving her higher and higher; in combination with what he was doing to her clit and his hot mouth on her nipples; it was almost too much. Her hand sank onto his neck, holding on for dear life. She had had orgasms, but never *never* had she ever felt like this. And then it all drew taut, her body waiting, and between one heartbeat and another, she came, waves of pleasure that he rode with her, continuing to stroke her, until finally, he slowed, following her down, soothing her, kissing her gently, taking her whimpers as his due.

Slowly, he eased his fingers out of her, bringing them to his mouth, and she watched as he tasted them. "Oh god," she moaned.

He grinned at her, but before he could speak, someone pounded on her front door. Drake cursed and yanked up his pants, carefully zipping them up. "Don't move," he told her. She just looked at him, still slightly out of it. Cursing again, he crossed the room and opened the door slightly.

Rachael sat up, resting her arms on her knees, trying to hear who it was. It was a man, she thought.

Drake closed the door and came back, running an aggravated hand through his hair. "Rachael, we need to get dressed. Come on, love." He found her pants and helped her put them on, and then her bra.

"I can dress myself, Drake," Rachael said, feeling sluggish and slow, but perking up a little.

"I know that," Drake said, fastening the hooks on her bra, and then sitting back to allow her to sit her breasts in the cups correctly before slipping her shirt over her head. "But I enjoy doing this. And you aren't all the way back yet. You're getting there, but you needed some care." And he looked extremely proud of himself about it, too, she thought.

"Hair brush?" He asked.

She blinked. "Uh, bathroom." He retrieved it and immediately started taking the tangles out of her hair. "It's like brushing rubies," he said, enthralled, and only then did she realize that her magic shields were still down. She started building them back up, and he sighed sadly.

"Are you ready?" At her nod, he stood. "Okay, a cop is outside."

"*A cop?!*" Her face reddened immediately. Rachael was convinced whoever it was out there knew what it was they were just doing. She stared at Drake in horror.

He burst out laughing. "It's okay, Rachael. We're both consenting adults, and he's not here to judge us." He sobered. "He does have news though, and it seems serious. Come on."

A white uniformed police officer stood just outside the door when Drake opened it for her. At their appearance, he nodded. "Rachael Knight?" he said asked.

Something about his demeanor made her stomach tighten. Short, with short-clipped dark hair, he had the physique of a body builder — bulky arms were crossed on his chest, his neck thick, and his legs toned under his uniform. His face was serious, solemn, no hint of a smile. Why would the police be here? The nature of her upbringing made her very anxious about authority figures and, on top of that, her conservative lifestyle had been deeply suspicious of government figures. They had not wanted anyone investigating, and perhaps ending, their way of life. The two completely different conditioning responses only caused her anxiety to spike, but she remembered her dad's advice on what to do when dealing with a police officer and kept her mouth shut.

"Ms. Knight," the man said, sounding put upon and annoyed. "I need to ask you a few questions about your location between the hours of 5:00 p.m. and 12:00 a.m. yesterday evening."

She narrowed her eyes at him and fought the impulse to spill all her secrets. The warring fear of authority was fighting with the fear of being falsely accused of a crime—if this man was asking her whereabouts, then they were looking for an alibi. She wasn't unaware of police tactics. "To whom am I speaking to, sir?" she asked politely. "And am I being detained?"

Drake let out a surprised huff behind her, causing the officer's eyes to bounce briefly to him, but he returned his focus to Rachael quickly. "Apologies. I am Officer Dalton." He was definitely annoyed now. "You are not being detained, but if you refuse to answer my questions, that circumstance might change."

Rachael smiled. "I see. Well, in that case, I'll see you if circumstances change. I'm sorry you came down here for no reason. Have a good day." She turned to go back inside.

"Ma'am," Dalton's voice was quiet, but not threatening. "Michelle O'Reilly's body was pulled out of the river by the Arboretum this morning."

Rachael carefully didn't react. "That's terrible," she said, not turning. "Have a good day." She listened as he walked down the corridor, his keys jangling and she went back into the apartment, Drake following, and locked the door.

Drake slid his arm around her, pulling her close, offering comfort. "Are you ok?"

"I am not okay." Rachael said, hiding her face in his chest, her voice muffled. "I was there yesterday. I *was there*. What happened, Drake?"

"I don't know, Rachael," he said, kissing the top of her head. "But we're going to find out."

LAYERS

In the end, Officer Dalton returned in an hour.

"They must really want to talk to me," Rachael said dryly, trying to cover her anxiety.

"Try not to assume anything," Drake said, soothingly. "It could be something else entirely."

She shot him an incredulous look, and he laughed softy while giving her a gentle hug. "It'll be okay, brightness. Open the door."

She sighed and opened the door to find Officer Dalton and his partner, a tall white man with ginger hair, standing there with serious expressions. "Hello boys," she said in greeting.

Dalton's face turned to stone, but the other officer grinned.

"Ms. Knight, we need you to come with us." Officer Dalton reached around and grabbed a pair of handcuffs from his belt and Rachael's stomach dropped, her mouth drying, making her swallow. Dalton didn't read her any rights, but Rachael didn't say anything. She knew better.

"I'll be behind you," Drake said. "Don't worry."

"We don't need those, Jeff," the other officer said, his voice gruff. "She's not under arrest."

Rachael's eyes flew to the one who spoke, his arms crossed across his chest, his eyes fixed on Dalton's back in an unblinking stare.

He had hazel eyes, very pale skin and seemed to tower over Officer Dalton's shorter stature. She re-evaluated his position here. Maybe not a partner. Maybe he was supervision.

Dalton's lips thinned, but he put back the handcuffs. Rachael raised an eyebrow in question and he glared at her, but answered. "You are a person of interest in the investigation of the death of Michelle O'Reilly. You will appear at the Davis Police Department in the next twenty minutes—"

"Twenty-four hours," interrupted the other officer calmly.

Dalton exhaled heavily out of his nose. "Twenty-four hours," he continued, "to answer questions or I will be forced to place you under arrest for obstruction." And he turned with no further words or waiting for her acknowledgement and walked out.

She, Drake, and the remaining officer watched him go, silently, until the outside door shut with a clang, and then they looked at each other.

"I am Officer Kyle Bleeker." He stuck out his hand, and Rachael shook it. At the touch of his skin, she knew he was a shifter, but how she hadn't felt his magic before was a surprise. She must have tightened up her magic more than she realized. "I was on the Shifter Patrol that found Ms. O'Reilly's body. If you can think of anything you saw yesterday, write it down. Come as soon as you can. Anything, no matter how small, can be important." And he handed her a piece of official looking paper, nodded, and walked away.

"Good cop, bad cop," Drake said dryly, once the door shut behind him. Rachael turned and looked at him in surprise, and he shrugged. "No matter how nicely he said it, he still wants you there as soon as possible."

She opened her mouth, and then she closed it again. He was right. She frowned and turned to look at Zakaria's door, which, for the first time since he moved in, had remained closed the entire time they stood in the hall.

Drake cocked his head and then said with decision, "I am going to call Mom."

"Wait, what?" She followed him back into her apartment, only pausing to lock the door.

Drake's eyes were black, a sign of his high emotional state, his motions jerky. "She is a person of note in town. Her presence will only be in your favor."

Rachael had forgotten that Diana had been on the city council. She was not a person who loomed large to her, but Diana was a person to be reckoned with. Realizing that gave Rachael an idea as well. "I'll be back." She turned and went into her room and quickly changed into a pair of slacks and a green blouse, slipping on a pair of strappy sandals with small heels. After, she immediately made a beeline for the bathroom where she wound her hair up into a bun and added mascara and lipstick.

Drake took in her costume change and smiled. "Perfect. Mom will be here soon. She's irate and said only that she needs to make a quick stop." His grin sharpened. "The DPD will have absolutely no idea what hit them."

Twenty-five minutes later and thirty-five minutes after the two officers had left the summons at her door, Rachael presented herself at the Davis Police Department in the presence of Diana Archer and Ms. Ivy Lee, Esquire, a tall, fashionably thin woman with curly sable hair artfully tamed, porcelain skin with natural looking make-up, a black pencil skirt and jacket over a lavender blouse, and black pumps. Diana was also armored in professional attire, and the three of them faced the front desk of the police station ready for battle.

"Ms. Knight, pleasure to meet you. Mrs. Archer gave me a run-down of what is happening. We don't have time for pleasantries, so I'll make this brief." Ivy had said when Rachael had gotten in the car.

"Oh! Er, okay?" Rachael nodding a greeting back. "Sure, that sounds fine, Ms...?"

"Ivy Lee, your lawyer." Diana had winked at Rachael in the rearview mirror, calming her nerves somewhat, while Ivy plowed forward. "The police do not have the evidence to arrest you or they would have. They have the legal right to lie to you and coerce you into implicating yourself into a false confession or giving them enough information to arrest you. Do you understand?"

Rachael's stomach felt like lead. "Yes, I understand."

Ivy nodded. "Good. You will answer all questions with yes or no. Do not elaborate unless I give you permission to do so. Did you kill Michelle O'Reilly?"

"No!" Rachael gasped.

"Good. How do you answer questions?" Ivy asked, looking back at her. Her eyes were a dark brown and fathomless, seemingly without a pupil.

"Yes or no. Do not elaborate." Rachael wanted to rub her palms on her pants, but settled for swallowing nervously.

Ivy smiled suddenly, and it changed her whole face. "Excellent. And don't let them sense fear. I heard you handled them well earlier. Just do that again."

Drake had told them that? Her shoulders went back and her

spine straightened. "I can do that."

"Good," Diana said. "Because we're here."

The interview room in the Davis Police Department looked like a cell. There were concrete walls, and a metal table that was bolted to the floor with handcuffs attached to the center surrounded by four metal chairs. Officer Dalton, the lucky man who had appeared to escort them back, gestured to the chairs on one side of the table. No one sat. He frowned. "You are here to be interviewed. Sit."

None of the women so much as twitched.

"Officer Dalton, there are only two chairs on our side of the table." Ivy left it at that, and Rachael applauded her restraint.

Dalton stared at them and then looked at the two chairs. "You can count. Congratulations." The sarcasm was so heavy, she was surprised the ugly grey paint didn't peel off the walls.

"I am sure you don't want to explain to the Commissioner why you forced Council Woman Diana Archer, the creator of the Archer fund, and the woman who runs the Magical Person Relocation Program, to stand?" Ivy cocked a slim brown brow at him, her voice smooth and calm.

Diana raised her hand and waved. "Hello." She smiled, the only one of them to do so, plying the skill of the politician. "It has been sometime since I held that seat, so you are forgiven for not knowing who I am. I look forward to seeing first-hand this part of the justice system and our proud police force at work."

It was all Rachael could do not to giggle. Officer Dalton's face paled slightly, and he looked between her and Diana, obviously wondering at the connection. "I—"

Before he could say anything else, the door opened loudly

and Officer Bleeker entered, carrying a chair and looking harried. "Ma'am, apologies." He rushed to set the chair down and indicated that she should sit.

"Well, thank you, Officer . . . ?" Diana asked with a smile.

"Now wait a minute!" Dalton finally found his voice, loudly. "She can't just sit in on this interrogation!"

Everyone looked at him.

"Well, she . . . she's," he stuttered, flustered once again at the lack of outrage he had seemingly expected. Diana smiled encouragingly and his face somehow became even more red. "She's not related to the suspect!"

"Officer Dalton, Ms. Knight is being interviewed and not interrogated and her summons made no indication that she was a suspect." Ms. Lee's voice was frosty.

Diana's smile had disappeared as well, her face now stoney. Dalton looked at her and straightened, blinking, swallowing. "Officer Dalton, Ms. Knight may not be my blood, but she is residing under my protection as is evidenced by her use of my lawyer. It should also have been obvious by the presence of my son at her home this morning at both of your unannounced visits."

Both officers went motionless at this information. "Your son?"

"My son." Diana didn't elaborate, her tone glacial. Both men turned to look at Rachael, and it was her turn to smile and wave. They didn't smile or wave back for some reason.

"Ah, I think she can stay, but you cannot say anything. Observe only." Dalton pointed a finger at her, only to lower it quickly when Diana looked at it like she would break it off.

"Of course. I would never dream of impeding an investigation," and with that, Diana sat, pleasant once more.

"Ladies, please, sit. We should get started." Officer Bleeker gestured to the remaining chairs, and Rachael and Ivy sat.

"This interview will be recorded. Please state your name for the record." Dalton completed the formalities and finally, they got down to the interview. After some basic questions about her name and residence and job, Dalton got to the meat of it.

"How did you know Michelle O'Reilly?"

This was not a yes or no question, so after a brief glance at Ivy, who nodded, she answered with the briefest of answers. "From work."

"Did you ever see her outside of work?"

This was a trick question—she did not see Michelle socially and her gut reaction was to say no. Rachael, however, was not stupid and knew if she said no, they would jump on that and start accusing her of lying, trying to fluster her.

"Once," she said.

Bleeker looked up, and Dalton blinked. Rachael waited for the next question.

"Just once?" Dalton asked, leaning back in his chair. "Two young women like you weren't friends?"

Rachael raised an eyebrow. "No."

Dalton's jaw tensed, and he shot Ivy a glare, which she returned calmly. "Okay. So the one time you saw her, when was this?"

"Three days ago."

Bleeker frowned, and it was his turn to lean back. "Was this the last time you saw her?"

"Yes," she said, unflinching. They were trying to make her feel guilty and in turn make her act guilty. Did she feel bad that Michell was dead? Yes. Was she responsible for her? No. If she kept repeating it, maybe she would believe it.

"Hmm," Bleeker hummed. "Was she with anyone else that night?"

"Yes."

"This is going to take forever if all you do is say yes or no," Dalton growled at her. Three sets of eyes turned to him from across the table and he grumbled and crossed his arms. "This is an active investigation. We do have things to do." Three eyebrows arched in response.

"Ms. Knight, who was Ms. O'Reilly with that night?" Bleeker asked, redirecting the interview.

"Zakaria Tate."

"Yes, Mr. Tate." Dalton sat up, like a hound with a scent. "Witnesses put him at the Black Bear during your shift, Ms. Knight. They said he was *very* interested in you and not so interested in Ms. O'Reilly, *until* she introduced herself."

Rachael didn't say anything, since that wasn't a question.

"You know what I think?" Dalton leaned forward over the table. "I think Michelle scored a date with the blond blue-eyed stud." His eyes raked over Rachael. "Not a surprise; they went together better, didn't they?"

Diana's gasp echoed through the room. Officer Bleeker blanched and Ivy glared. Rachael, knowing that Drake was waiting for her at home, took a breath and waited.

"It must have hurt," Bleeker said, shooting a repressive look at Dalton, who shrugged. "To have your advances rebuffed." He was all conciliatory kindness, blue eyes wide, and a soft smile on his face. It was just as derogatory as Dalton's barb. She looked at Ivy, who nodded.

"Officers, it may be a shock to you, but I turned Zakaria down." Her tone was icy. Both men blinked.

"You turned him down?" Bleeker asked.

"Our witnesses claim—"

"If your witness is Mr. Tate, I suggest you examine his reliability." Rachael said, and the men gaped at her. She rolled her eyes, but stayed silent. Men!

"She has answered your question, moving on." Ivy ordered.

To expedite things, Rachael gave a brief and factual summary of what transpired that night after she got home from work.

"You weren't friends, and she stole your man, but you helped her?" Dalton asked skeptically.

Rachael sighed, pinching her nose. "He is not, nor has he ever been, my man. And yes, I helped her. He locked her out of his apartment in her underwear." She couldn't keep the disdain out of her voice, at both Dalton and Zakaria.

Bleeker cleared his throat. "What was her demeanor, Ms. Knight?"

She sobered and looked at him bleakly. "She was very upset. Enough that I asked if he had hurt her."

The men shared a glance, and notes were taken.

"Did she file a report.?"

"No." Both men shook their head, and she had to force herself not to retort. File a report on what? Icky feelings? She would have been laughed out of the police station.

"Were there any obvious injuries?"

She shook her head. "No."

"What are your own magical abilities, Ms. Knight?" Bleeker asked.

"I can sense magic and the type of magic a person has."

Bleeker stared at her. "Thatt's . . ."

Ivy cleared her throat.

He glanced at her and changed whatever he was going to say and instead asked, "what am I?"

She let down her shields, her glowing skin reflecting off the table slightly. Both men gave a startled gasp, and even Ivy inhaled sharply. She was fae and something else, but Rachael wasn't sure what. It was something she had never felt before. "You are a shifter, Officer Bleeker, but I knew that from this morning." She cocked her head and held out her hand. "May I touch you? It helps some-times." He hesitated, but let her take his hand.

She nodded. "I thought so. Bear." She grinned suddenly. "You watch from the University field." He stared at her and pulled his hand back. He looked at Dalton and something passed between the two of them.

"Please wait here, Ms. Knight." And then they got up and left.

"Well, what the hell?" she asked, frowning.

Diana was also frowning. "Ivy?"

"They don't mean any ill intent. Now." Rachael looked at her, eyebrows raised. Ivy raised her own in response, obviously not about to expand on that.

"What on Earth is going on?" Diana wondered, staring at the two-way mirror opposite them. She reached over and patted Rachael's knee. "You were wonderful, love. Honest and to the point."

Rachael smiled at her warmly. "Thank you. Still, we haven't left yet."

The door opened and Bleeker came back in with a tall, curvy

woman in a grey pant suit. "This is Ms. Fernanda Flores, and she is the forensic pathologist assigned to Ms. O'Reilly's case. She has some questions for you."

Ivy frowned, and Rachael shook her head in confusion. "What questions could you possibly have for me?" she asked.

"I don't know. Who are you?" A perfectly waxed black brow arched up, and Rachael grinned at her.

Bleeker cursed. "Sorry. Fernanda, this is Rachael Knight, her lawyer, Ivy Lee, and this is Diane Archer."

Fernanda shook everyone's hand before sitting down in Dalton's vacant chair. This gave Rachael time to look her over. She was taller than Rachael by several inches, approaching 5'10", and with dark tan skin, lush lips, and dark, almost black eyes. She had long black hair with an undercut and braided into a thick braid and then wrapped around her head. Her figure was plus-size, yes, but she wasn't soft. If Rachael had any guess, she would say Fernanda could punt any of them across the room easily. Despite the formal-looking pantsuit, she wasn't wearing heels, opting instead for comfortable looking sensible shoes that suited standing for long hours.

"Rachael is the woman I mentioned." Bleeker added.

Fernanda nodded. "Ah. Yes, this is the problem I have, Ms. Knight. Michelle O'Reilly, from all accounts, was not a depressed or suicidal person. There is no reason to believe that she was harboring thoughts of self-harm and it makes her death . . . well, it makes it weird."

All three women glanced at each other and then back at Fernanda.

"Weird," Rachael repeated.

She spread her hands and shrugged. "It makes no sense. Why did she drown herself in that river? Three days before that she was a perfectly normal young woman, and she was living a perfectly normal life and she was neurotypical, as far as we know."

Diana leaned forward with a frown. "Is it possible she had been depressed and never sought treatment?"

"Of course," Fernanda nodded. "But even so, there are markers, certain behaviors that we can use to identify depression or suicide. Michelle exhibited none of these. There is absolutely no reason to believe that she would have killed herself."

Rachael was shaking her head. "But . . . what does this have to do with me?"

Fernanda turned her dark eyes on Rachael, and Rachael swallowed. "You can feel magic."

Rachael nodded.

"Even glamored magic?" Fernanda leaned forward slightly, her dark eyes piercing.

Suddenly it clicked in her brain, and she let out a soft breath. "You think someone hurt her and hid it? That they glamored her body to hide the evidence."

Fernanda nodded. "Yes. More than that though, we have had other people look at her and they have found nothing, not even a *trace* of magic on her body. Our best magical experts, who specialize in breaking glamor, can not find any magic."

At this point Ivy shook her head and said, "that's impossible, Michelle had Fae magic. She would have had magic on her body, regardless. She wouldn't have been able to help it."

Fernanda nodded. "Exactly."

Silence fell. Rachael took a deep breath. "You want me to go look at her."

Diana inhaled sharply and Ivy sat back in her chair. Fernanda nodded again. "Yes. Something happened to her, Rachael, and I cannot find out what until I can see the evidence."

Rachael looked down at her hands, thinking. This was a lot of pressure, and she had no idea if she could even do what they were asking of her. Diana put her arm around her shoulders in support, but stayed silent, letting her make her decision. Ivy was the one who spoke first.

"If she does this, I want it in writing that she is cleared of any suspicion and removed from the list of suspects. She has committed no crimes and is now an active member of the investigation."

Bleeker narrowed his eyes at her, and a low growl rumbled in his chest. "Unless new evidence comes to light that implicates her."

He and Ivy battled, and Rachael finally raised her head. "I'll help."

"Once he agrees," Ivy said sternly. Rachael turned to look at Officer Bleeker.

"Officer, Michelle left my home and my care and then turned up dead. She had been abused and used and now probably murdered. She deserved better. Let me help her rest. Please."

He stared at her for a moment and then threw up his hands. "Oh fine. I'll go get the paperwork."

She smiled at him. "Thank you, Officer." He and Fernanda both froze for a moment at her smile, and Bleeker rubbed the back of his neck.

"I'll be right back," he muttered, and left.

Fernanda watched him go and made a humming sound. "Rachael, that smile would blind the sun itself."

Diana chuckled and gave Rachael a squeeze. "I'm proud of you, hon."

She took a shaky breath at those words and then sat up straight. "Okay, give me the address."

MAGICAL DISCOVERY

There was no official morgue in Davis; it was too small of a city to boast a fully stocked hospital, although it did have an emergency room and several urgent care centers. And while they did have a police office, there was no detention center or coroner's office either. That all fell under the jurisdiction of the Sacramento County Coroner, and so they had to drive into Sacramento.

The coroner was between the DMV and a bakery, and across from the California Department of Justice. Upon parking, Sam and Drake flanked her automatically, scanning the area.

"Uhh, guys?" Rachael started looking around, too.

"Don't worry." Sam said, soothingly. "It's just that Sacramento doesn't have as much . . . comaraderie between people as Davis does. It's just better to be wary."

It was then she realized they were both armed, and she swallowed. She didn't sense any magic nearby, but her shields were up tight out of fear. Protection for her had always been to hide her magic. She had to learn that it wasn't always the best option. Had she really gotten so used to how safe Davis was that she had forgotten the common safety measures she needed in Los Angeles completely? The idea made her uncomfortable and happy at the same time. She made a mental note to learn how to shoot or fight or something. It wasn't deemed appropriate in LA, but here, here they would teach her.

The inside of the building seemed like a normal bureaucratic building—flickering lights, white tile, dingy, and uncomfortable. They waited in a room after signing in at the front desk and then were escorted down a hallway. Rachael tried to pretend there wasn't a dead body at the end of it. The body of someone she had known. It didn't work.

No one after the Convergence was unfamiliar with death or dead bodies. Law enforcement and coroners were luxuries that many smaller cities and towns didn't have. Funeral homes made a lot of money immediately following the Convergence, either from the deaths caused by Shifters who went feral and killed people, or people who had taken their own lives, or died of hunger or thirst, or in the Earthquakes or fires. But when the energy crisis reached its peak, refrigeration became coveted as much as gold. Replacement parts were hard to find, and a lot of the funeral homes closed down. California became its own country from sheer necessity. Still, money and power didn't trickle down, and the people with the money didn't give up their power easily. Riots, violence, disease, poverty, hunger—death became very well known indeed.

"Here we are. When we go in, you will see that she hasn't been examined yet, but she is nude. She is under a sheet, which you may move to find any injuries or hidden magical marks. As far as we can tell, there is nothing extraordinary about her death and it looks like she is sleeping, so there is nothing obviously wrong with her, but witness reports led us to believe that an investigation may be required."

"Witness reports?" Rachael asked sharply.

"I'm sorry, I cannot tell you at this time, as it is under investigation." Fernanda shook her head and shrugged.

"Then you shouldn't have said anything about witnesses, then, huh?" thought Rachael, but she nodded. "Okay. I'm ready."

Fernanda opened the door, and they entered the examination room. Michelle was laid on a steel table under a white sheet. Her pale skin was even paler, although her blood had started to collect on her lower half turning her skin the blue-black of a bruise. Rachael slowly approached, letting down her shields as she did so, her glowing skin reflecting off the shining surfaces in the room. Fernanda gasped.

"I've never seen anything like that before!" she said. "What magic is that?"

It was Sam who answered, allowing Rachael to focus. "No one knows yet."

"It's beautiful. Can you feel it?" Fernanda had no magic of her own and so couldn't feel anything herself.

Both Sam and Drake nodded. "It's almost like static electricity," Sam said.

Rachael was looking over Michelle's face because it looked like there was *something* there. She dropped her shields even more and scanned down her shoulders to her chest. Bruises and scars were there, some new and others were faded green. "There is something here," she said.

"You're sure?" Sam came closer, Drake beside him.

"Yes," she pointed, but didn't touch. "Here along her face, it's almost like a lattice. I can see it over her face and neck. It's covering her; I can't see underneath it."

"Can you remove it?" Fernanda, asked excitedly.

She shook her head. "My magic has always been passive, not active. I can see it, but I can't do anything about it. Surely you have someone who can?" Magic breaking had become a standard operating procedure in criminal departments since magic appeared.

"We didn't even detect there was anything here to begin with," she said with frustration. "You're sure there's something there?"

Rachael nodded. "Yes, the more I look at it, the more obvious it is, actually. It's definitely on her face, but I'm not sure if it's anywhere else. Well, her head. It's on her head," she corrected, seeing that it did indeed wrap around Michelle's whole head.

Fernanda reached out and lowered the sheet and Rachael scanned Michelle's body, trying to be clinical about it, but her stomach clenched at the sight. "Yes, there's more. Breasts and groin," she swallowed at those implications, "and her hands and arms."

"Maybe hiding defensive wounds?" Fernanda murmured.

Rachael stepped back, at a loss. She badly wanted to help, but she didn't know what else she could do. She focused on the lattice on Michelle's face, studying it. glamor and fae magic had a certain feel to them that was different than shifter. This had a different feel than both of those magics. This was slick, like oil, almost, like it was unnatural in origin. Rachael frowned. "Have you washed her yet?"

Fernanda looked up, startled. "No, but she was found in the river. Any make up would have washed away."

"Yes, but what if magic was applied topically?" Rachael asked slowly. "Witches can make potions, right?"

"Yes, but we can sense those, and they are usually connected to talismans or pouches near or on the body. We didn't find anything like that or sense any magic on her at all." Fernanda had turned back now, her face close to Rachael's.

Rachael lapsed back into thought. Drake pressed against her in silent support. "Can I touch her?" she asked after a minute.

Fernanda stood up. "You think you can do something?"

"I won't know until I try, and I can't try until I touch her." Rachael said with a shrug. "I want to help. She didn't deserve this."

Fernanda nodded. "We have already collected the physical evidence, but wear these gloves first, just in case there's something under this magic you see."

Rachael took a deep breath. She really did not want to do this. She needed to do this, but her stomach was threatening to climb out of her mouth and she clenched her jaw. While she was familiar with dead bodies, she hadn't had to *touch* them. Viewing one and touching one were two very different things. "Let's give her some privacy," she said softly, pulling up the sheet once more. "I can try this on her head and if it works, move it later." No one argued.

Once she was standing at Michelle's head once more, Rachael lifted her hand and lightly touched Michelle's forehead. The lattice was tacky, like tape that had lost most of its glue. She frowned and cocked her head. "How *odd*. It's like . . . ." She pinched her fingers and took a thread of the lattice between her fingers, to see if she could hold it. She could. She lifted slightly and the whole lattice lifted too, like a blanket, sliding over her features. Her skin crawled at the feeling; it wasn't natural, and it wanted to stay on Michelle's face, but it would go where Rachael wanted it to go.

"It's like someone knitted a glamor together and attached it to her face," she told her waiting audience, still studying the magic. "I think I can take it off, but I want to make sure that however it's attached is loose before I do. I don't want to tear it off."

Fernanda was on the other side of the table, watching avidly. She heard a disgusted sound from Sam and Drake behind her. "It's the oddest feeling. The magic is fae, but wrong. Let me see where it's..." she followed the lattice carefully, trying to find where it was fastened on, gently skimming Michelle's hair, her beautiful pointed ears, and the lattice bent under her fingers sliding around easily until the crown of her head. "Here, the crown. It's here." Rachael moved to the head of the table and bent down, and then gasped. "Oh, Michelle. No."

"What?" Fernanda demanded.

Drake was beside her again, offering silent emotional support. "It's fae magic because it's hers," Rachael whispered. She cleared her throat and repeated it louder.

"What do you mean it's her magic?" Fernanda shook her head impatiently. "We would have detected it."

Rachael shook her head. "It's . . . corrupted. Twisted. I'll try to remove it, but it'll be hard. It's very attached to her, both physically and magically. She wove this to herself so tightly I think she must have . . . I don't know." She frowned in concentration, picking up the bundle of threads that connected the lattice to Michelle's head, her own magic seeming to flow in and out of her body.

Fernanda backed up. "Your eyes are yellow."

Rachael didn't know what to do with that information, but she was too busy to think about it, so she dismissed it for now. If she could just cut these threads, that would be so perfect. She sighed and took one fingernail and imagined using it to slice a thread. A small bolt of energy shot from her finger into the thread and it was cut, the ends slithering away. "What?" Her eyebrows drew forward. Could she do it again? She moved her fingernail, imagined cutting a a thread—Yes! "I can do this!" she said, and went on, strand by strand, until the bundle was severed. She stood up, her back aching and gently, ever so gently, pulled the magic blanket off of Michelle's face.

Gasps of shock echoed off the tiled chamber. A brand had been seared into Michelle's face, new, still red, and it stood out starkly from her pale skin. "It's a Z. A stylized Z," Drake said darkly, his hands curling into fists.

Rachael shook her head. "Not exactly though. It could be, but it's not *quite*, is it?" She understood the impulse. She wanted to blame someone and Zakaria was an easy target. But the brand didn't look like a Z to her.

"Can you remove the rest of the magic?" Fernanda asked, never taking her eyes from the brand.

Rachael nodded and lowered the sheet. The magic here was larger, but connected to her heart. It was all one large sheet that wrapped around her torso, from her breast to mid-thigh. "I know I have to, but I don't want to see," she said softly, already touching the magic web in preparation.

Drake nodded. "I know."

This one went faster, now that she had some idea what she was doing. It was like her magic absorbed and returned the magic she touched, allowing her to use it a little. This was a new level of heretofore undiscovered magic ability and Rachael had no idea what it meant or if she could replicate it elsewhere. At least here, for Michelle, she could help. "Okay." she said and took a deep breath before slowly pulling off the glamor. "Oh, my god. *Michelle.* Why didn't you tell me!" Tears started falling down her cheeks.

Michelle's body was striped with red and black bruises from some blunt instrument. Here and there, it looked like a knife had cut into her, deeply, and her nipples were swollen from some kind of clamp that had been left on too long or too tight. Her thighs were bruised with finger print sized bruises and - "We did a rape exam, but we will have to do another one." Fernanda said, darkly.

Rachael backed away and then turned away, trying to give Michelle some dignity. The men followed suit. She remembered what she had told Rachael, the morning after. "I will give a witness statement for rape," she said shakily. "It started out consensually, but I think he tricked her or used magic to force her into things. I don't know. She wasn't . . . right the next morning. She said that he made her feel dirty even though he was an enthusiastic participant."

"Asshole," both Sam and Drake said at the same time.

Fernanda nodded. "I'll be giving you a call. Do you have a name to give me?"

Everyone nodded and Fernanda raised a beautifully arched eyebrow. "Excellent."

In the car, driving back to Davis, Rachael sat thinking. "I think that fucker twisted her magic somehow and made her ashamed and, at the same time, made her compliant."

"I agree," Sam said, tapping one finger on the steering wheel. "And I am not taking you back to Primero Grove. You will go in, pack a bag, and stay with us." For whatever reason, Zakaria had not been arrested. He had been interviewed just like Rachael, but had also been released. No one would tell them why. Rachael, in the privacy of her mind, wondered if he had charmed the police. But surely, if he had, the magic breakers on staff would have detected it? Whatever the reason — lack of evidence or malicious magical usage — Zakaria remained free.

"What?" Rachael looked back and forth between Sam and Drake.

Drake nodded. "Absolutely. There is no way you will be that close to that asshole. I'll stay with you while you pack."

Rachael could see the wisdom, but didn't want to impose. "Maybe a hotel or something. . ."

"And deny Diana the chance to cook for you again? Are you trying to get me in trouble?" Sam asked.

Despite herself, Rachael laughed. "Oh okay, fine."

For the second time, Zakaria's door remained firmly shut, which merely cemented suspicion in Rachael's mind, and she hurriedly packed a bag while Drake waited, leaning against her kitchen counter. Rachael was ready to go in fifteen minutes flat, eager to be away, and as she moved to the door, Drake her took her hand, pulling her towards him.

"Hey," he said, nuzzling her hair. "Before we go down, I wanted to say that you were amazing today."

"Oh." Rachael felt a glowing warmth from his praise and smiled. "Thank you."

He pulled back, snagged her bag neatly from her, and stood up. "Let's get out of here." Zakaria was there when they left, staring as Drake and Rachael left together, eyeing the bag they carried with a smirk.

Drake tensed, but Rachael just shook her head and sighed. "Oh Zakaria, really. It's all so *old-fashioned*. Any minute now, you're going to actually use the word "harlot," and then where will we be? Or even *worse*, 'Jezebel.'"

Drake started laughing behind her and Zakaria's face turned a very gratifying shade of purple and Rachael turned to leave, saying. "I'd take a deep calming breath. Try some meditation. You're going to give yourself an aneurysm."

Back in the car, Drake asked her as he was buckling his seat belt, "how is he not affecting you any more? Two days ago, you could barely stand to be in the same room as him."

Rachael smiled to herself and then at Drake. "I realized something last week, before he came here, and it was that my conservative upbringing had no hold over me here. That I was an adult and I could do what I wanted now." She absently rubbed her arm where the burn from the cast iron pan had healed.

Frowning, Drake nodded, slightly confused, but willing to go along. Sam, older and wiser, patted her knee in a fatherly manner. "Good for you."

She straightened slightly, proud. "When Zak-the-liar arrived," Drake snorted at the nickname, "he acted just like the people I grew up with did. My parents. My pastor. My neighbors. Everyone."

Understanding dawned on Drake's face. "You wanted to move on, but he pulled you back in."

Rachael nodded, tucking her hair behind her ear. "He made me doubt myself. Doubt what I could see with my own eyes." Drake reached over the front seat and squeezed her shoulder. "I knew that magic itself wasn't bad. I knew that I wasn't evil. I *knew* this. But then at the bar . . ."

Drake cursed. "That asshole tricked you, and then convinced you that *you* were the problem."

Rachael nodded. "Yes. And I started spiraling. After I freaked out in the Black Bear, your mom found me." She laughed softly.

"She found me and helped me see things from outside my own head. She helped me put things in perspective." She took a deep breath. "I am not all better and I will probably freak out again. But. Zakaria? That fucker," she relished the profanity, the forbidden words coming easier now, "he has no power over me."

NORMALCY LESSONS

L ife on a farm was much more what Rachael was used to than living in an apartment in town. The large farmhouse was full of laughter and shouts and normal sounds of a boisterous family—the difference for Rachael was that it was a loving and accepting family instead of a scared and frightened one. She had never realized how much she had walked on eggshells around her own parents until she got to stop doing it. She was free here to be herself. All of herself. And it was giddying. She was free to laugh and play just as much as she was to cry or pause. Dinners weren't silent affairs where they had to listen to scripture or judgments or lessons. Instead, everyone shared what had happened during their day and if someone didn't want to talk or had a bad day, their reticence was respected or their problems listened to. Space was respected. It was such a simple concept, yet Rachael was so grateful for it.

And to watch Diana and Sam together—two people who were very obviously loved and respected each other—be together and work together. It was just as enlightening.

"I don't think my parents were very happy," she said one night to Drake, sipping tea on the front porch.

They were wrapped in light blankets and were on the porch

swing together, enjoying a moment of privacy. Living with his parents was great, and it was also not so great. The house was busy and full and there were rarely moments where it was just the two of them.

"No?" Drake never pressed for more information than she was willing to give, but she knew he was curious about her life before she came here.

She shook her head. "My Dad was not a forgiving man, or a happy one. He demanded my mom and sisters behave as 'good women should,'" she quoted, anger riding under her words. "Submissive and quiet, biddable and stupid." She couldn't hide the bitterness.

Drake kissed her temple. "Boring. And how on earth did you pretend to be any of that?"

She laughed. "Poorly, it turns out," she replied wryly. "I got in trouble a lot." And she had, too. The consequences had gotten more severe as she had gotten older until she had learned to hide herself better. Still, she had never been the submissive or biddable type and her dad had known it. She had taken to hiding early on, avoiding him as much as possible. This had been easy — he was often out of the house doing "men's work" leaving her and her sisters at home with their mother. Because of her magic, Rachael had self-isolated a lot, especially on days she was tired or emotional when the risk of discovery was higher. She became very good at pretending and very good at watching others' behavior so that she could fit in. But pretending doesn't make one belong. Rachael had felt the sting every time curses were cast at magic users. How could she be evil when she cared for her family and sisters as she was supposed to? She tried to follow the rules. She tried to do everything right. What made her any worse than anyone else? There was no one she could talk to about this, no help to seek, no solidarity. No one to trust except herself. As jarring and startling as it was to leave, doing so had allowed Rachael to become more herself than she had ever been before.

"I think he hurt her," she said softly. "Never where us kids could see, but kids know. We all knew. And I hated him for it." And she had, while still craving his approval. Approval that she now knew was never going to come, no matter what she had done or how she had behaved.

Drake kissed her again, squeezing her tight, but said nothing. She snuggled in to him with a sigh. "Why did she stay?" he asked finally.

"Oh, there was no other option. It was stay or leave the whole compound and if she left, Dad would keep us, the kids. And if there was one thing mom loved, it was us." And that was true, too, she supposed. *Then why didn't she take you and run?* a small voice asked. Rachael tried to ignore it, but it pricked her like a thorn.

"I like it here," she said. "I thought it would make me sad to see a happy house, but it doesn't. It's healing."

Rachael listened to the soft sound of Drake's heartbeat, the bleating of the goats and the wind through the fields. This is what home should be, she thought, relaxing, starting to glow as her shields dropped. Home should be safe.

She cheered as a bobcat raced across the grass in front of the house, chasing a large black raven.

"RUN DRAKE!" she called and then, feeling like she should also lend her support to her friend, yelled "GET 'EM EMBER!" It wasn't really a contest, Drake could *fly*, but he dive bombed Ember, calling in croaking caws, giving Ember the illusion she could grab him.

Diana came out, shaking her head. "Those two will never grow up, I swear. There's a pile of clothing in my kitchen and new scratches on my hallway floor." For all her grousing, Diana's eyes were sparkling, and she watched the chase. "I'll miss Drake, when he goes, though."

"Goes?" Rachael's stomach clenched. What was this? He was leaving? Why hadn't he said anything?

"Oh, not far. There's an old manager's house a few acres down the way. No one has lived there for ages, not since the kids have gotten old enough to take care of the managing duties. Sam's been cleaning it up for Drake." Diana was very carefully not looking at her, and Rachael felt her cheeks heating up. "Kids need their own spaces, you know. Ember has an apartment in town she goes to a few days a week, but Drake, well, Drake's a country boy. He likes the space out here." She put her arm around Rachael's waist in a motherly hug. "You can take his room if you like and stay as long as you need to."

Rachael had been sleeping on the couch, not feeling ready to share Drake's bed yet, and now she would have a room. In their house. And there would be no pressure to move in with Drake or to go back to Primero Grove. They had figured out a solution that didn't involve pressuring her at all. "Oh." She ought to say thank you, but anything else would end up a teary mess. She sniffed and blinked a lot.

Diana gave her a little squeeze. "Exactly. When you're ready, come on in. I have a bit of something for you to try." And with that, she went back inside, as if she hadn't just destroyed Rachael emotionally in the best way possible. She found herself humming as she went inside to try the latest bit of confection that Diana had cooked up, even while wiping away tears that had found their way down her cheeks.

It wasn't all fun and games, but it was pretty good. Besides farm chores, Diana tried to learn what she could do with her magic. She had always just thought it was passive, but discovered that it had at least somewhat active properties in Sacramento. So she went around without her shields as much as possible at the farm, just to practice feeling it. It turned out that living things had a basic magic of their own, animals, humans, and very old trees. The goats, flighty creatures that they were, loved it when she went into the barn, but were easily startled. She found that if she had her magic on she could find them more easily and calm them more quickly. It was as if she could tune into them somehow, like a dial on a radio. She started practicing every time she entered the barn, getting the right 'frequency' right away, and soon she could hit it almost immediately.

Horses weren't quite as flighty, but they weren't far off, and some of them were jumpier than the goats. A misplaced bucket or bag could make them startle in a way that could injure a person, so she worked on their natural magic as well. Over time, using her magic became as natural as breathing, something she had never thought possible. She found while she glowed naturally; it was more like a dayglow stick in daylight: perceptible, but only if you were looking for it. If she started using her magic, or as Ember called it, her "universal translator," the glow got a little brighter, but for the most part, it was just a soft radiance. Drake theorized that by bottling it up all the time she had created an echo chamber of sorts, which caused the glow to be brighter than it was naturally. Now that she was using it, all the extra was gone, making her light much dimmer. Dropping her shields led to a relaxation that she didn't know she needed, and that too made her days much easier.

Rachael didn't know how to thank this family that had accepted her so readily. She knew she pulled her weight and more on the farm and with the house, but her gratitude and a driving fear that one day they would wake up and ask themselves why they let her stay drove her to do more and more acts of service. It was one of the few stresses of her stay there, and she worked tirelessly to ensure that she was indispensable. This did not go unnoticed by the very intelligent Archer family.

"How was your shift at the Black Bear today?" Diana asked, as Rachael served herself from a bowl of steaming mashed potatoes. Rachael had kept her job there, both for the money and to keep an eye on Zakaria if he popped in. It was a busy place and full of gossip. She heard lots of great stuff about all sorts of people there.

"Oh, fine. Long. Nothing interesting, at least, so that's good. I did get a great tip off of one table though!" She was saving up still for an apartment of her own, refusing to live on the Archer's charity forever.

"Wonderful! With the breakfast shift, you must have been there so early!" Rachael nodded, her mouth full of food. "And then you came back here and helped Drake and Sam clear a field?" Rachael nodded again, proud. That had been hot and hard work, but it had been so sweet when completed.

Sam passed the salt to Ember. "She worked without complaint. Did more than Drake." He bumped his son with his shoulder.

Rachael glowed at the praise, even while discreetly trying to stretch her aching legs and feet under the table. And maybe her back was a little sore.

"And *then* you helped Ember break down the rotted boards on the back porch so we can redo the steps?" Diana asked.

Rachael nodded. That hadn't taken but a moment and Ember had really done most of it with her shifter strength, although, she did seem to have several splinters in her hands, come to think of it, she mused, looking at her hands.

"Wielded a crowbar like she was born to it," Ember said, raising a toast at Rachael.

Rachael eyed Ember suspiciously. What was that look? "What . . ."

"Such a busy day! And such hard work!" Diana beamed at Rachael.

Rachael stared. "Uh, thank you. It wasn't much . . ." her plate was whisked away. "Hey! I wasn't done!"

"You stopped eating five minutes ago," Drake said, a large grin on his face. Was he laughing?

"What is going on? Y'all, what are you . . ."

"Let me see your hands." Diana demanded.

"My hands? What? Why?!" For some reason, Rachael refused, clutching her hands to her chest as if they were precious.

Not to be dissuaded, Diana tsked and held out her hand as if Rachael were a child. Rachael found herself putting her hand in Diana's calloused ones. "Splinters." Diana said, running her hand over the palm. "You feel like a porcupine. Gloves," she said, looking at Rachael, "gloves."

Rachael flushed. "I . . ." She was twenty-five years old, damn it, why did she feel like a child?

"And no sunscreen, either. Your face and arms are red as a tomato. And on your feet all day long. They must hurt like hell." Diana crossed her arms. "Drake, you have your orders."

"Orders? Orders?! What orders? Drake?" Rachael's chair was pulled back, and she was picked up bodily, cradled in Drake's arms. He grinned at her. "What in the fuck are you doing?" Rachael asked, incredulously. No one picked her up. Ever. Certainly not like she weighed nothing when she knew for a fact she did weigh quite a lot of somethings.

"You are coming with me. For rest and relaxation." His arms did feel nice, Rachael thought, and the thought of walking had been rather daunting.

"But . . . the dishes!" She said, looking at the remnants of dinner.

The entire family groaned, and someone threw a roll at her. "Ow! Hey! What was that for?"

"Get out of here, Drake! Go on! Rachael, no working, you hear me?" Diana called as Drake walked out the back door.

"But . . .where are you taking me? And I can walk! I'm too heavy to be lugged about!"

"You are not, and I'm not lugging you. And the house is done. I want to show you." The night air was cool as he walked toward the manager's one-bedroom house, out of sight of the Big House. It was a far enough walk that she put her head on his shoulder and started to doze a bit, the day catching up with her.

At the door, he set her down, opening it for her. The front

room was cozily lit with a small floor lamp and simply decorated with a love seat and overstuffed chair around a TV. There was a small kitchen connected to a small dining area, checkered drapes framing a window that reflected her face back at her. To her left, a staircase led upstairs to the one bedroom and bathroom. It was simple, clean, homey and perfect.

"Oh, it's lovely," she said, kicking off her shoes with a groan of relief, only to give a holler as she was once again lifted to be carried upstairs.

"Bath time, love." Drake said, kissing the top of her head.

Once in the bathroom, Drake methodically stripped her and then wrapped her in his bathrobe before planting her on the closed toilet while he started the bath. While the water was running, he gathered materials, kneeling before her. "Give me your hands," he ordered, shaking his head at her. Placed her hands in his and he turned them over, shaking his head and tsking, making her grin at how much he sounded like his mother. "Gloves," he said sternly, his blue eyes flashing up to hers and her grin faded.

"Yes, sir," she said, automatically, and then flushed. *Sir?!* Where the fuck had that come from?

He snorted. "I'm not your boss, but I don't like seeing you hurt." He pressed a kiss into her palm, making her stomach flutter, and then grabbed the tweezers. "You need to take care of these hands, please." Her heart ached, and she took a deep breath. After shutting off the bath, he took his time, plucking slivers of wood from her hands with remarkable skill and gentleness. "There. I think that's all of them." He ran his thumbs over her palms, rubbing in the muscles between her fingers, massaging them while checking for further splinters. She gave a soft moan as the aching muscles relaxed. He grinned and moved forward a bit. "This is just the beginning, love." He tipped her face up slightly, even kneeling before her he was slightly taller than she, and kissed her gently, licking and sucking her lips, teasing her.

He pulled her up and untied the robe, helping her into the bath.

"I can take it from here," Rachael said, sighing at the hot water, and trying to pretend that she was comfortable with him seeing her completely naked. While they had kissed and touched a bit more in the week and few days since she had moved in, they had had no time to be really alone since her apartment and that seemed an awfully long time ago. This all seemed so intimate.

"I am sure you can," Drake said, sitting on the floor and grabbing a washcloth. "Have I mentioned that you are gorgeous?"

Rachael eyed him. "Not today."

"My mistake." He soaped up the cloth. "Hands." He washed her hands, under her nails, and between her fingers. Then moved up her arms. He was completely focused. She had never felt such attention on just her before and in such a way. He wasn't hurried, nor did he make it sexual; at the same time, he made it obvious that he enjoyed doing it. He examined her toes, her ankles, marked the scars on her knees from when she fell as a child, and cleaned the space behind them, which made her squirm and his blue eyes sharpen on her. The cloth got more soap and his hand disappeared under the water, up her thighs to her hips. He lifted one leg and slid it up the inside of one thigh and she caught her breath, but he stopped short of the crop of curls there, giving her a mischievous smile. More soap. The other leg. Her hips lifted this time, trying to get that cloth to touch her, just there, a little closer.

"Tsk," he said, his eyes sparkling with humor. "Rachael, I do think you're trying to seduce me."

Her jaw dropped before she caught herself, and then she glared at him and crossed her arms. "I'm trying to seduce *you*?"

His eyes dropped to her breasts, wet and glistening and pressed together by her crossed arms. "Ah. Touché."

She smirked. He had her sit forward, and he washed her back massaging her shoulders a bit, but making sure to get her neck and behind her ears, then the cloth went down her side to her round stomach, under her breasts, around her naval, up the other side, always circling, until she thought she would scream. Finally, he ran the cloth over her breasts and she arched up, the feeling bliss after waiting so long for it.

"One last place, love." he said, his hand sliding down, his eyes on her face.

"Ahh," her legs fell open, her hips tilted up, and he cleaned her, every inch of her, and then down to her ass, making her gasp. "Drake!"

"Gotta clean you properly," he whispered in her ear, biting her lobe as she squirmed.

And then he was pulling her up out of the water, running clean warm water over her, wrapping her in a dry towel, and once more setting her on the toilet. "Time for your hair," he said, pulling the stopper on the dirty water. "And me."

He started the shower, and then stripped, taking off each item slowly, and Rachael enjoyed every second. His dark skin was speckled with dirt from his long day, just as hers had been, and she longed to touch it, to run her fingers over the muscles and feel his body heat. She did not care if he was sweaty or dirty. The slickness between her legs didn't care either. He undid his pants, and she leaned forward, stopping his hands.

She looked up at him and just shook her head. "I want to." She tucked her hands into his pants, pulling him a bit closer, and then pushed down, her hands running down his ass cheeks. Then she moved them forward and grabbed the band of his boxers and pulled it out, gasping as his cock jutted out, and his pants fell to his feet. She sat back and just looked at him. After a bit, she looked up at him. "Have I told you you're gorgeous?"

He laughed. "Not today."

"My mistake," she breathed back, finding it hard to get enough oxygen. He pulled her into the shower, letting it wet her hair and rubbing her scalp. She moaned at the delicious feeling of someone else doing her hair as he scrubbed in shampoo, rinsed it and repeated the process with the conditioner. And then came his turn.

She washed him with the same thoroughness as he had shown her. Every muscle, nail and finger was cleansed and inspected. And soon his hips, too, were thrusting, longing for her to touch. She ran the cloth around the shaft and he groaned, his hand on the wall of the shower. She moved it lower, to get his balls and she thought his legs would give out, but he remained standing. She washed the area between his balls and ass and he moaned loudly, thrusting, and she looked up at him to find his eyes on her hands and she felt herself get even wetter, if that were possible.

"If you don't stop that, I am going to come on you now," he grunted. "And I will love every fucking second of it, but we might regret it later."

"Hmmm," she hummed, thinking about it, making him moan, but stopped. He sagged, grabbing his cock and backing up, his eyes slightly wild, like he wanted to do something shocking and wild with her, and her nipples hardened even while her pussy clenched.

"Don't look at me like that," he warned.

"Like what?" she asked, licking her lips as she watched him squeeze his cock and take deep breaths.

"Like you would take anything I would give you."

Her eyes rose to meet his. She was so new to this; she didn't know what that meant and he knew it, but her body was aching and she *wanted* it. She swallowed.

He turned the water off and soon they were both wrapped in towels and out of the slippery bathroom. He sat her on his bed, towel dried her hair, and brushed it, giving them both time to cool a bit. But his final hurrah more than made up for it. He pulled the comforter off the bed and laid her on her stomach on the sheet. He then started massaging her back, working the knots out of her shoulders and neck, rubbing in lotion as he went, and then down to her hips, even her feet and calves. She was in bliss, melting into a puddle, while at the same time groaning at the sensations he was causing her.

"The sounds you make drive me wild, woman," he groaned, as he dug a thumb into the arch of her foot.

Finally finished with the back, he flipped her and worked his way back up, stopping to tease the crease of her pussy with his thumb, making her gasp, and then he was resting on top of her, nose to nose. "Time to make you as wild as you were making me, Rachael," he said, his eyes alight with glee.

Rachael looked at him and felt such happiness and appreciation and . . . could it be love already? He had been so good to her, and this evening had been so amazing. She grabbed his head and kissed him. It wasn't sexy or hot, just a kiss, but he groaned and cupped her face.

And then suddenly it was more. His tongue licked her lips, and she opened for him, groaning at the feeling, wrapping her arms around his neck, brushing her nipples on his chest, feeling the coarseness of his chest hair. "Oh!" She gasped and did it again. He growled, and kissed her jaw, then her neck, moving so his leg was between her legs, pressing against her and she cried out, grinding against it as he bit her shoulder, his hands moving up, so so slowly.

"Drake, you've teased me enough, don't you think?" she whined, arching up, hands gripping his biceps.

He laughed, his breath ghosting her collar bone, tickling her hair. "Not nearly enough," he said, blue eyes flashing to hers. His thumbs rubbed the underside of her breasts, and he kissed the tops, neatly avoiding the nipples. "I think I can tease you plenty more," he grinned at her, even while pressing his leg tighter against her pussy.

She groaned, her body twisting. "Damn it, Drake!"

He groaned back. "I love it when you swear. I know you're really losing it then." He nipped the side of her breast lightly and then covered one with his hand.

She sighed and moaned, pressing upward. "Yessssss." She hissed happily, still grinding herself against his thigh.

He massaged one breast while he rubbed his stubble over the other. The conflicting sensations caused Rachael's mind to blank, and all she could do was moan.

"I can feel how wet you're getting," he said. "Like this, do you?"

"I think 'like' is too mild a word," she managed to gasp.

He chuckled. "Let's see what else you 'like.'" He lifted his hand and switched breasts, only to pinch her nipple, rolling it, gently at first, watching her face carefully, and slowly increasing the pressure.

"Ohhhh goooood," she moaned, her hips lifting, "Owwwww," she cried, twisting.

"Should I stop?" he asked, lightening the pressure.

"Yes!" she said. And when he did, she shook her head. "No!"

He bent down to the other nipple, using his teeth, until her body was rolling, her pussy rocking against his leg, hot and wet and her moans were constant. He sucked, easing the pain, and she moaned. "Drake, fuck!" He groaned against her, sliding his hand under her ass, helping her grind against him. He moved back to the other nipple, tender and swollen, and sucked that one too. "I could do this forever," he groaned into her chest.

"I'm going to die," Rachael panted, her body writhing. "You are trying to kill me by denied orgasm."

Surprised, Drake let out a laugh. "Feeling needy? Okay, okay." He sat up, leaning onto his side and she moaned at the loss of his knee. He bent down and kissed her, hard. "One orgasm, coming right up." He sank between her knees and she gasped, rising up on her elbows, looking down at him over the rise of her stomach.

"What? You don't have to . . ."

"*Have to?* Love, this is the *prize*." Her eyes widened and fuck it was hot, her watching him open her thighs, and damn, she was so sexy. "Hmmmm, you are so sexy," he said aloud, and was rewarded with her smile.

Rachael stared at Drake, at his hands on her thighs, and then he nuzzled her curls and licked her, and her head fell back. "Holy. Shit."

"Mmmm hmmm," he agreed, sending vibrations through her

sensitive flesh.

He settled into his work, spreading her open with his fingers of one hand while pressing down on her mound, and then finding her clit peeking out from its hood with his tongue. Her arms gave out, and she put her hands on his head, resting them there, even while her hips were grinding into his mouth. It felt *so good*. He slid a finger inside of her, bending in a "come here" motion, and her whole body jerked. "Ah!" He lifted his head. "Play with your breasts for me, Rachael."

She didn't hesitate, her breasts ached to be touched, and so she rolled her nipples, and he groaned into her, making her squirm. He slid a second finger into her and she started panting harder. Suddenly, he sucked on her clit and *bit* it gently while fingering her and she cried out, her thighs lifting and tightening around his head. And then she knew nothing as the world exploded and she was coming in waves and waves that he rode through and stroked her through until she pushed his head away, rolling onto her side, gasping for air.

"Mother fucking shit oh my GOD."

Drake curled around her back, tucking his legs into her, his erection sliding against her ass, and he nuzzled her neck. "I think they heard you back in town," he said, pride ringing in his voice.

"I'm going to slap you when I have bones again," she said, her eyes closed.

"Worth it," he smiled, palming one breast. "Totally worth it."

The only response was a soft snore. Drake lay for a moment and then laughed to himself. Gently, he unwound himself from her, covered her with a blanket, and locked up the house for the night. Returning to the bathroom, he did his own lotioning routine and wrapped his hair for the night. He needed to wash it tomorrow. As he climbed back into bed with her, she rolled toward him with a happy sigh, cuddling in like she'd done it for years. He grimaced at his aching cock, but he said again with a grin into the dark room, "totally worth it."

THE PLOT THICKENS

Rachael awoke almost instantly, her heart pounding. She lay there, still, waiting, every nerve tense, waiting for an attack. The room was dark, the outside the still quiet of the deep night. Her gut clenched. Too quiet. In the country, the night was never this quiet. There were crickets and toads, or the goats or horses, or *something* was making noise. Owls or night birds hunting. There was *noise*. It was silent. She released her magic, her subtle glow brightening a bit, but she was afraid to let it go too much—what if whatever was out there saw?

"Rachael?" Drake's voice was rough with sleep.

"Shhhhh," she hissed. Her breathing came fast, she couldn't help it. Every nerve was on edge, trying to sense what the danger was. Every muscle tense.

"What." She could feel him tense next to her.

"I don't know. I woke up, and I felt scared. And listen . . ."

He was silent. The night remained so still. He didn't say anything else, merely slipped out of bed and shifted without a word. The bedroom window was open and out he went. Oh Gods, Drake . . .

Rachael couldn't sense any magic but his, nothing. She couldn't lie there any longer and got up, put on the discarded robe and stole downstairs, using her dim glow to light the way. Still, it was only Drake. He was skirting the perimeter of the adjoining field. Wait. What was . . . there was *something* else out there. Barely anything, it was like a smudge or smoke on her senses; as soon as she sensed it, it was gone. What was it?

There was Ember. They must have felt it, too, the weirdness, up at the main house. She was going in the opposite direction from Drake, and they would meet up, having scouted both sides of the field wasting no time. Rachael started pulling on her shoes and then opened the front door. As soon as it opened, the smudge solidified.

Ember snarled, and Drake cawed, abruptly changing directions and charging at the solid point of magic. It took off running and then it was gone, smoke-like once more.

Back at the main house an hour later, Rachael sipped a mug of tea, warming her hands. Ember and Drake had searched and searched, but after that brief appearance, the trail had gone cold.

"It was definitely Zakaria," Ember snarled, her teeth elongating slightly. "But how he just disappeared is anyone's guess."

"And what made him appear?" Diana set down another mug of tea in front of Drake, who was sitting next to Rachael dressed only in a pair of jeans, and was so close that she could feel his body heat through her robe.

Rachael stared into her mug, rolling it back and forth. "I think I know, or at least, it happened at the same time."

Everyone looked at her expectantly.

She shrugged. "I opened the door."

Nothing. Sam asked, "You opened the door?"

She nodded. "I was going to go out and look. I could sense

that something magical was out there, but I couldn't tell what. It was so faint and it was almost like smoke. So, I opened the door." Ember and her mother shared a look. Rachael exhaled hard. "Look, I know it sounds silly, or like a long shot, or circumstantial or SOMETHING," her voice somehow was very loud and she took a deep breath and began again. "But as soon as, and I do mean, as soon as that door opened, that magic became solid. And you guys scented him. It was instantaneous."

Silence reigned once more. Finally, Ember yawned hugely, and Diana started chivvying them all back to bed. "It's still a few hours until dawn; go on, back to bed with you all. Off with you! Rachael! you're with Drake! You are to rest the whole day, no exceptions!" Rachael thought of Drake's idea of resting and blushed bright red, running out the door so that Diana didn't see it, but Sam's low laugh chased her out. Damn it, this family was a menace.

She and Drake walked together, Drake's head scanning for danger, back to his new home. Her magic felt nothing, no smoke, no magic but his, so she wasn't as worried. The sounds of the night were back. But . . . "What does he want with me?" she asked softly?

"I don't know," Drake said, his voice lower than usual. "But I'll be damned if he gets you."

"And now I've put all of you in danger, too."

"Nonsense. We put us in danger. You didn't make our decisions, brightness." He put his arm around her shoulder and pulled her close to him. "Tomorrow, we'll talk. Tonight we're going to go back to sleep."

Rachael nodded, but the worry gnawed at her. These were people she cared about and all she could see was the damage done to Michelle. Zakaria was the last known person with her. Who else could have done it? Why was he lurking around the farm? The small house was a spot of dark amongst the stars as they approached, and she allowed herself to glow a bit more brightly to light their way. She regretted it almost immediately.

There, scrawled on the door in dripping red, were the words "go home whore."

"That fucking *bastard*," Drake said, with feeling.

Rachael just sighed. "He forgot the comma."

Zakaria seemed to be losing it. Rachael was working her shift at the Black Bear and watched him almost *hit* his server for bringing him the wrong drink. All of his suave arrogance was gone and was replaced with anger and rudeness. What on Earth was he so angry about? Rachael didn't really care except that he was maybe out bespelling women and killing them, so she watched him carefully. Still, she was overjoyed that he was having a bad day. Just thrilled.

She was exiting the restaurant to walk to Diana's office when she felt a presence behind her. "Look, if you're going to lurk, be less obvious about it," she said irritably. "I've had a long shift and you're really annoying."

"You are the most vexing female," Zakaria said.

"Of course it's you," Rachael said, turning. She kept walking backwards, aiming for a busy corner. Snarky and confident she may sound, but she was not keen on being alone with a potential murderer who was also stalking her. "And vexing? What is this? The 1800s?"

"Have you no sense of self-preservation?" Zakaria really looked flummoxed by her, which almost made her laugh.

"Oh, and you really shouldn't call women 'females.' It's insulting." Rachael was almost at the corner.

"I mean to be!" Zakaria's hands clenched in frustration.

"Oh? You are terrible at it. You know, they have this thing called the internet. If you go on it, there are 'trolls.' They can give you lessons." Just a few more feet.

He lunged at her, grabbing her arm, hard. "I don't need lessons from fucking trolls, whatever those are," he snarled, shaking her for good measure. He studied her face carefully. "You really aren't afraid of me. How did you do that?" And then, suddenly, as if he revealed too much, he stood up straight and a mask of calm descended over his handsome face. "I see you are just using your magic openly now."

Rachael pulled back, but he was holding her too tight. There was no getting out without a fight or the element of surprise. "Why should I be afraid of you? You're just a giant prick who is afraid of magic." And she released more of hers.

He hissed.. "Magic is a drug. The more you use, the more you crave."

She laughed. "Still believe the lies, huh?" Something was happening though; it felt like ants crawling up her magic. This needed to end. She leaned forward slightly. "I think you like the magic. A lot. You liked Michelle"s. Does it turn you on, Zakaria? Is it forbidden? Taboo?" She lowered her voice. "Dirty?" His eyes widened, and he blanched.

"You are sick," he spat, and his hand loosened, just a bit.

"Am I? Do you wonder what magic users do with their magic?

How it feels? I think you're jealous." She brought up her hand, as if to touch his face. "I think you *want*, Zakaria."

"Whore!" he shoved her, backing away. "You will not use your power on me!"

She cocked her head at him. Interesting. He had no problem with Michelle's glamor, and yet he was afraid of her magic. He had held her arm, but her sleeve covered her skin. "Oh, I won't?" She stepped closer, now the one chasing him. "What is going to stop me?"

"Rachael!" Diana called to her from the street, pulling up in the car. "Come on, it's time to go home."

"Mommy's calling. Oh wait, not yours." Zakaria smirked.

Her heart gave a pang, but she showed nothing. "Saved by the bell, Zakaria." She turned away and got into the car, her mind running through all of her past interactions with him. Had he ever touched her skin? Had he?

"What was that about?" Diana asked, tense, her hands white knuckled on the steering wheel.

"I am not sure. He wanted something, but I don't know what." She shook her head, absently rubbing her arm where he had grabbed her. "That whole thing was . . . weird."

"Well, he's out of Primero Grove now, in his own apartment elsewhere. I do not want him anywhere near anything connected with us."

Rachael's stomach clenched. Did that mean she was expected to leave? Was that a hint?

"I hope you don't mind, I had Drake stop by and pick up some more of your stuff while you were working, but I think we need to just make a final run now that Zakaria is officially out. You can pack up the rest of your clothes and stuff."

Rachael's body relaxed. She didn't have to leave. She had spent her "day of relaxation" in Drake's new house, helping him clean the graffiti off the front door, to his extreme irritation. She smiled, thinking about how she had made it up to him later.

"I haven't ever done it," she said, her hand pressed against Drake's chest, backing him up to the bed.

He looked at her, her green eyes alight with determination, her hand warm on his chest. "Ah, but, you, I . . ."

"You are not making any sense." Rachael smirked and his cock twitched, hardening even more. "Do you not want me to?"

"I want you to," he said definitely. "If you want to. But you need, I should see to you first." There, he made some kind of sense that time. They had cleaned the brushes and paint cleaning supplies, him grumbling the whole time because she was supposed to be resting, when she had just looked at him and said, "I would like to give you a blow job." And then somehow they were up here and he was backing up and he honestly had no real memory of how that happened.

"Maybe after. But you have seen me come more than I have seen you, and that doesn't seem fair. And I haven't gotten to touch you nearly as much, and that doesn't seem fair either."

She was really making some excellent points. His knees hit the bed. She slid her hands down his shirt, grabbed the hem, and then slid her hands back up underneath, lifting the cloth. He had to help her get it over his head as she was too short, but she thanked him by kissing his chest. And then she unbuttoned his jeans.

Somehow, his pants were off and she pushed him down onto the bed. He sat naked, his cock as hard as it had ever been. She walked to him and kissed him. "You are so beautiful," she said, between kisses. He pulled her over one of his knees, having her straddle it, and she rocked on him, moaning. He groaned. "Hmmm," she said. "Yes, I want to hear from you this time." She said in his ear, still rocking her hips. "Will you moan?"

"I will make all sorts of noises," he assured her, his hands on her hips, and then her breasts, making her gasp. "Strip." he demanded.

She stood and backed up. Feeling confident after the night before, she lifted her shirt slowly, watching his eyes follow the hem. She turned, giving him her back, and then bent as she lowered her pants and he groaned, reaching out to palm her ass. She stood back up and looked back over her shoulder as she unhooked her bra and then turned, clad only in her underwear.

"Fuck me," he said.

"Maybe later," she quipped back. "I have something else in mind right now." She looked at his penis and idly brought up one hand to play with one breast as she imagined him jerking it at her apart-ment. "Lean back on your arms," she said.

He swallowed hard, but did as she asked. She knelt on the floor and moved between his knees and looked up at him, her hands on his ankles, and slowly sliding upwards. "Again, totally new to this," she said and he could feel her breath on his balls. Dear god, he had died and gone to heaven. "Advice is appreciated and if you like or dislike something, tell me." Her hands were on his thighs now and her eyes were on her goal.

Rachael's hand closed around him and she smiled at his grunt and the way his hips moved forward a little. She moved her hand up and down it a little, just enjoying how it felt, soft and hard at the same time, so different from herself, and then brought her mouth down to lick the tip.

"Fuck, that's . . .do that again." She did it again and then licked the length from the bottom to the top and he made a strangled sound that made her pussy wet. He was breathing faster.; was that good? She kept her hand tight around the base because he seemed to like that, and then she slowly lowered her mouth down the crown.

"Rachael!

Rachael blinked. "Oh, yes, Diana?"

"What on Earth were you thinking about? I called your name three times."

Rachael shook her head. "Nothing. Not a thing."

Diana glanced at her. "Oh, I see. Well, we're almost home. Nothing should also be there."

Rachael laughed. "It all feels too fast and also not fast enough."

"You've been in town for months now. You two should go out. Let him take you on a date. You don't need to eat every meal with his parents." Diana shook her head. "Even I think that's weird. It's a weird situation and I don't want you to feel trapped. If you want out, you tell him so, you hear me?" Diana's voice brooked no opposition, so Rachael nodded. "AND, if you decide you want to live elsewhere, you just say so. I know you enjoyed your independence, as well you should!"

Rachael shook her head. "You give me plenty of independence," she countered. "Far more than I ever experienced with my family. I am very happy at your house."

"Well, then," Diana said, clearing her throat. "Good."

They turned the last corner and headed up the long drive to the farm. Rachael saw another car up ahead. "Who is that?"

"I don't know," Diana replied. "It can't be good. Visitors rarely are."

The car was a beat up converted relic of a vehicle. "Is that a classic Beetle?" Diana asked, impressed. "I haven't seen one of those in forever. And it has solar? Wow."

Rachael had *never* seen one, even the more modern ones were rare, and she was awed as well. "Actual metal, not fiberglass." She couldn't help peering inside. "Look! Stick shift! Do you think it really works?! I've only read about those in books!"

The front screen opened and Sam called out, "Rachael, you have company!" Pixie barrelled out of the door, barking ecstatically in greeting, running straight to Diana who was making cooing noises. Rachael shook her head fondly before responding to Sam.

"Me?" She looked up and saw Fernanda standing behind Sam carrying a mug, black hair loose and dressed in black jeans, and a ripped t-shirt, and wearing a spiked collar around her throat. Her make up was heavy and dark, and she emanated a "don't fuck with me" air that was very impressive.

"Hello, Rachael," she said in her slightly accented voice.

"Fernanda," Rachael crossed over the porch and shook her hand. "What on Earth brings you all the way out here?"

"Murder, of course. What else?"

HAPPINESS

"The second body came in yesterday," Fernanda said, back in the kitchen. The three of them were at the table, focused on the coroner as she studied the liquid in her mug. "At first, I thought it was just a suicide. He had jumped off the roof of his apartment building."

The front door opened and they heard Drake and Ember entering, taking off their shoes, and walking down the hall. They entered the big kitchen and froze at the sight of Fernanda. Drake immediately came to sit next to Rachael, taking her hand, because he knew who she was and what she did for a living. Ember cocked her head, her locs falling to one side, as she studied Fernanda, and came over to sit next to her.

"Hello, I'm Ember," she said, sticking out her hand, never breaking eye contact.

Fernanda returned the perusal, but seemed less intense about it. She merely cocked an eyebrow back, briefly shook the offered hand and said, "Fernanda, Yolo County Coroner."

Ember's eyes widened in surprise, and Fernanda smiled a bit.

Rachael, impatient, sat forward. "So, second body, yesterday, assumed suicide from roof jumping."

Fernanda cleared her throat. "Yes. Nothing seemed out of the ordinary and nothing seemed to contradict that conclusion." She shook her head. "Nothing, that is, until I looked at where he was found. Here, in Davis."

"Two suicides? In the span of a couple of weeks?" Diana asked. "Here?"

Rachael looked around. "Is that unusual?"

Fernanda nodded. "The statistics for suicide in a town the size of Davis are fairly small, an average of two to three a YEAR, certainly not that many in a few weeks. Two suicides in just a couple of weeks is exceptional and noteworthy. And since it turned out the last death wasn't actually a suicide . . ." Fernanda shrugged.

Rachael sighed. "Do you need me to come and look at the body?" she asked reluctantly.

Fernanda gave her a sympathetic look. "I'm sorry, but yes."

"Ok, I'll be there tomorrow morning." Drake squeezed her hand.

"Since you're here, how about staying for dinner?" Diana asked, standing.

"Actually -"

"I know," Rachael said, looking at Ember. "Why don't we go to Woodstocks? I haven't been out in ages."

Fernanda frowned. "I really should get back."

"We have an extra room here, if you can't drive," Drake said to her. "We can drive together tomorrow."

She raised a black, perfectly arched eyebrow at him. "All of you are potentially suspects in a murder investigation."

"*Potentially*," Rachael said, raising a finger with an arch look.

Fernanda blinked and then laughed. "Ok, I'll admit, I find myself dying to get to know you better."

"And you're punny, too," Rachael said.

Drake groaned, clamping a hand over her mouth. "Do stop now or she'll run away."

"Give me a moment to change and shower," Ember said, her eyes having never left Fernanda. She turned, as if reluctant to leave the room, heading upstairs.

Drake kissed the top of Rachael's head. "Yes, I'll be right back."

"So, you're with Drake," Fernanda said. "Is Ember single?"

Rachael stood to go get ready to go out as well. "Ember? Oh yes, I believe so."

Upstairs, Rachael slapped on some make-up and a new shirt and then ran to Ember's room. She was trying on outfit after outfit, frantically.

"Oh, whoa." Rachael said, taking in the chaos. "Breathe, hon."

"Have you SEEN her?" Ember threw on another outfit, dismissed it immediately, and dived back into her closet. "She is so fucking cool. And the most confident person I have ever met. How do I even compete with that?!"

Rachael blinked. "Is it a competition? And by the way, when I first met you, I thought *you* were the coolest most confident person I had ever met."

That brought Ember up short. "What?"

"I mean, have you *seen* you?" Rachael gestured to Ember, from her locs to her feet. "Are you fucking kidding me?"

Ember stood up a little taller. "Ok. You're right. I am cool."

Rachael nodded. "Absolutely!"

"I can't be too alt, though. She's already got that look covered. But . . ." She started pulling things out again, but this time the frantic energy was focused. She had a plan. In the end, she was in a leather mini-skirt with chains dangling from the pockets, thigh-high boots, and some sparkly backless shirt that tied around her neck and back. Honestly, Rachael thought it was likely held on by magic. She looked like alt plus.

"Amazing. Ready?" Rachael held up her fist for bump and Ember took a deep breath and bumped it.

"Let's do this."

Drake was already downstairs. He and Fernanda were waiting, chatting quietly in the front room while they waited for them. He looked up and grinned as they came down the stairs.

"Ember looks ready to either go to war or vomit." He whispered in Rachael's ear.

She poked him. "Hush, she's nervous." She kept her eyes on Fernanda, who kept her eyes on Ember. Good.

"Why don't we take two cars?" She suggested, already moving toward the door. "That way, if I Drake and I end things early, you too can stay out longer." And she was already out the door, Drake right behind her, thank God, before either of the other women could offer up a protest.

"You are mean," Drake said, pulling out of the drive and onto the road heading to Davis proper.

"Well, yes and no," she said thoughtfully.

"Oh?"

"I have plans for you, Mr. Archer, and they require energy and time. I don't plan on staying out too late."

Drake's hands tightened on the steering wheel and his eyes darkened. "Oh? Plans?"

"Hmm hmm. Plans. Good ones, too." Despite having the house ready, Drake had been taking things slowly with her physically, which she appreciated, but she was ready. More than ready. Past ready. And with things in Davis looking so grim, she really wanted to find something pure to celebrate.

"Did you want to, maybe, share some of these plans with me?" Drake's voice had dropped an octave, and Rachael smiled.

"If you're good, maybe."

"If I'm *good*?" Drake shot her a look. "But you like it when I'm not."

Oh, she really, really did. She reached over and patted his thigh, feeling it clench under her hand, and smiled. To think just a few months ago, the thought of just this touch would have made her blush and run. "Better try hard then."

"Being hard won't be a problem," Drake muttered.

Rachael giggled and Drake muttered an oath and adjusted himself in the seat, trying to find a comfortable position, which just made her giggle again. "Okay, no more giggles or I'm turning this car around now." Drake threatened.

Rachael burst into laughter.

Dinner went well. The atmosphere of Woodstocks and the clientele lent enough material for there to be a steady stream of conversation. Fernanda was sharp witted and dry humored, with a piercing gaze that missed nothing. Her entire being oozed confidence. Coupled with her height and dress, that confidence caused people to give her a wide berth. Her and Ember together? The crowd parted before them like the Red Sea.

"I think Ember has met her match," Drake mused, watching as the two women went to the old-fashioned jukebox to select some music. "Fernanda is no pushover and she's smart."

"Does she usually date pushovers?" Rachael couldn't see that happening at all. Ember needed a strong personality, someone who would challenge her, but not break her.

Drake snorted. "Not by choice. But men can act tough only to run when she won't back down. And women . . . Well, she hasn't found one that fits yet. She's been looking for a long time."

As they watched, Ember reached over in front of Fernanda, pointing at a song, and the other woman wound an arm around Ember's waist, pulling her in close. Drake's eyebrows climbed to his hairline. "I have never seen a woman make the first move on her. Ever."

Rachael was beaming. "It's so sweet. I do hope it works out. We should go. Leave them to it."

Drake's head swiveled back, having not forgotten for one second their conversation in the car earlier. Only to find Rachael staring at someone off to her right. "What are you . . . oh." There was a man, very fit, with a woman, her arm around him, and he was wearing a cropped t-shirt and a short pleated plaid skirt. "Have you not seen a man in a skirt before?"

"Nooooo," Rachael said slowly, turning back to Drake, a strange look on her face. "I have. Just not that kind." She gazed at Drake thoughtfully.

"You. . . you can't mean, really?" Drake gaped. "I wouldn't have thought that was your thing?"

"I don't know if it is all the time," she mused thoughtfully, her teeth chewing on her lower lip. Drake sucked in his breath, his eyes glued to her mouth. "But, you kneeling while you are wearing it, and reaching under it—"

"Jesus Christ on a fucking . . ." Drake shoved a slice of pizza in her mouth, and her eyes widened. He leaned forward so that his mouth was next to her ear. "Rachael, when is your birthday?"

She giggled, and he swore some more. It felt like all he had been doing was swearing and his cock had been hard since he got in the car. "What did I say about the giggling?" he told her darkly.

Reaching up, she took the pizza out of her mouth, and gave him a scorching look. And she giggled.

Drake swore, threw some money down on the table, grabbed her hand and hauled her from the table. He stood there, breathing hard and holding her to him for a moment, letting her feel what she was doing to him. "I am going to tell Ember we are leaving." He tilted her head up and gave her a hot, wet kiss. "You are going to wait. Right. Fucking. Here. If you are not here, there will be consequences." He gave her another kiss, his mouth taking full possession of hers, her knees going weak, and then he was gone, leaving her gasping.

"Hot DAMN," someone said next to her. Looking over, she saw it was the couple she had been staring at before, the woman and the man in the skirt. It had been the woman who spoke. "That has got to be the best kiss to go down in the history of best kisses."

Rachael blushed. "It's why I keep him around."

The woman pulled her companion in close and he put his head on her shoulder. "I totally understand. What I had originally meant to ask you was, are you guys leaving? We're looking for a table."

Rachael told her that Ember was remaining, and as the woman

was leaving, Drake reappeared. "Damn," he said. "I was half hoping you had taken a step to the left." His eyes twinkled at her.

She laughed. "I think we will have quite enough going on tonight. Like I said. I have plans."

"Did he just growl?" Rachael wondered as he once again grabbed her hand and hauled her away. She was laughing though, finding this teasing fun. Who knew what tomorrow would bring, but she knew that the days ahead would be darker and tonight, well, tonight she wanted light and passion.

Back at his house, the car had barely stopped before he was out, leaping across the hood with shifter strength and swiftness, and opening her door almost before she had removed her seatbelt.

"Drake!" Rachael laughed as he slung her over his shoulder, slapping her ass, and took off toward the house. "Honestly!"

"This is what you get, teasing me all night!" He slapped her ass again and a bolt of pleasure shot through her, dampening her underwear.

Drake stopped, his head turning toward her jean covered ass as he took an audible sniff. "Hmmm, you liked that. We may have some consequences tonight after all."

"Damn your shifter senses!" Rachael yelled at him, swatting *his* ass, which only made him laugh.

He carried her straight upstairs and dumped her onto the bed, sending her sprawling, and then immediately began removing her shoes and clothing, dropping kisses upon each new bare patch of skin.

"Drake," Rachael said, as he kissed her navel.

"Hmmmm?" Drake's rumbling inquiry made her squirm.

"Plans," she managed to get out, as his mouth traveled up to her bra covered breasts.

"Plans," he repeated, his mouth covering her nipple through her bra, making her gasp.

"I went to the doctor the day after you made me come in my apartment," she said, and this time, he stopped, his mouth hovering over her neck. "I went on birth control. Implant." His hand ran over her arm, testing and finding the tiny, tiny implant. "It's always only been you, Drake. And enough time has passed since it was inserted . . ."

"You want me inside you tonight," he said into her ear, nipping her earlobe. "And you are asking if I want to wear a condom."

"Yes." Rachael felt herself blushing, which was ridiculous. This man had had his fingers and tongue in her most private places, but somehow this felt even more personal. More real.

"Plans indeed. This is relationship talk, Ms. Rachael Knight." He kissed her tenderly and deeply, his hands cradling her head, his hips settling between hers. Leaning back so he could look at her, he said, "I was tested before I started seeing you and I haven't been with anyone else since then. No condoms. Is that okay?" And then he waited, his finger teasing the edge of her ear.

She nodded. "Yes."

"Hmmm, Rachael, you are full of surprises." He pressed his jean clad hips to her, and she moaned as the ridge there rubbed against her thinly covered pussy. "I don't want to share you, so if we are doing this, it is only my cock in here, only my hands, only my mouth. Are we clear?"

"Drake, if you fucking touch another woman I will shoot you dead," Rachael said with no hesitation. "And as for me wanting another cock, why would I?" She moved her hips, rocking against him. "This one feels really good." She arched up, rocking some more, using him for her pleasure.

Drake groaned at the sight and feel of her grinding herself on him. "Fuck, you learn fast. No! Don't you dare stop, that's it." She had slowed, afraid he hadn't liked what she was doing. Now, seeing the heat in his eyes, she reached behind her and unhooked her bra. "Drake, please."

He lowered his head and sucked her nipples, using his teeth to apply pressure, his tongue to sooth the bite.

"Oh, Gooodd," she moaned, grinding faster, harder.

"Are you going to make yourself come?" Drake asked, using his fingers on her breasts, whispering in her ear. "Do it. Use me to pleasure yourself."

Her arms grabbed his hips and her legs wrapped around his. "Drake, please!"

"Please what? Tell me what you want." He rocked his hips gently back and forth while she went up and down and she cried out. "More, I . . . I need more." He pulled back, and she moaned at the loss of contact, but all he did was pull down her underwear. He stood and started to undress. She watched him, panting, her hips still jerking, needy. "Touch yourself, Rachael. Show me how you do it, what you like."

One hand went to her breast, her fingers rolling a nipple, the other parted her labia, and he groaned as he unbuttoned his pants, his eyes glued to her body. She dipped her fingers in her wetness and then returned to her clitoris, rubbing in light circles. A light blush started to spread from her chest up to her face.

"You're close, Rachael."

"Yes!"

Now naked, Drake moved her farther up the bed, lying beside her, his hand cupping her, his mouth on her other breast. He inserted one finger, and she moaned and removed her hand from her clit.

"I didn't tell you to stop. Put that hand back," he ordered.

She put it back. He added a second finger and her back arched, her breath coming faster and deeper. He found that spot inside, swelling now, and she let out a sharp cry.

"That's it baby, let go. We'll do it together." And between one breath and another, her orgasm roared through her and he drank the cries from her mouth while he rode the spasms with his hand.

"I should be embarrassed at what you get me to do," she said, finally lifting her hand from her body.

"Never." He captured the hand, brought it to his mouth, and licked it clean. "I love what I get you to do." He put her hand on him. "I present the evidence."

She wrapped her hand around him, and all she wanted to do was roll him over and ride him. Instead, she hooked her leg over him and rubbed her wetness over him, letting it slide over her.

"Not yet, greedy thing." Drake said. "I get to warm you up again and this time, it is all me."

"What? What was it last time?" Rachael gave a surprised cry as he rolled over on top of her with surprising speed.

"A joint effort." he nuzzled her neck and gave it a biting kiss. "A gentle introduction. And we both know that while you like gentle, what you really enjoy," and here he bit the side of her breast, hard enough to leave an imprint for a second, the pain shooting straight to her pussy and making her buck beneath him, "is a bit of pain and roughness. And that," he said with such a heated look that her hips wriggled under him, "suits me just fucking fine." He bit the other breast and then blew on it, the differing sensations making her moan. "If you don't like something, say no. If it's something I think is truly shocking, I will ask." He looked at her, his eyes blue fire. "And if you want me to do something, *ask*."

And then he set to work. Rachael fell into a world of sensation. It wasn't all pain, but it was all passion. His hands took what he wanted, first her mouth, holding her head still while he claimed it, his tongue dancing with hers, his teeth biting her lips, until they were both moaning and her hands were in his hair as well, gripping handfuls of his short twists. He kissed his way down her neck, biting wet kisses, using her hair to turn her head, biting her shoulder, and suddenly her wrists were held in one of his hands over her head.

"Oh!" She tugged, but they didn't budge. He waited, watched. "You okay?"

She nodded. "Yes."

He kept his eyes on her face as he used his other hand to bring a nipple to his mouth. She closed her eyes, moaning at the hot wet heat, arching up as much as she was able, twisting to get closer to him. He groaned at her response, rubbing his erection along her pussy, making her cry out.

"Yes, that's new, isn't it?" he said, repeating the movement, while moving his mouth to the other breast. "Feel how hard I am for you?"

Beyond words at this point, Rachael panted, wrapping her legs around his hips, rocking herself along it.

"Hmm, too much movement." He unwrapped her legs and straddled her, depriving her of his erection and she thrashed against his hands and cried out in disappointment. "Oh no, Rachael. This orgasm, this one is *mine*." Her eyes widened at his tone and she stilled, moisture seeping from her pussy and her thighs clenching. He chuckled. "I see you're getting it now." He let go of her hands, burying his in her hair, kissing her deeply. "You can touch me, but if you do anything to yourself without my permission there will be consequences."

Rachael shivered, her eyes closing, and she ran her hands down his back, his shoulders, and around to his chest. "You are driving me mad," she whispered.

"Yes," he replied. "And you're loving it." In demonstration, he bit the joining of her neck and shoulder sharply and her hips bucked, or tried too, under him. His hands were back on her breasts, kneading and pulling. "I love the noises you make," he said, as he slid down her body, taking care to keep her legs closed. "Especially as you get more desperate." His mouth did something sinful to her nipple, and she made a keening noise as her hands clenched on his shoulders.

"Please, Drake," she said. "Please!"

"What do you want, Rachael?" Drake knew she was still shy about verbal requests. She wasn't shy with her body or her desire, but actually making the request was hard for her. He blew on her damp nipple, watching the skin pebble around it.

"I need your . . . touch my pussy, please." The words came out in a breathless rush. Rachael's mind was in turmoil, a mix of desire and fear. God, had she really said that? Drake grabbed her hair and kissed her fiercely while rolling off of her at the same time.

"Good girl, Rachael," he said. Her whole body clenched, desire and pride pooling together inside her. "I want nothing more than to touch you."

"GOD," she said. Desire and pride now warred for dominance in her as his hand skated down her stomach to cup her between her legs. "Yessss," she hissed, raising her hips.

"You are so nice and wet for me," he said into her ear, biting her earlobe. "Just soaking."

His words only made her more wet, and he knew it, the bastard. He slid one finger inside and then another. "Please! Oh, god, Drake." She strained against him and put her hand on his wrist, not to stop him, but to hold him there, while she rode his hand.

"Please what, love?" His fingers slowly moved in and out, keeping her on the edge. He moved his mouth back to her neck and then her breast.

She gasped, trying to twist so that his fingers hit that spot inside her, but he was too smart.

"Tsk, naughty. You need to ask, Rachael." And he pulled his fingers out, slapping the inside of her thigh.

Her back bowed at the sharp sudden pain that had turned into the most intense pleasure, coming back down only to find Drake looking at her, considering. "Almost sent you over," he said with a smirk. "Good thing I didn't smack your pussy."

"The fuck," she exhaled sharply, and he laughed, kissing her and then his fingers were back and she lost her concentration. In and out, so slowly. It felt *so good* and yet was so damn frustrating, too. She just needed *more*, and he knew it too, damn him!

"Drake, please! I need…" she groaned in frustration, knowing what he wanted. He nuzzled her neck.

"You can do this. What do you want, Rachael?" His voice was warm and loving and gentle. "I want to give you what you want."

He thrust his cock against her hip and she groaned, her hips jerking. "Yes, feel how hard I am for you? God, I've been like this since you started talking in the car. And your pussy is so wet and hot and you are making the most amazing sounds. What do you want, Rachael?"

And suddenly it was easy. He was right. Everything else she had been doing had been open and honest; she could do this too. "Drake, please, I need you. Will you make love to me?"

He groaned, grinding against her. "Fuck yes, I will. God, it's sexy when you ask."

She moaned, loving his response, as he rose above her and got between her legs, his hand on his cock. Her breath caught at the sight; it was so hot, everything about it, the passion in his body and face, his hand on himself, the look he was giving her. She never wanted to forget it.

He put a forearm beside her and kissed her while he pressed the head of his penis against her and they groaned together as they slowly merged. "God, so tight," he said.

"It's been a while," she replied, resting her head on his shoulder. "Give me a sec." They lay there, connected, and she had never felt so full. "Okay," she said, kissing his shoulder, his neck, his chin. "Now."

He pulled out just as slowly, his eyes never leaving her face, and then pushed back in. Her eyes slid shut on their own accord at the delicious feeling, and her head fell back. "*More.*" She demanded.

"As you wish," he said, nipping her chin. And then he started really moving, a steady hard rhythm that made her moan. He paused, but only to shove a pillow under her hips, tilting them and the next time he thrust, he hit that spot inside her and her whole body lit up. "There it is," he said, and he grabbed her waist, thrusting slightly faster as she flushed, getting closer. "Come for me Rachael."

Rachael heard the command, but she had no control over her body. His cock was hitting her g-spot with every thrust and she was on the verge, his words, given in the command and said while his body was inside hers, just drove her over the edge. "Drake!" she cried as she fell over it, pleasure cresting.

He groaned, feeling her pulsing around him, and he drove into her, chasing his own finish, which wasn't far. Rachael felt his thrusts become slightly erratic, and then he was pressing against her, his cock pulsing inside, and he was groaning into her hair. "Oh, Drake," she sighed, wrapping her arms around him, just as tightly as her legs, and they lay there breathing each other in.

An unknown amount of time later, Rachael found the strength to go clean up in the bathroom, Drake following soon after she returned, and then they collapsed together in bed, falling asleep, naked, limbs entwined, and whispered words shared between them.

Rachael had this moment of happiness at least.

STOLEN

"**G**ood morning."

Rachael grinned and rolled over. "Good morning," she said, blinking her eyes at the bright sunlight. Drake was propped on his elbow, smiling down at her. "Have you been watching me sleep?"

"Only a little," he said, bending down to kiss her nose. "How are you feeling?"

In answer, she pulled him down for a kiss, hooking a leg around him, and then reaching around to fondle his ass. He deepened the kiss, his hand massaging her breast, his erection hard on her stomach.

"You're not too sore?" he asked, his hand working its way down her stomach.

"No," she gasped, as his finger found her clit and his mouth her nipple. It was slower than the night before, but no less passionate, rocking together as their need climbed; until Drake reached between them and circled her clit with his finger and she came with a cry. He let himself go, his orgasm waiting there, and they lay there, gathering themselves in the morning sunlight.

"I didn't think I could get any closer to you," Rachael said into his chest.

Drake gathered her to him and kissed her head. "You always had me, from the start. From that first lunch, watching you look at ketchup like it was gold."

She laughed. "You treated me like I was a deer about to bolt."

"You seemed like it." He kissed her head again. "Hey, before we get busy this morning, I need to tell you some—" his phone rang. "Damn."

"They're waiting for us," Rachael said, climbing out of bed and heading for the shower. She didn't let his words freak her out. At all. Really. She was sure what he was going to tell her was something totally innocuous and fine and nothing serious.

"Rachael," Drake, attempted to stop her as she headed directly downstairs after his shower.

"I have to grab—"

"Rachael," he hooked her around her waist, and put a hand on her face, making her look at him. "Breathe."

She huffed out a breath. "You're dripping." She wanted to hide and run, her whole body tense. If she didn't hear the bad news he was holding on to, then it didn't exist.

"Deal with it." He kissed her, gently. "I'm not running away and I'm not mad, okay?" He pulled back, looking into her green glowing eyes, so full of fear. "I am so sorry someone made you feel this afraid."

She shuddered, her anxiety disappearing. "Okay. Thank you."

"Give me five minutes and we'll head over together." He kissed her again, rubbing his nose on hers, before disappearing to get dressed.

Ten minutes later, they walked into his family's kitchen, hand in hand, and Rachael nearly groaned as the smell of coffee and bacon slapped her in the face. Then she caught the underlying thread of tension and froze, looking around. Everything seemed fine, everyone was eating at the table . . . no, wait, Fernanda wasn't here. She shared a glance with Drake, but didn't say a word; she wasn't an idiot.

"Here, dear," Diana handed her a mug of coffee, and pulled out a chair for her.

"Oh, I love you," she said, sipping it and sitting. Suddenly both Sam and Ember froze and turned to stare at her, their eyes changing to their animal form briefly. Ember's turning golden, Sam's black.

Rachael paused, one hand frozen, lifting a piece of bacon to her mouth. "What?"

Sam turned and pierced his son with a hard look. Drake looked uncomfortable and shrugged his shoulders. "You called before I could bring it up," he said, somewhat defensively.

Ember's look at Drake was disgusted. "Honestly, Drake, this needs to happen BEFORE not after. As we TOLD you."

"WHAT." Rachael's voice was getting louder, and she was definitely not appreciating feeling out of the loop.

"What do you know about shifting mating rules, brightness?" Drake asked, his hand reaching out to take hers.

"Mating rules? There are mating rules?" Rachael frowned.

Sam cursed. "Drake, she was isolated from magic her whole life; you are going to have to tell her. Your mom and I lucked out, plain and simple, but a good many people didn't and got trapped. She deserves to have the option."

Drake's hand tightened. "I had hoped to do this without an audience," he said, throwing his family a glance, "but you are carrying my scent now. It's obvious to anyone who is a shifter."

"WE'RE MATED?!" Rachael asked wildly.

"NO." Drake turned her to face him. "I would not do that to you, do you hear me? I would not just spring a lifetime commitment on you with no warning. We are NOT mated, but it has started."

"How?! What? How does it just START?!" Rachael was gripping his hands like he was a rock in the sea.

Drake shook his head. "It's exceedingly easy to start. In fact, after the Conversion, many couples were mated without even intending to be." He nodded his head at his parents. "Mom and dad being two of them."

Sam and Diana nodded. "It's true, surprised the hell out of us." Sam said.

"But . . . what DOES start it then?" Rachael's eyes were bouncing from person to person.

"Well, frankly," Ember said, "sex."

"Not just sex," Drake said, squeezing Rachael's hands, pulling her attention to him. "Meaningful sex."

"Ooookay," she said. "If that starts it, how is the process completed?" Rachael should have been mortified talking about sex with Drake's whole family, but the idea that she may have been mated without her knowledge somehow outstripped that.

"Well, more," Drake said with a small smile. "Which is why I needed to talk to you. There's a bit more to it than that. I'll explain on the way to Sacramento."

Rachael managed to stuff some food into her mouth and swallow some of it, but her mind was whirling. She fluctuated between anger, excitement, and anxiety and she had so many questions. By the time they got in the car, she was about ready to explode.

"You knew this was a possibility before last night." It wasn't a question.

Drake was driving, which was probably best, considering her emotional state, but he shot her a glance. "Yes. I wasn't lying this morning when I told you how I felt about you and how long I've felt that way. Depth of emotion goes a long way; it's one of the reasons meaningful sex matters and not just a one-night stand. The magic," he rubbed his chest, "it senses the connection. And you cannot deny we have one."

"No, I don't deny that." She never had denied that. It was the intensity of it that scared her, actually, and why she had taken so long to do anything about it. She had felt railroaded into it from the beginning and now magic was doing it again, trying to force her into a commitment she wasn't ready for. She shrugged her shoulders, trying to loosen muscles that felt too tight. "You should have *told* me, Drake." She clenched her fists. He knew how she felt. He *knew*.

"I know. I'm sorry. I messed up." Drake reached out a hand to her, but she refused it.

"How is the mating completed? I need to know everything." She kept her voice steady, but he flinched as if she had yelled.

"The magic sees the act of mating as Mating," he said. "So, sex is how it is done. One partner, during a meaningful act of lovemaking, asks their partner, or partners, if they are consenting. Magic doesn't differentiate between the act of sex and the lifetime bond. If you consent to one, you consent to both. That's how it starts."

She thought back. "When you held my wrists."

"Yes," Drake said, his hands gripping the wheel. "That was the start. It takes three consecutive consents to seal the bond and make partners Mates."

Rachael took a deep breath. If he had asked her two more times last night . . . "So, we have two more times," she still wasn't yelling.

"Rachael," Drake's voice was soft. "I promise, I would never—"

"Stop. Talking." Rachael snapped her mouth shut before she said anything else and took a deep breath. "Let's just get to Sacramento and then I can . . . I don't know. Process this."

"Okay." Drake nodded. "I know, it's a lot—"

She slashed her hand in a silencing gesture and turned to face out her window. She couldn't speak without crying and if she cried now, she wouldn't stop, and she had to be in control to do right by a dead man. God. Damn. It.

After the longest twenty-minute drive in her life, Fernanda escorted them back into the morgue. She was stony-faced as well, inviting no questions about Ember, so they were a silent party, their steps the only sound as they walked down the tiled hallway.

"Here," she said, gesturing. "His name was Jamie." He was young, as young as Michelle had been, with neat black hair and a tan complexion. "He landed on his back, so most of the physical damage is underneath. You should be able to do your examination without too much trouble."

Rachael swallowed. She hadn't thought about the fact that he had jumped from a building and what that would mean for his body. Still, she approached and studied him, looking for traces of magic, releasing more of her own.

"I'll never get used to that," Fernanda murmured as Rachael gave off a soft glow.

"There's something here," Rachael said, nodding. "Absolutely. Now that I know what to look for, it's easy to spot." She lifted her hand and gently grasped the netting of magic. "What magic did he have? It isn't glamor; it feels different." It had that same wrongness to it as the magic that had been on Michelle's body . . .

"Shifter." Rachael and Fernanda spoke in unison.

"He was a Bear," Fernanda said quietly. "And your eyes, they are a bear's eyes, Rachael."

Her eyes had glowed yellow when she had done this with Michelle. And her glowing, dimmer now that she had been using her magic, was dimmer still as worked with the magic on Jamie's body. Rachael filed that all away to the back of her mind to be dealt with another time.

Drake let out a soft sigh. "There are not many of the large predators," he said sadly. "The poor kid and his family. Mom and Dad probably know them. We'll reach out."

Rachael kept busy with the job at hand, her heart aching under its iron casing of anger and hurt. Yes, Drake was a kind man. He also had almost entrapped her in a lifelong commitment without her knowledge.

"It's much the same as with Michelle," she told Fernanda. "A lattice of magic woven out of a combination of the person's own magic with some unknown type and then overlaid on the body. I'm removing it now." She gently grasped the fine strands and pulled. First, she revealed the face.

"The fuck," Drake swore darkly.

Rachael swallowed. His face had been severely beaten, the nose broken, the lips split, and both eyes blackened. The bruising had started to fade to a sickly green color, but the lips had continued to break open due to the severity of the cuts. There was a wound on his jaw, some sort of round scab. "What is that?" Rachael pointed. "It's not a cut."

Fernanda donned a pair of gloves and magnifying glasses. "It's a burn," she said, examining it. "Whoever did this branded him."

Rachael backed up a step, breathing deeply. It was exactly like with Michelle. Exactly. "Can you make out the symbol?"

Drake moved closer to her, his arm stretched out, but she moved away. He wasn't a comfort right now. His lips tightened, but he dropped his arm. Fernanda didn't miss the byplay, but she didn't say anything.

"The burn was sloppy this time. It was too hot and pressed too deep." she straightened and moved around the lab. "I can try and figure it out digitally. I'll take a photo. Can you finish removing the magic cover?"

Rachael really didn't want to, but she also knew that the brand was a piece of evidence. There could be more. "Yes." She switched to fresh gloves and resumed, carefully dragging the magic web down Jamie's chest and arms. More bruising appeared, although not as intense as his face. There was more around his genitals, just like with Michelle, signs of rough sex, possibly non-consensual, and his legs bore marks of restraints. "Okay, there's no sign that there's any more. I think that's all." She brought up the sheet to cover his body before stepping back and removing her gloves.

Fernanda nodded. "Thank you. I know this can't be easy; you're not used to being around, well, this." she waved her hand to encompass the morgue, Jamie's body, and possibly murder.

Rachael gave a tight grin. "I'm not, but it helps to know I am trying to stop it from happening again. Can you tell us if you identify the symbol on his face?"

Fernanda shook her head. "Not unless the police release it. Active investigation and all that. I'm barely allowed to let you in here and that's only because you can do what you do."

Rachael nodded. She hadn't thought so, but she had had to ask. "Okay. Well, good-bye then. And Fernanda," the tall woman raised an eyebrow in question. "Whatever happened, I'd like to hang out with you some more. Don't be a stranger."

Her face softened a hair. "The dance has just started. The next step is hers." She gave Rachael a brief hug, something Rachael felt she didn't do often. Then she turned to Drake. "I don't know what you did, but I feel like I should punch you. Fix it."

Drake's face closed off and his back straightened. "I don't know you."

"I don't give a fuck." She pointed at Rachael. "This woman is walking sunshine, and you dimmed her." Her dark eyes glared daggers, full of malevolent promise. Rachael, touched, placed a hand on her arm. Fernanda stared at Drake for another long moment before turning away. "Make him work for it," she told Rachael, throwing Drake a glance.

Despite herself, Rachael smiled. "Yes, ma'am."

"Walking sunshine." Fernanda shook her head. "Okay. Off with you. I have work to do" She shooed them out of the room, turning to get back to work.

The car ride back wasn't quite as tense and quiet as the ride to the morgue, but Rachael wasn't ready to talk to Drake about the mating bond yet. The whole thing still made her feel twitchy and betrayed, bringing up feelings about magic that she had thought buried. As soon as they pulled into the drive of the farmhouse, she jumped out and bolted, heading into her room upstairs in the main house. Ember was waiting.

Rachael stared at her for a moment and then said, "I can't be here."

Ember nodded. "I'll take you to my apartment in the city. You can stay there for a bit."

Rachael sagged in relief, taking a shaky breath. "Thank you."

"He should have told you." Ember's eyes flashed dark gold. "I don't care if he is my brother. You cannot do that to a person without talking to them first. And he knows your history."

The tears that had been threatening all morning prickled the corners of her eyes and she blinked. "I have to go. Now."

Ember didn't ask questions or hesitate; she just helped Rachael pack a bag and then they were downstairs and in the car. "I'll tell Mom and Dad. Did you want me to talk to Drake or will you tell him? I'll do whatever you want."

Rachael dropped her head back against the seat. "I'll tell him. I'll call tonight. I just need a few hours of space first. If he asks, you don't have to lie, you can tell him, and tell him I'll call tonight. I don't know what I'll say, but I'll call."

They drove in silence for a bit. Rachael noticed Ember seemed on edge, but then saw her open her mouth to say something only to close it before she did. "Fernanda looked well this morning."

Ember's mouth, open again, shut with a snap. "Oh?"

"No, she didn't ask after you. And I had the distinct feeling if I had mentioned you, she would have shot me down instantly. She is a very private person." Rachael didn't mind. She liked that Fernanda had respected Ember's privacy.

Ember smiled, her body relaxing. "Yes, she is."

"I don't suppose you will tell me . . . ?" Rachael left it hanging suggestively.

Ember snorted. "Not much happened, but it's started." She smiled a feline grin. "The fun has just begun."

Rachael didn't understand, but Ember seemed content, so she let it go. "Thank you again for lending me this apartment."

They were pulling into the parking lot before Ember replied. "Sometimes distance is the best remedy. Take some time to think; I'll be here when you need me."

Rachael entered the one bedroom, cozily decorated apartment, appreciating the comfy over-stuffed couch and the throw blankets. She dropped her bag, collapsed on the couch, and let herself cry. The pent up emotion broke out in sobs and didn't last for very long, but it left her feeling tired. She pulled a blanket over herself and fell asleep, her eyes swollen and nose red, curled up on the couch.

Something was wrong. She wasn't sure what it was, but she knew something was wrong. She didn't move, trying to take stock of where she was. She was in Ember's apartment, wasn't she? No. She wasn't. She was moving. She tried to open her eyes, but the lids wouldn't lift. What was going on?

"The drugs should wear off soon. I couldn't risk you waking up while I was carrying you to the car. Screaming would have drawn too much attention." The masculine voice came from in front of her. Car. She was in a car? "I didn't give you a lot, but it was an injection, so it knocked you right out. Time to wake up now, though."

She was sensing more of her surroundings. Yes, she was in a car. She could hear the road noise now, feel the bumps in the road. But who was that speaking? Who would have taken her? She tried to move her arms and nothing happened. The car turned and the noise of the road changed and the bumping increased. They were no longer on a paved road. Where was he taking her? She tried lifting her lids again and this time they worked.

"Ah, there you are." Zakaria's handsome face looked at her from the reflection in the rearview mirror. Icy terror slid down her spine, but she tried to keep her face still. "I was wondering when you'd rejoin reality. Sleeping Beauty never really held any appeal for me."

"No," she thought to herself. *"You like them awake and aware you creep. Bluebeard in the flesh."* She tried her hands again, but still nothing. She was lying on her side across the back seat and she felt way too exposed, but she just couldn't make her body *move.*

"I did have to tie your hands and legs together," he said, almost apologetically. "If you got lost out here, you could hurt yourself."

Right. That's why she couldn't move. Okay. Well, this was bad. This was really pretty damn bad. "You seem to be taking this rather well, Rachael." Zakaria said, cocking his head quizzically.

She remained silent, but he was right. She felt no fear, not yet. It was there in the back of her mind, but her brain was busy, and right now it was busy telling her that talking to him was the wrong thing to do, as was panicking. Panic made people make mistakes. She needed to think.

"Well, we'll have time to talk," he said, unconcernedly. They drove for a bit longer and then he turned, bringing the car to a stop.

"Here we are. Home sweet home. Now the fun really begins."

No Help Is Coming

Zakaria opened the door and pulled her from the seat, standing her up and propping her against the car. "If I release your legs, you can't go running off. There are no people anywhere near and you'll get lost or hurt."

She stood there, docile, looking around. They were in a small clearing, paved with gravel, in front of a small house. Where the hell had he taken her? Davis was smack in the middle of a flood plain and there just weren't a lot of wooded areas. Had he taken her all the way to the coast? Or the mountains? California was broken up after the Convergence and if he had, she may very well be out of state or even country. It had simply been too big and too diverse politically to survive the chaos after magic had been released and the aftermath when all reliable methods of fuel were destroyed. The entire United States had started to collapse from the middle toward the edges as well. Still, that was neither here nor there.

"Where are we?"

"Far enough to not try running, love," he said, kneeling down to release her legs. She dearly wanted to knee him in the face, but she also knew that he was petty enough to make her pay for that later. So, she waited. It was far better for him to think she was calm and to underestimate her and to trust her a bit.

"But the trees."

"Oh, it's just an old family place. We've owned it for years. Planted the trees when we bought it originally. Helps keeps out prying eyes." He stood and grabbed her arm, pulling her forward. Her legs were still wobbly from the drugs he had given her and he had to drag her more than she would have liked. Maybe he hadn't taken her that far then, if the trees had been planted around the house.

"Vacation home, huh?"

"Feeling chatty?" Zakaria asked, seeming amused.

"It just feels a little rustic for a vacation place. Please tell me there's running water and flush toilets."

"Little princess needs flush toilets?" He sneered. "Too bad. There's an outhouse, and I brought water with me." He turned and raked his eyes over her. "I'd be happy to give you a sponge bath, though."

Her mind recoiled from *that* thought, but she didn't react beyond saying, "no thank you."

They climbed the stairs, and he unlocked the door. She saw that the windows had bars on them, which seemed odd way out here, and the deadbolt was one of three locks. "Take your security pretty seriously."

"You never know what you need to keep out," he said ominously. She shook her head. Probably people looking for him, she thought. This was a bolt hole if she had ever seen one.

"Stay here," He sat her in a straight-back chair at the back of the main room as far from the door as possible, while he went and closed it. Returning, he waved her to follow him. "You will have this room."

Her own room, huh? She looked in. There was a cot, some stacked milk crates, a battered dresser, and a bucket. "How lovely."

"You will stay in here unless told otherwise. Give me your hands." He didn't wait for her to follow his instructions, just grabbed her wrists and then removed her restraints. There was a deep bruise around her wrists and part way up her arm; he had tied her tightly, and he traced it with a finger. Rachael's jaw tightened in an effort to not jerk back. His eyes . . . the look in his eyes as he looked at her wrists. Ice slid down her spine. She never wanted to see him look at her like that again.

"Am I to sleep on the cot as is?" She asked. "No blanket? A pillow? What am I to do for clothing?" She did not care, at all, but she knew it would anger him and distract him from whatever he was thinking right now and she *needed* to get his hands off of her.

"Spoiled brat." He shoved her inside the room and shut the door. After a few seconds there was a click and she knew he had locked her in. She stood, waiting, until she heard his feet walk off and only then did she allow herself to shudder.

"God," she whispered. "Fuck, that was gross." She wrapped her arms around herself and paced the small room that was her cell. Now what? She had no doubt that her absence was going to be noticed soon. But how would they find her? Why did Zakaria take her? What did he want with her? It occurred to her now that the graffiti on Drake's house had been literal— Zakaria had wanted her to go home so he could abduct her. As soon as she was outside of the protection of the Archer ranch, he had struck.

Well, she had nothing but time it seemed, and she could either panic or do something. So, she looked around the room. First was the dresser. She opened every drawer and examined every corner, even pulling it out from the wall to look behind it. On the back, there had been several sets of initials carved on the bottom. She traced them, wondering who they had belonged to. Thinking of Michelle and Jamie, she pushed the dresser back and turned to look at the door, wondering if Zakaria was a serial killer and this was the next progression. She was not the first person to stay in this room. Had he killed Michelle and Jamie with a strange magic suicidal spell? If so, why would he kidnap her? If he was going to kill her, why not just do it the same way he had Michelle?

She expended a bit more magic. The walls around her room reflected back at her. She got close to them, wondering why they would do so; there were no mirrors in here. Rachael had just lifted her hand to touch when she heard the door being unlocked. She turned to face it, hands folded primly in front of her.

Zakaria entered, laden with bags. He threw them on the floor in a heap and then stared at her.. "Ah, trying some magic huh? won't work," he delighted in telling her. "The room is warded. Nothing you do in here will be able to be seen, felt, or noticed outside of this room."

She made a pretense of frowning in consternation, but this was hardly something that was a hardship. Her magic was passive. The most active thing she could do was act as a lightbulb. Or peel off glamor shields on dead bodies. Or collect stray goats. Maybe talk to old oak trees. Apparently Zakaria didn't know that though, so she made an effort to keep it that way.

"Here you go, Princess. Toilet paper, clothes, sleeping bag, toiletries. I even left a few magazines. Say thank you,"

"Thank you," she said immediately. She imagined pulling his hair out strand by strand and it helped ease the sting a bit.

"So biddable," he said. "I must say, this is a side of you I didn't expect. You were so corrupted by your new friends, I thought for sure you would make this whole experience harder for yourself, but I can see you're very smart about your circumstances."

She bowed her head to keep him from seeing her grimace. Biddable. Yuck. "What experience is this exactly?" She asked as neutrally as possible.

"Tsk tsk," He wagged a finger at her. "Curiosity killed the cat, Rachael." And the door was shut and locked once more, leaving her alone and with no more answers than before.

"Ugh." She stared at the pile of shit he had thrown at her. There seemed to be a sleeping bag, some sort of disgusting looking pillow, and bags of soft looking items, maybe clothing. She sighed. Well, she had more exploring to do; this would keep. The bars on the window were on the outside *and* inside of this room, which was odd, and the soldering was solid all the way around as far as she could reach. Not even a hint of rot or weakness.

She plopped on the cot with a sigh, staring at the pile of stuff on the floor. Whatever Zakaria had planned, they were going to be here for at least one night. At some point, he was going to have to feed her. Would he just throw food at her like he did these supplies? What did he *want* with her? None of the other victims in Davis were removed from the city, as far as she knew. And Michelle had been willing, by her own admission. There was no reason to think Jamie was any different.

Well, Rachael was definitely not willing, and they were not in Davis anymore. So either Zakaria was not the killer or his M.O. had changed drastically.

Did Ember realize she was missing yet? Were people looking for her?

What if she was never able to work things out with Drake?

Emotion drove her to her feet once more, and she paced the room like a caged animal; she let her magic surge. The reflective surface of the shield around the room looked like water or molten metal; liquid and blurry she could just see her glowing skin, hair, and eyes as she moved about the room. It was reflective enough that it bounced from one wall to the next. The sun had lowered toward the horizon and soon would set, the day having passed and she was bright enough and the walls reflective enough, that she could light the room.

Suddenly, she stopped. Glamor shields. She could remove glamor shields.

"Fuck me, I'm an idiot," she murmured.

"No argument from me," Zakaria said behind her.

She turned, forcing herself to do it slowly and not spin suddenly. He was standing in the doorway, casually leaning against the doorjamb. Why he had to be so good looking was a great mystery of the universe. "Can I help you?" she asked politely, acting as if this was her home and he was invading it.

He frowned. "You really are something. It's no wonder you were exiled. I am more surprised it took so long." He straightened. "Dinner. You will eat with me."

She didn't move. He had taken several steps before realizing that she wasn't following and was forced to turn and come back. "Was something I said unclear?"

"No." she said, simply.

He looked at her. She looked back. "What are you doing, love?" he asked after a moment. "This won't end well for you."

She didn't reply. She had been accommodating so far. What would he do if she weren't accommodating? Would he starve her? Hit her? She needed to know the rules if she was going to break them, and since he wasn't being very forthcoming with them, she would just start with defiance.

"Last chance. You will eat dinner with me." He gestured toward the room where there was, supposedly, a meal waiting. She didn't move. His eyes narrowed. "I see." He approached her, his eyes full of dark anger, but otherwise calm. He grabbed her chin in his hand and lifted her face, forcing her to look at him. "If," he said, with quiet menace, "you do not eat with me, you will not eat. In addition, for refusing to follow instructions given, there will be a consequence." And with no further words, he grabbed her hair at the crown of her head and dragged her from the room.

She bit back a pained and startled cry, her eyes pricking with tears, as she bent over to try to relieve the pain on her scalp. He made no effort to help, only continued to walk. Once they were at the table, he forced her into a chair. Then he tied her hair to the chair back, making it so she couldn't bend her head more than a few inches forward. "Hair really is pretty good for temporary restraints."

She lifted her hands only to hear him "tsk" behind her. "Don't even think about it or it will go much worse for you." Her hands dropped.

"Good girl." Those words from Zakaria made her skin crawl, and she clenched her jaw to keep from saying something sarcastic as a reflex.

"You will eat dinner, but now you will have to do it as you are." He moved away and then returned, placing a bowl of chicken soup in front of her with a spoon next to it and then sat across from her with his own bowl. He grinned at her. "Bon appetit," he saluted her, raising his spoon.

She stared at him in chagrin and then turned her gaze to the soup. Swallowing, she raised a hand and reached for the spoon. She had to really stretch to reach it, her hair keeping her from bending forward. Carefully, she dipped it into the soup, tried to wipe the excess broth off on the side of the bowl, and then brought the spoon slowly to her mouth. Half the soup fell on her and half ended up in her mouth. Zakaria watched the entire process with undisguised entertainment.

"I was really afraid you were going to make this a boring assignment for me," Zakaria said, leaning back in his chair.

Assignment? Rachael tried not to react to his statement and just continued eating. Her shirt was damp with cooling soup, but she was managing to get at least half of the soup into her mouth. Zakaria's comment had allowed her brain to ignore his staring and her embarrassment because now she had something to think about. He was on an assignment? To do what? And what did it have to do with her? And why the *hell* couldn't she feel what kind of magic he had?! She knew he had used a glamor, but there was no way for her to tell that he had magic at all. If he hadn't done that at the bar, she would never have known he was capable of it.

After an interminable period, the meal ended with her wearing half of her soup. She was starting to shiver from being wet and cold, and she was stiff from being forced to sit in the same position for so long. She lay down her spoon and waited.

"All done then?" Zakaria was grinning at her brightly, the asshole. He rose and removed the soup and spoon. As for her hair—

"It is just tangled beyond fixing, I am afraid," he said, not sounding at all apologetic. There was the unmistakable sound of scissors as he cut her hair free from the chair back. "There, all done." He didn't set down the scissors.

Rachael stood up carefully and turned back to her room.

"Ah ah ah," chided Zakaria. Rachael froze. "You didn't thank me for dinner."

Rachael closed her eyes for a moment and then turned slowly to face him. He stood there, scissors held in one hand and his face avidly watching her for some sort of reaction. She smiled and said, "thank you for dinner." And then waited.

He kept her standing there for a long time before finally saying, "you are excused."

She turned and went into her room, but didn't shut the door. Rachael had figured out the game now, and it was one she had played before. She had lived it. Hell, she grew up in it. It was her life before she was exiled. It may not have been this extreme, but it felt very very similar to her home life under her father's rule. She would have to wait for permission for privacy, and then that privacy could be revoked at any moment. The only difference here is that Zakaria also wanted privacy, and he wanted to ensure she remained secure.

Sure enough, here he came. If she had any guess, there would be some punishment for playing correctly as well. There was never a reward. "You will not be visiting the outhouse today. The bucket will do if you need to relieve yourself." And the door shut, and the locks clicked and she was alone.

She sagged onto the cot. "Mother fucker." All that time she spent healing and finding people who treated her with respect and love, and here she was, dumped right back into the shit. Tears started streaming down her face unbidden, and she wiped them angrily away. She didn't have *time* for this! Self-pity solved nothing, and tears only made things wet. Well, in this case, wetter. She plucked at her shirt in disgust, making a face as the scent of drying soup wafted at her.

"Once more into the breach," she said bracingly and took a deep breath, which she instantly regretted as she once more smelled soup, and stood up. First things first, she decided. She dug through the pile of stuff on the floor, wishing for the first time that her magical glow had remained brighter, and found a cleaner shirt. Once she had changed, she looked at the walls.

"I can remove shields," she repeated to herself. This shield differed from the ones on the bodies, true, but she approached the wall and carefully reached out a hand. She couldn't see anything to grab onto and she didn't want to touch the wall in case there was a trap there. Her hand hovered over the wall for a moment, but she didn't see or feel anything.

"I'm going to have to touch it," Rachael said softly, in lieu of sitting in silence. Her hand was glowing brightly now, her magic burning, and she slowly set her hand on the wall, bracing for something.

Nothing happened. At least, nothing happened *to her*. Rachael let out a sigh of relief and then stared at her hand because something had definitely happened *around* her. The reflective/liquidy surface of the wall disappeared where her hand was and in the immediate surrounding area. She could see the magic underneath and then the wall under that.

A scuffling noise near her door caused her to jump, and she jerked back her hand, quickly stepping away from the wall and closer to the window, pretending to look outside. Rachael could see Zakaria's shadow under the door as he paused there, listening. What he was expecting to hear, she didn't know, but he stayed there for several moments before he left, walking away. Rachael's whole body was jumpy and twitchy; how she was going to survive this without punching him from sheer fight or flight, she had no idea.

She returned to the wall and set her hand on the shield. The magic was a lattice, very fine and woven tightly together. Rachael pulled her hand back, frowning. There was no weak point to grab onto and move it. But . . . her eyes moved to the floor, which was not shielded. How did the magic connect to the floor? Whoever had constructed the shield had to have secured it somehow, or it would have moved when she had touched it. Maybe it was tied to the floor?

Rachael got onto her hands and knees and started crawling around the floor, running her hands along the baseboards. The lattice was uniform all the way across; it was a really neat bit of magic. It felt fae, but it wasn't a glamor. She didn't find anything until she hit a corner.

"Got you," she hissed. And she did. There was a knot there, something she could pull on. She tugged gently on a line of magic, watching it slither free from its neighbors, the end waving in the air.

A thud by her door made her jump and spin, sitting with her back to the wall. She watched Zakaria's shadow move past the bottom of her door again and ground her teeth. The bastard was doing it on purpose, just like he was denying her any sort of light. She had looked for a flashlight or lamp in the pile he had dumped on her floor, but there had been nothing. Rachael supposed she was supposed to ask for it; he would love for her to come begging. Well, she didn't need it. Feeling somewhat silly, she stuck her tongue out at the imaginary shape of Zakaria in the other room and waited for him to move on again. It took him longer this time; who knows what he was doing out there, but she really wished he would just hurry up. Now that she had found a knot, she wanted to untie it.

Just when she thought he had moved on, she had in fact gathered her legs under herself in preparation to move, her door flung open hard enough to bang against the wall. She didn't jump, prepared as she was for something like this, just froze and stared at him. He was looking at the cot, obviously expecting to find her there, and when he didn't, frowned. Rachael crossed her arms and waited for him to find her.

"What are you doing on the floor?" He asked, shaking his head.

She shrugged. "Cot or floor, it's all the same."

"Hardly," he replied dryly.

"Yes, well, I'm not the one who tried to catch me doing something illicit on the cot, pervert." Rachael said, trying to be calm, but knowing that's what he was doing. He was just looking for ways to terrorize her, whether it was keeping her on edge or meting out punishments for perceived wrongdoing.

"And now you've earned yourself a punishment," he said, rather too gleefully. Rachael would have rolled her eyes if it wouldn't have gotten her into more trouble. Honestly, was there a handbook somewhere? Because she talked back, she was guessing it would be a gag or some other means of keeping her from talking, which would be fine. She needed her hands free. This way she was controlling the scenario and could still work on the damn shield.

"Come here." Zakaria pointed imperiously at the floor in front of him while reaching into his back pocket.

Rachael rose and crossed the small room and stood exactly where he pointed, not saying a word. Now that she had given him what he was looking for, she would cooperate so he would fuck off.

He pulled out a black piece of fabric from his pocket and grinned evilly at her. "Sass gets you gagged. Turn around." For fuck"s sake, he really was this unoriginal. She barely managed to force down the eye roll. She turned around, and he wrapped the fabric around her head and into her mouth tightly. As her saliva wetted it, though, she caught a taste of something and swallowed, stiffening.

"Ah, noticed that little extra surprise, did you? I coated it with cayenne pepper. You'll be a little uncomfortable for a while."

What an asshole, she thought, her eyes watering, her mouth on fire. Maybe it would go numb? Zakaria grabbed her shoulder and spun her around, studying her face. Her eyes were teary, she couldn't control that very physical reaction, just as she couldn't help the extra saliva her mouth was making. He smiled. No, he *beamed* at her. "Ah, very nice. Now, I don't plan to keep you completely in the dark forever." Her ears perked at that, even as she was trying not to blink too much or sniff back the snot her nose was making. "We will be staying here for a couple of days. I have to make appearances in town. Alibies you know." He grinned at her, blue eyes sparkling in the light from the door. "After that, we're going on a little trip."

Fuck, this was awful. It was so damn *spicy.* Just concentrated spice in her mouth and every time she moved her tongue or tried to find a new area, she got a fresh mouthful. She tried to moan a question, and he knew damn well what she was asking.

"Nah ah, it's a surprise!" He took in her red face, and she crossed her arms, trying to hide the fact that she was starting to sweat. He chuckled darkly. "The sooner you learn to cooperate, the sooner I won't have to do all of this. When we are on the road, you cannot be acting up." He leaned in. "It won't matter to me if you remain in the trunk of my car the entire way. It will be entirely up to you."

She swallowed and then winced at the burning pain and the resulting flood of tears and snot. He reached behind her and untied the gag, pulling out several strands of hair as he did so. "No more sass."

"Okay."

He nodded, turned, and locked the door.

The knot in the corner was the same as she had left it—one thread was waving around loose, the knot ready to be picked apart. She found another thread and picked at it, pulling it out and the knot loosened, causing the whole spell to shimmer. She froze, but then went on. After the third thread, the knot came undone, and the threads waved like fronds in water from the corner. Rachael sat back and grinned. She could do this!

Okay, time for the other corners. The cot would be last, after Zakaria was asleep. Too much risk of discovery if she meddled with the cot to get to the corner. And the one behind the door was out for the same reason. So, she went to the safest remaining corner and started there. After about ten minutes, she heard movement in the outer room, so she turned around and sat.

"What *are* you doing in here?" He asked curiously after finding her sitting on the floor again.

She shrugged. "Waiting. It's very boring."

He handed her a glass of water. "I don't believe you. If you are not in that cot when I come in next time, I'm going to tie you to it." He watched as she drank the water greedily, washing the remaining taste of cayenne out of her mouth.

Well, being tied up would be inconvenient. It would let her work on the knot there, though. He closed the door, locked it and then said through the door: "you have about twenty minutes before that sleeping pill takes effect. I suggest you make up that cot, or you'll be very uncomfortable."

What. An. Asshole. She glared at the door and resisted the urge to toss the empty water glass at him. Pawing through the bags on the floor she hastily made a bed *under* the cot (why make it easy for him if he came in looking for her in the middle of the night?) and squeezed in. The fit was very tight and uncomfortable, but it felt a bit safer knowing that she would be knocked out and incapacitated. While she waited, she worked on the knot in the corner, working on it until her eyes closed and she knew no more.

BECOMING

The next couple of days were very bland punctuated with brief periods of fear and anxiety. Her world was a tiny room and only the brief interruptions of Zakaria when he decided to make her life more miserable. He would disappear for several hours each day, going, Rachael assumed, back to town to make an appearance and buy supplies. She used this time to disconnect the shield from the wall completely and start attempting to unravel it, but it was beginning to look like she was correct in her assumption that it was also attached to the ceiling.

After his trips, he would come back and inevitably force some evil punishment on her for her behavior. These she could handle. These tiny injustices and discomforts only added up and cemented her dislike. They played along with who she thought he was. It was when he had her come out and sit with him and play games like chess or cards that she hated. She didn't want to play nice or act happy or see him have fun. She didn't want to appease him or smile. It made her feel gross and fake and anxious. And he knew it. She also knew that he was doing it so that she would become used to being around him. He could take that notion and go straight to hell with it. Wherever they were going, it was not a vacation, she was not going to go peacefully, and the first opportunity she saw for freedom, she was going to take it. There was no way she was going back into a situation like her childhood. None. She would die first.

It was the middle of day two when Rachael just got angry and desperate and she decided she would give up on the corner idea. She stood in the middle of the room and stared at the walls with her hands on her hips. She was dirty, her hair was hacked to different levels, her arms were sore from holding books at shoulder height, her thighs ached from doing wall squats for who the fuck knew how long, and she was just *so tired.*

Marching to the wall, she slapped her hand against it and, as usual, the silvery sheen of the shield parted to reveal its matrix. Rachael cocked her head and studied it more closely. She brought up her other hand and closed her eyes. What if she was relying on her sight too much? She had always *felt* magic before. It gave her a feeling or a shiver; she could see it too, but she felt it first.

Fae. It was definitely fae magic. It jangled against her skin, vibrating, almost humming. Each strand was vibrating different-ly, but together they made a sort of chord. *Hmm,* she thought. *"What if I put it out of tune?"*

Opening her eyes, she picked a strand at random and hooked a finger around it, trying to pull it out as much as possible. Okay, now, how to go about changing it? She released a bit more of her magic and concentrated on that one strand. She felt the vibration going through her finger and her magic dimmed. In fact, the whole wall did a bit. She frowned and let out some more, and the same thing happened, the reflection fading so that the matrix was clearly visible. The vibrations grew stronger.

"Huh, that's weird." Rachael flashed back to when Ember startled her when she was running from Zakaria when he first moved to Davis and she had dropped all of her shields so quickly. She had almost turned, her claws, teeth and eyes *had* turned. Rachael had just assumed it had been a defensive maneuver, but what if her magic had caused it?

She started feeding her magic out in a slow but steady stream, attempting to keep it focused on the one strand, but knowing it was spilling out everywhere, anyway. The strand started vibrating faster and faster. "Oh God, it's working!" she said. "Fucking hell, it's actually working!"

And then suddenly the strand broke, the ends slithering away, and the shield looked like an old mirror, the silver aged and marked. Rachael stood there, breathing hard but grinning. "Hot damn, look at that! I can actually *do* something!" Unable to contain herself, she danced a little jig, stopping when her sore muscles complained. "Ow." Rubbing her thighs, still grinning, she went on, burning out thread after thread, watching the mirror dim and then "poof" out it went.

Rachael looked at the bare wood wall of her room and laughed. "I did it! I actually fucking did it!" She may still be behind a locked door, but now she knew how her magic worked and the shield to her room was gone. At the least, she could feel other magic users and maybe, somehow, they could find her. Maybe.

Too full of energy to sit still, Rachael paced her small prison, giddy and grinning, allowing herself the occasional twirl. Active power, she could buoy power! She had never heard of anything like that before, and she really wished she had someone here to ask about it. She went to the window and stared out at the trees. The bars were sturdy, she knew that, and she would bet money there was iron in them. Fae magic users, she'd heard, were sensitive to iron, just like in the old stories. What she would give for that Viking she had seen that one night out with Ember. He looked like he could bust through one of these walls with no problem.

A crow landed on a tree outside and goosebumps erupted all over her body, causing her head to jerk up. *Shifter*, she thought. She stared at it, hands curling around the bars and gripping them tightly. The crow turned its head, looking at her, but before there were any further developments, a gunshot rang out.

"No!" she cried, as the crow disappeared in a flurry of feathers. Had it been hit? Where was it?

Zakaria came into view holding a pistol, looking in the direction of where the bird had been, and then he turned to look at Rachael. She swallowed nervously, but he only turned on his heel, returning back the way he came.

"Rachael, it's time to go." He called as he entered the cabin. "It seems we have been discovered. Come on, we have a long way to go."

He unlocked her door and beckoned her with a crooked finger.

She slowly walked toward him, everything in her screaming to run, but her eyes watched the gun in his hand. "Where are we going?"

"Oh, well, that's a surprise now, isn't it?" He grinned at her, his handsome face bright and happy. "I told them I would let it be a surprise."

Oh, she didn't like this at all. She did not want to be moved, and she did not want to go to wherever *they* were. He was hired by someone. For what purpose? She kept moving though, her breathing speeding up as the adrenaline sped through her system.

"Hurry up, girl," Zakaria snarled, finally losing his patience and grabbing her arm. What she had forgotten in the bright light of day was that she had her magic burning and the instant he touched her, she felt it. He was magic. *He had magic.* She flashed back to his glamor in the Wunderbar; she had known rationally he must have cast it, but she had never, ever felt his magic. She had been too drunk and upset to detect it then. And since then she had never felt it. Ever. But now she had finally touched his skin and there it was, and it was powerful.

He cried out and flung her away from him, causing her to fall back several steps, hit the cot with one leg and spin, arms windmilling to help catch her balance. "What was that, you magic using bitch?" Blue eyes blazing, he advanced on her.

"Nothing!" she said, which was true. "I didn't do anything!"

"You used your disgusting magic on me, I felt it." he was there, his hand in her hair, lifting until she was on her toes, her hands on his arm as she tried to pull it away.

"No! I can't!" she said, on a sob of pain. "I can't do anything with it but sense other magic! Please! I swear!" She had dampened her magic now, but not completely. She could see the shield he had around himself now, how it lay over his body to prevent anyone from sensing his magic. The sneaky lying bastard!

"Why were you using it, anyway? You are going to ruin everything!" Spit hit her face as he spoke, and she could feel his body tremble with emotion.

"No! No, I won't ruin anything! Please!" The gun was there, but he wasn't raising it.

He lowered his arm and her scalp stopped screaming in pain, but he kept his grip on her hair. "Ah well, I suppose I'll just have to say there was an accident in your retrieval." A calm came down over his features that sent a stab of fear into her gut and she felt her bladder want to release. If she had ever seen a man look at her with death, this was it. "Yes, this will be much more fun for me." The gun did come up this time, but only so she could see the handle descending. There was a flash of pain on her temple and then darkness.

Her head throbbing was the first thing she noticed when she came to. The second thing was that she was outside; it was cool, and the wind was blowing her hair. The third was that she was sitting up and her head had been lolling, causing her neck to pull painfully. She knew she would have to lift it and the desire to do so was almost irresistible, but she also knew if she did, Zakaria would start whatever he had been planning.

"You can stop pretending. I know you are awake." Zakaria's voice whispered in her ear and she flinched.

Groaning, she lifted her head, her neck complaining loudly, and her eyes squinted against the pounding in her skull. Gods above her head hurt. She was in a . . . field? Yes, she was in a farm field. The night sky stretched above her and something tall grew around her, whispering in the night breeze. The watering apparatus lurked like some dark monster over them all, waiting to bestow its life-giving moisture after she was offered as sacrifice.

"What are you doing, Zakaria?" she asked incredulously, staring at what could only be a pyre.

"You know what I am doing," he replied, still whispering creepily next to her head. "You know what that is."

Rachael clenched her jaw in annoyance. "Fine, I'll play. *Why* are you doing this?" She pulled on her arms and she wasn't surprised to find them tied behind her.

Zakaria stood and walked around in front of her and she saw that he was dressed in dark clothing and sported a wicked-looking knife in a sheath on his hip. All evidence of the decadent man in Davis was gone; this man strode with the knowledge of how to use that blade and his face was sharp with the knowledge of death. Dread slid down Rachael's spine. "Since you ruined the original plan, I've decided to go with the plan for you from the very beginning."

What the fuck was he talking about, the plan for her from the very beginning? But as she looked at the pyre, suddenly the pieces fell into place. "No. You can't mean from—"

"You were meant to die, Rachael. That was the plan. You were sentenced to death by fire." He turned and looked at the pyre thoughtfully. "A little drawn out for my taste, really, and impersonal. And more clean-up than I like. Still, I am not the one who decided it," he finished with a shrug.

"But *why*?!" she cried, pulling at her bonds. "I don't understand why I need to die *now*, you absolute bastard!"

"Tsk tsk," he tutted at her. "You really should watch your language. It could get you in trouble." And he backhanded her across the face.

She breathed heavily through her mouth, trying to keep awake. Her head pounded and now her cheek and nose also ached. Blood ran down her face from somewhere. She tried to ignore it.

"But, those sentenced to death are told of their crimes. Magic,

Rachael," he said, arms opening wide, as if that explained everything. "Your fucking magic is why."

Rachael stared at him blankly. Finally, spitting blood out of her mouth first, she said, "that doesn't explain why now."

"Hmm," he crouched down in front of her, his eyes black in the night's darkness. "You touched me with your magic and you saw. I know you did because I am not stupid either." His voice was full of dark menace and intelligence that had not been there before.

She frowned. "The shield? But that's all I saw! I swear I don't know what it hides!" But what did it hide? She wanted to know that, too. And she was dead anyway. Her shields were impossible to hold with the pain she was in and her soft glow indicating that she was a magic user diffused into the night. "I can't even see it from here! See? You're safe!"

"I am a Tracker, Rachael."

Her mind went numb, and she stopped breathing for a moment in shock. Trackers were essentially bounty hunters, sent out to collect magical beings for money. They were often used by law enforcement, but sometimes they were used by colonies like the ones Rachael came from, to hunt and bring back or kill those who used their magic against the colony. "Wh-Why are you after me?" she whispered. And unvoiced, she wondered, "*what are you hiding from the people who hire you?*"

"I was hired to return you, originally," he said. "That was the contract." He stood and went to the pyre, checking the post and the fuel around it before returning to her. He said as he lifted her to her feet, "your mother wanted you brought home. She felt she could convince them of your innocence, or at least, of your inability to harm."

Her mom? Her mom had hired this man? She could see the shield around him as he walked her to the pyre. Anger overtook the numbness that had descended upon her at his news and she started to tear through the threads of the shield as they walked, trying to pace slowly, pretending she was still in shock.

"What-what are you doing?" Zakaria suddenly stopped, shaking her, but she didn't stop, not when she was so close. It wasn't nearly as complicated as the shield that had been in her room. "Stop it!" He gathered his arms to push her away, but it was too late; with one last surge, she burned through the last thread and the shield disintegrated. "Ahh, fuck!" He shoved her anyway, and she sprawled on to the ground, tripping and out of balance because of her bound hands.

"You're shifter and fae, together!" she laughed. "You can't have anti-magic colonies finding out their Tracker uses *magic* to collect his bounties. Or worse, to seduce and kill magic users."

With the shield down, his anger turned his eyes golden as his shifter magic burned. "The rebound from that hurt, damnit." He rubbed the side of his head.

"I am so sorry," Rachael said sarcastically, rolling her eyes from the ground, her face covered in blood and her body aching. She inched her legs under her, trying to get onto her knees. She released more magic, uncaring now what he did to her. In fact, he was going to kill her anyway, let him try to get close to her when her magic was at its strongest. "What is the Fae magic? Is that the shield?"

"Not that it matters, but no, I can Track magic with it. Once I find it, I can follow it wherever it goes." She stared at him in horror. With that magic and a shifter's senses, no magic user would ever be able to hide from him. Hell, no criminal would have a decent chance, really. "The shield is a basic glamor, but it works well enough. Fae magic is pretty adaptable. The tracking ability is the strongest of it all." He stopped rubbing his head and glared at her. "I think the shield masks the magic somewhat actually, I can sense you a bit stronger now that it's gone."

Rachael said nothing, secretly hoping it was because she was slowly increasing the strength of her magic. She managed to gain her knees, but then Zakaria grabbed her, impatient. "Come on." He lifted her and began dragging her toward the pyre once more, forcing her over the pile of wood and newspaper and other tinder, growling as she tripped.

The hair rose on her nape. "That sounded real growly there, Zakaria," she said. "What animal do you turn into?" She kept releasing more magic, just a bit at a time.

"Lynx," he snarled, backing her up to the post. He went behind her and she heard him rustling in his clothing, then felt him tying her hands together around the post. "Watching you mingle with lesser shifters was difficult."

"Lesser?" She snorted. "Because one can fly and the other is smaller? Is a lynx better than a bobcat somehow? I can absolutely believe you think you're better than a squirrel." Her ire at his dismissal of her friends and what had felt like family made her hands shake.

He was growling constantly now, a low rumble in his chest. Something scraped the skin on her wrist and she knew his claws had emerged. "Small and pitiful." He rubbed his cheek on her cheek, much like a cat marking territory and she jerked away. "I could have made you very happy on the trip back home. I know Michelle enjoyed our time together."

Her skin tried to crawl off her body this time. He had admitted it now that he thought her defeated. He had the magic and the inclination. He could put the glamor on the bodies and he could glamor himself. But how did he make them hate themselves? "I like myself too much, though, don't I?" She tried to meet his eyes, but he was still behind her. "Can't mess with my mind the same way, can you?"

"Clever girl," he ran his fingers through her hair, pulling on it, bringing his face to her ear. "Next to Tracking, Charming is strongest."

Revulsion made her stomach clench. He had placed those ugly insidious thoughts inside Michelle's head and probably Jamie's. He had destroyed them and killed them for no other reason than he wanted to. "Why kill her, though?"

"She knew, of course. The shield doesn't hold through touch, and a Fae especially can feel it. I couldn't have her tell you and she was a friend of yours. So I charmed her to forget and then she had to disappear as well. Charms fade after a time; it's a sad truth. It was how I had planned to get away after I returned you. Once the charm had worn off, causing you to forget I had used glamor on you, I would have been far away. That plus your lack of credibility with your own people and the high probability that you would be killed by them anyway—" He stepped back and then off the pyre and shrugged. Rachael ramped up her magic faster now.

"And Jamie?" Rachael threw out the name like a dagger, angry and sharp.

Zakaria froze for a second, surprised. "Well, look at you. How well informed." Rachael kept releasing magic; she was on borrowed time now. He could light this thing at any second. More, she needed to give out *more*. "Jamie was mine. He was a weakness." Was that regret on his face? Indeed, Zakaria's face had softened for a brief moment as he thought back and sadness echoed in his golden eyes.

Suddenly, he groaned. "What is happening?!" His words were muffled as his teeth became fangs and fur erupted from his body.

Rachael could feel the magic pouring off of him now and she threw everything in her out, but instead of using his magic she threw it back at him so that her eyes never changed. No, her eyes glowed like green fire.

"Ahhh, it's you!" he gasped, bending over. He wasn't shifting completely, but his hands were paws now, his ears tufted. He raised his hands to his head, scratching it as he grasped it, moaning in pain. "I can't . . . every magic I tracked . . . I feel."

She kept it up, forbidding herself to feel bad for him as he fell to his knees. He had killed. He was going to kill her. She steeled herself; with her magic she could feel it all.

"Stop!" He screamed, his hands/paws gripping his head, digging deep furrows in his skin, blood running down his pale skin and darkening his blond hair. Zakaria, once so handsome, had lost all good looks, beast and human fighting for dominance on his body, and he fell over on his side, writhing in pain. It couldn't last much longer; Rachael closed her eyes, unable to bear it, and finally, everything went still and quiet.

She stood there, sobbing quietly, unmoving for a long time, afraid to look and afraid to stop the magic. Finally, she took a deep breath and slowly opened her eyes.

THE RETURN

Zakaria was on the ground, but he was still alive. Rachael couldn't stop crying and she was afraid she was going to hyperventilate, but she didn't lower her magic. As she watched, Zakaria lifted his head, just enough for her to see his face. Blood was leaking out of his eyes and nose and ears and it was apparent that he was almost beyond moving, but with whatever he had left in him, he twitched a finger and a flame caught on the tinder beneath her feet.

"NO!" Rachael screamed, her agonized sobs turning to screams of rage. Zakaria's head fell to the dirt, and he moved no more, but now smoke curled in front of her and she had a new battle to fight. She wrenched at her hands, but there was no give at all in the ropes. Her feet were untied, and she kicked at the ground, trying to move the stake she was tied to, throwing herself side to side, while also trying to upset the placement of the fuel the fire was trying to burn. "God damn it all to mother fucking hell, I will not die NOW! You fucking asshole!" She screamed obscenities until words failed her and she was just screaming in rage, yelling as she rocked back and forth, feeling the stake move, but so, so slowly. She felt blood run down her fingers as the rope rubbed through her skin and her shoulders wrenched, but she didn't stop. She couldn't. She had to break free.

Smoke started billowing up and blowing into her face and she coughed, but kept going. She would not die because some man thought she needed to die so he could make money killing people. No. She deserved better than this!

"I am better than this!" she screamed at the heavens. "I was free! I cannot die trapped back in this hell, I can't! I won't!" She shoved harder, heat touching her toes now. And then she felt a drop on her face, cold and wet.

And then another.

She froze, hardly daring to believe it. Rain? Was this some deus ex machina bullshit come to save her? God was real and had been listening all the time? And then the sprinkler system that stood watch over the field came to life and water rained down on her, dousing the growing fire, and plastering her hair and clothes to her body.

She stood there, gasping with relieved laughter, her head leaning back against the wooden post as she let the water wash away the remnants of smoke and tears, the water glittering on her skin and hair. Vaguely, she heard someone calling her name, but now that she was done fighting, she just didn't have the energy to move. It was over; she was done.

Hands were untying the ropes behind her and there were flashlights flashing into her eyes and the blue and red of police cars and ambulances before long, but she wasn't seeing faces clearly or understanding what people were saying. Some things stood out: Zakaria's unmoving form covered with a silver reflective blanket while men in black coats with FBI stamped on them stood around it, a gentle hand urging her to stand, red-tipped locs sliding over a shoulder as an arm wrapped around her shoulders protectively, a blond curvy woman hugging her in a motherly embrace. Nothing broke through the icy shield that Rachael had around herself until a tall man with piercing blue eyes called her name.

"Oh, god, Rachael!" Drake held out his hands towards her, needing to touch her to see that she was whole and alive.

Rachael jerked at his voice, remembered pain and betrayal piercing the fog that surrounded her, somehow combining with what had happened to her. She stepped back. "No!" She shook her head frantically.

Drake froze. "Rachael?" His heart broke at the look she gave him, broken and fearful, and he dropped his hands as she retreated from him. He stepped back, knowing he was causing her pain and distress and desperately wanting to tell her she was safe. "Oh, Rachael," he whispered. Her scent, when the wind blew it his way, was full of panic, acrid and nose stinging, and iron, from the blood of her wounds, and despair. If Zakaria hadn't already been dead, he would have killed him himself.

"We have her," Diana said softly, her eyes so full of sorrow. "I'll come find you."

He looked at his mother, then back at the woman who had stolen his heart. He couldn't just leave her like this!

"Drake, we have her. You are hurting her." This was from Ember, on Rachael's other side, her eyes golden from emotion.

"Come on, son," Sam placed a hand on Drake's shoulder, pulling him away, and he let his father lead him away, every step taking him away from where his soul cried out to be.

Rachael felt the panic leave her as Drake left and she sagged against the two women, bracketing her, her eyes once again leaking tears.

"Come on, love," Diana's soft voice, oh so gentle, soothed over the jagged edges of her mind and she turned with her, to find healing.

The hospital was bright and airy, with a large window overlooking Davis. If she lifted the bed, Rachael could see the tops of the university buildings. She couldn't stand to have the blinds shut, for it to be dark, so they stayed open all the time, letting in beams of sunlight for the dust motes to dance in. Rachael had a lot of time to watch them dance. She couldn't focus on anything for more than a few minutes at a time anyway, so she just stared out the window, letting her brain drift.

Not that she was alone a whole lot; nurses came in to take her vital signs every thirty minutes and her I.V. kept beeping at her if she moved her arm wrong (they said they would remove that soon, thank god, it was annoying as hell), and morning and evening a doctor came to check on her. Rachael kept insisting she was fine and could go home, but because she lived alone (she had given her apartment as her address), they insisted she stay until they were sure the concussion Zakaria had given her wasn't severe enough to cause problems.

Rachael sighed as she remembered the look on Diana's face when she rattled off the apartment's address instead of the farm's. Guilt tightened her stomach, which, she thought, was probably good, since that hadn't happened the moment she had done it.

"Are you sure, Rachael?" Diana had said, her voice kind, belying the hurt in her eyes. "I only think that you might not want to be alone?"

But she did. She really, really wanted to be alone. Every time someone walked into the room, her brain jumped a little and it took her a long time to settle again. Finding the words to respond to small talk seemed to take a monumental effort, and when people weren't talking, Rachael could feel them looking at her when they thought she couldn't see them. If a nurse was too chatty during vitals, it was all Rachael could do not to scream at them to shut up. All she wanted was quiet.

And Drake would be at the farm. She would see him every day. Feel every day. No, better to be at the apartment.

An hour and two nurses' visits later, Diana and Ember appeared in a burst of energy, right at the beginning of visiting hours.

"Oh, you look so much better." Diana stroked Rachael's hair off her forehead and smiled. "All clean at least. Here," she gestured to Ember, who hefted a small bag. "We brought some of your things so you can change and brush your teeth before you leave."

Rachael felt her eyes burn, and she found herself on the verge of tears. Diana merely squeezed her shoulders, smiling softly, and changed the subject. "Exhibition Day is just around the corner."

"Exhibition Day?" she asked.

Ember snorted indelicately, making Rachael smile. "It's a U.C. Davis thing. They set up booths up on the quad and there are demos in some of the buildings. It's a huge event and everyone goes. It used to be called something else, but it was changed for the better some years ago. Mom has a booth for her wool and yarn." This last bit of info was given with a proud look at her mother.

"She's settled on a name for her business: Pixie's Purls!"

"Oh, well, it's just tucked into a corner. We'll see how we do," Diana said deprecatingly, but Rachael could tell she was nervous, yet excited.

"I bet it's great. That's wonderful news," Rachael reached out and squeezed Diana's hand, trying not to wince as the movement hurt her sore wrists. Diana's blue eyes were sharp though, and she chided Rachael gently for causing herself pain.

"Where is that nurse? You should have a higher dose of pain meds!" And out she bustled, all maternal anger and energy.

"She has been fretting over you all day. It was all I could do to make her wait until visiting hours to leave. We've been in the parking lot for an hour." Ember leaned against the end of the bed and shook her head, but her eyes were watchful.

Rachael gave a little laugh. "What have you been doing for an hour?"

"Pacing." Ember said definitively. "Lots of pacing. She should be exhausted. And yet."

Both women huffed a laugh together, but Rachael knew what was coming.

"Can you talk about Drake?" And there it was.

She sighed. "I don't know what to say and I can't say anything that will make anyone happy." She looked at Ember miserably, who returned her look steadily, waiting. "It's . . . it's just all mixed up. In my head. The last memory . . . no that's not right. The last *feeling* I have about him is betrayal."

Ember's face changed. "Oh."

Rachael's fingers plucked at her blankets restlessly. "When I saw him, when I think of him now, I just feel fear. Somehow, it's all connected to Zakaria even though I know, I *know,* he had nothing to do with it." She shrugged and shook her head, as if trying to dislodge the feelings. "But what he did, that whole mating thing, was such a breach of trust for me, you know that."

Ember nodded. "I do. And he does too."

Rachael nodded. "But it wasn't resolved. Fixed. So, he . . . that feeling, it was there and then I was kidnapped. My brain just can't separate it." She closed her eyes and turned away. "I am so angry, Ember." It was a whisper of sound. "It scares me how angry I am."

"Rachael," Diana's voice was next to her, quiet and calm, and it hurt Rachael at how accepting it was. She should be raging at her, at how hateful she felt toward Drake. Those days at that cabin she had been so focused on surviving that she hadn't given any thought at all to Drake and then seeing him had brought it all back. She knew she was focusing on that anger instead of dealing with how she was feeling about being actually *kidnapped,* but knowing something rationally and then convincing your brain to do the right thing didn't always work. So, she sat here, numb, unless she thought of Drake. And then she just felt an all-consuming rage.

Rachael opened her eyes and looked at Diana, the woman who had taken her in and accepted her into her family; this small woman who had forced a whole town to her whims in order for the people she loved to have a safe place to live.

"I love you." The three words hit Rachael like bullets and she sobbed out a breath. "I love you and Sam and Ember love you."

Ember nodded. "You bet I do."

"Drake made a mistake, and no one here is forgiving him or excusing him. Nor are we going to force you to do anything you don't want to do." Diana's hands came up to cup Rachael's face gently, mindful of her bruises. "This experience you went through was awful and anything you are feeling is valid, my love. Anger too. Even if it seems wrong. We'll find someone you can talk to and I am always here. Always."

Undone by her kindness and acceptance, Rachael sobbed, allowing herself to be embraced by this gentle and wonderful woman she wished had been her mother. Ember came in from the other side and wrapped her arms around her too, and the three women held tight together until a soft knock on the door.

"I'm so sorry to interrupt," a nurse waited until Rachael, blotchy and stuffy nosed, looked at him. "This came for you. You have some mail!"

Groaning inwardly at his cheery demeanor, she smiled her thanks and then looked at the envelope he handed her.

"What is it?" Ember asked.

"I don't know. I don't recognize the return address. And it's addressed to the hospital?" Rachael turned it over and saw that it was actually an outer envelope for a smaller one. She tore it open and found the inside envelope, which had been addressed to her. Via Zakaria. Sweat broke out on her forehead.

"Rachael?" Diana was there immediately and Ember's eyes changed to gold.

"Someone wrote a letter and left it with Zakaria. And now it's been forwarded here. Someone knows where I am. They are at the cabin." She dropped the letter. "Shit. This is evidence." The three women stared at the envelopes lying on the blankets in silence. Rachael finally took a breath and reached for the phone, asking the weary voice on the line to connect her to the Davis police department.

"You know they are going to take it," Ember said, bitterly. "You aren't going to get to read it."

"I don't know if I want to read it," Rachael replied. "Zakaria was an asshole just to be an asshole. He took great pleasure in psychological torture and if he had held this letter in reserve, I can only assume it was because he knew it had some sort of emotional impact." Her hands were shaking. When did her hands start shaking? She tucked them under her arms, staring down at her lap. It was only paper, but it might as well be a bomb for all the adrenaline her body was producing.

Diana made a very guttural and feral noise that made Rachael look at her, startled. "If that man weren't dead, I'd kill him myself." She looked like she could do it, too. Short, plump, and blond, no one usually described Diana as "fierce," but if Rachael had been standing, she would back away from the woman right now. "I don't know why he felt the need to kidnap you and keep you locked up and torture you. His job was to return you to your family. His jollies were not included."

Ember, looking at her mother with a mixture of awe and fear, blinked at the end of that speech. "Jollies? *Jollies?*" She started laughing. "Oh. My. God. Say it again, please?"

Diana just gave her daughter a look of exasperation, which only encouraged her, and Ember doubled over, snorting, unable to stay still.

Rachael felt her lips twitch, and Diana threw up her hands, huffing. "Oh, not you, too!" Rachael laughed, and even Diana started to chuckle. The air in the room lightened and Rachael felt the knot in her chest ease, her hands stopping their shaking.

A knock sounded at her door, and she turned her head. "Ms.

Knight?" A detective stood, badge flashing, at the door to her room, her partner standing behind her. She was a short woman wearing a hijab and a gray suit, her brown skin and eyes complimenting the emerald green of the head covering.

"Yes." The laughter fled the room, leaving ghostly echoes in the corners. Her voice was flat, her face unsmiling under the bandage that circled her head. Rachael had been prepared for uniformed cops, or perhaps the FBI, not yet another new person flashing yet another badge at her.

"I'm Fatima Edris and this is my partner, Chris Smith." She gestured to the white man behind her in khakis and a navy blue polo shirt. "I've been assigned to your case, and I heard you had some new evidence."

Chris crossed his arms, his face impatient. Rachael narrowed her eyes. "I see. Why a detective? I thought the FBI was involved?"

"It is a homicide investigation and I am a homicide detective. Do you mind going through some things with me first, and then we'll look at this new evidence? Do you need anything before we get started? Water? Tea? Coffee?" Ms. Edris moved into the room, smiling at Diana and Ember, who took positions at either side of Rachael, and stood at the foot of the bed, completely at ease. Chris rolled his eyes at her offer as he entered and Rachael narrowed her eyes at him. "Yes, some water would be great."

Fatima turned slightly and gestured at Chris, without speaking, just assuming he was watching and knew what she meant. Rachael smiled slightly. He scowled, but said calmly enough, "I'll be right back."

"Your partner seems a bit impatient to be dealing with victims of violence, Ms. Edris," Rachael said, turning to the detective.

"In order to speak to a victim, you need to understand what it means to be one," Fatima said softly. "He is a good man, but he is new at this still. He merely wanted to catch the bad guy, and these niceties make him impatient. He'll learn or he'll return to being a uniformed cop."

"What can I do for you?" Rachael asked. "Somehow, I don't think it's really to rehash my entire statement."

"Fernanda said you were smart," Fatima said, smiling broadly. Ember straightened suddenly and Fatima's eyes went to her.

"You know Fernanda?" Rachael sat up a bit, eyes brightening. "How is she?"

"Concerned about you. I told her I would report in; she seems to feel you may have a few too many visitors at the moment. She'll come by in a few days." Rachael felt a rush of affection for the tall and imposing forensic pathologist. Ember made a harrumphing noise at the comment and Rachael could have sworn Diana chuckled.

"I would like that." Rachael said softly.

Fatima nodded. "I came because after I read your statement, I went and looked at Fernanda's reports. She had made some progress with the brand on Jamie."

Frowning, Rachael nodded. "I remember. On his jaw."

"Yes," Fatima opened the slim folder she carried and pulled out a colored photo, holding it out to Rachael. "It seems to be a symbol that we have seen before. One that is actually emerging across Northern California on bodies of magic users, as well as in graffiti on houses of suspected magic users." The hairs on the back of Rachael's neck stood up at that statement, and she bent her head to look at the photo.

"What is that?" she asked, unable to really identify it.

"From what we can tell, a horned demon."

Rachael sat back and looked grimly at Fatima. "A hate group."

"Possibly. I think it's something a bit more focused and skilled."

Rachael frowned and thought for a moment and then stared in horror. "You think it's a hate group composed of Trackers."

"Yes. An anti-magic group," Fatima said. "Or at least run by them. I need you to think back and tell me if you saw this symbol anywhere in that cabin. Or did Zakaria mention it?"

"Wait, wait, why do you think that?" Diana's eyes were wide, and they were bouncing from Fatima to Rachael and then to Ember.

Rachael held up her hand in the sign her whole cult had used against evil. "If you had magic, you were evil, wrong, cursed. And contagious."

Fatima nodded. "The extremist groups, like Rachael's old one, shun all magic and often use symbols like this to mark the homes of people they target."

"They also use it to protect themselves from 'evil magic'" Rachael couldn't stop the bitterness from seeping into her voice, and Diana's hand squeezed her shoulder.

"This symbol has been cropping up in Sacramento and now it's in Davis. One has been reported in Fairfield. Usually, they are isolated to communities. The fact that it's so widespread is concerning. That there was a house with a room that was shielded and had been in use for some time is especially concerning. This is an organized group that has been trafficking for years and now they are escalating." Fatima looked at Rachael and repeated. "Did Zakaria mention this symbol or this group or did you see it anywhere in that cabin?"

Rachael shook her head. "No, I don't think so. I know he confessed to both murders—Michelle's happily, Jaime's with some other emotion. But at the cabin, I was kept in that one room the whole time, except to eat or play games, and then I was at the kitchen table." She closed her eyes, trying to picture it. "Not on the table, no carvings or decorations there. The whole place was exceptionally plain, on purpose, I think. The room was just the walls, cot, and the dre—" Rachael's eyes shot open. "The dresser."

Fatima leaned in but said nothing, pen poised over a notepad.

"I searched every inch of that room looking for some weakness or way out. The back of the dresser had some stuff marked on it. I thought maybe some other victim had scratched it in there, counted days or something. But . . . it was that. It was a crude sketch of *that*." Rachael pointed at the photo of the brand. Zakaria's glee in her suffering made more sense now. He couldn't kill her; he had a contract for her safe return. But nothing in that contract said he couldn't torture her while he had her. If he were involved in a hate group. . .

"That doesn't make any fucking sense," Diana said loudly. "Trackers use *magic*. They *are* magic users. How can they be in a hate group biased against magic users?!"

Rachael was shaking her head, as was Fatima. Rachael was too tired to explain, so she let Fatima take the lead. "You are applying logic where there isn't any. Zakaria had magic, and he used it as a bounty hunter. That's how he made money. But he took joy in hurting people. He was able to do that by joining a hate group. They let him hurt, maim, and kill people and he got to use his magic to do it because sometimes when he found people, he gave them to this group to do who knows what with. When Rachael destroyed his shield, when she learned just how much magic he had? Zakaria panicked. Something about this organization terrified him, and keeping the extent of his magic secret was paramount. Tracking is one thing, but being able to glamor *and* shift? No, he wasn't just shielding to protect his bounty hunting income. He was protecting his magic use from this group. Suddenly, Rachael knew way, way too much."

Rachael added, softly, "Hate always has room for hypocrisy. I know, I lived where hate thrived for twenty-five years."

It was time for Rachael's letter. Chris had been waiting patiently, if you could call sighing and tapping his pen every time Diana asked a question patient, and he and Fatima donned gloves. They gingerly picked up the letter and looked it over carefully.

"Did you touch it a lot?" Chris asked.

"Of course. So did the nurse who brought it in and the postal service." Rachael supplied.

Chris' mouth dropped open slightly, but he nodded at her, acknowledging the point. "Okay, here we go."

They slit open one side over a clean, and empty plastic bin borrowed from the nurses. A smaller envelope fell out, and Rachael's heart skipped a beat. She recognized the handwriting.

"Do you want to read it?" Fatima asked, waiting neutrally. Rachael nodded. Chris cut a careful slit down the side of the envelope while Fatima handed Rachael clean gloves. Chris pulled out a small rectangle of lined paper and handed it to her.

It was a simple piece of notebook paper, pulled from a school notebook, like she had used all her life. Unfolding it, her breath caught in her chest.

"This . . . this is my mom's handwriting." Rachael's voice shook, and she felt the supportive press of Diana and Ember on either side of her.

Dearest,

Oh, my dearest one, how I have missed you. Every day that has gone by has been darker because you weren't here; you were always the heart of the family. Your father is quiet, and I know he worries, but you have my fire in you. You always have. I am sure it is serving you well. The village is slowly starting to work with us again, now that you are gone, but without your trial, your forgiveness, we have lost the support of key income and good will. Food for the winter is going to be thin this year and we may lose access to the gardens if your dad can't convince the Council that the magical taint left with you. Your sisters are not allowed back at school yet, and no one will touch anything I cook or sew. It has been difficult.

I know why you ran, my love. I understand. But you must come home and repent of your sin. It is for that reason I have hired Zakaria to bring you home to face your trial. Until you are forgiven, they will see us as tainted. No one trusts us. They think we helped you escape! And I know they look at your sisters and wonder if they are also hiding evil under my nose; how could I not have known that you had it! Our reputation has taken a serious hit. I know you don't want us to suffer, my darling girl. You were always so good to us and worked so hard. I know you have our best interest at heart. We shall see you soon,

Mom

"Damn them," hissed Rachael.

Diana wrapped an arm around Rachael's shoulders, her blue eyes filled with quiet anger. "She thinks she's doing what's right," Rachael said, unsure if she was defending or explaining her mother's actions.

"By condemning you to death?" Diana spat. "Her own child?" Blue eyes blazed as she let her rage spill over. "What kind of mother does that?" She took a deep breath, trying to rein in her anger.

"One who is protecting her other children," Rachael sighed. "Or at least she thinks she is. By saving my eternal soul, as well. In addition, the goodwill of the community is key. They could starve them, kick them out. Ostracize them." She was suddenly exhausted and overwhelmed, and she leaned back in bed and closed her eyes. Ember murmured something, and she felt a gentle kiss on her forehead.

Fatima and Chris bagged up the letter in an evidence bag and carefully labeled it. Fatima remained carefully stoic, but Chris's face showed emotion for the first time: pity.

"We are still looking for that cabin. If you can think of any other clues, please give me a call." Fatima handed over a business card. Rachael took it and Ember slipped it from her numb fingers to place into Rachael's overnight bag.

"We'll be back tomorrow to help you get back to your apartment." Diana squeezed her hand, and Rachael let herself drift. It was all just too much. Every time she thought she had escaped it she was pulled back. Was she ever going to be free?

PAIN MEANS YOU'RE ALIVE

T wo weeks after she returned to her apartment, Rachael still felt numb. She went about her life as if everything was normal: she woke up and went grocery shopping and went to work. Mr. Barlett tried to tell her she didn't need to come to work, but she honestly couldn't stand the idea of sitting around at home by herself. She wanted to be alone, and there was nowhere more alone than working a shift as a server. The small talk with strangers was the most banal and empty of all small talk and no one asked her personal questions. At least working she was busy and didn't have time to remember.

It was nighttime that was dangerous, the creeping hours after midnight when her mind would bring up memories for her to replay. Sometimes it was playing monopoly with a dead man, sometimes it was seeing Drake's stricken face when he realized she was afraid of him.

Diana and Ember called daily with updates about the farm and the family businesses. Rachael missed living there with an ache she could feel constantly. Sam would yell commentary to their stories that would always make Rachael laugh, but she never heard Drake's voice. She knew they were still being careful with her and she couldn't bring herself to ask after him. Was he okay? Had he moved on? He should move on. She was sure she was too broken to ever be worth it now. Who knew how long this healing would take?

And that anger, that roiling rage, was still there, under the surface of her skin, and she was so afraid that if she saw him, she would attack Drake and he didn't deserve that either.

So, she talked to his family, and they invited her to dinners and lunches and she politely passed on all of them. She wasn't ready. She just wasn't ready to pop the bubble of numbness yet. It was safe in here.

A month after her hospital release there was a knock on her front door. Rachael felt a brief flash of irritation at being interrupted; she was in solitude and enjoying it. How dare someone intrude without asking? But all emotions didn't really stay for long anymore. If they did, there was the real risk that the bubble would pop and she would feel again for real, and that was something she just didn't want.

She opened the door. She should smile, probably, but she didn't. "Sam?"

Sam was there, all six feet of him. He had never knocked on her door before. Diana ran the refugee business and Sam tended the farm, only occasionally helping with things when needed. Not having a close relationship with her own father, she had been unsure how to act around him generally and he had sensed her skittishness, so he had respected her space. What was he doing here now? Had something happened to Diana?

"Hi, Rachael," Sam smiled warmly at her, his salt and pepper hair and beard neatly combed and trimmed, his clothing tidy. Rachael thought he must have taken some time because there was no way he came straight from working on the farm to her apartment. He put some thought into his appearance. "May I come in?"

She wanted to say no. Something about all of this made her uneasy, and she didn't know why. Sam was always so kind and gentle and understanding. Her hand tightened on the doorknob, and she nodded. "Yes, of course. Come in."

He came in and looked around. Rachael looked too, suddenly afraid that she had let the place go. She had, a bit, but not too much. It had been hard to get all the dishes and laundry done, but she had managed to keep the living space clean. Most of the mess was confined to her bedroom, at least. "You seem to be doing well." He looked back at her. "I promised I would report how you were doing. If it looked like you were struggling, I was to tell Diana and she would send out a cleaning service."

And this is why Rachael had always liked Sam. He was so honest. Diana wouldn't have said anything, but Rachael would still have known what she was checking on. Sam just said it right out, but with no judgment, just honesty. It was love, too, and acceptance. Her chest tightened, fighting to contain the feelings. "Oh, no, I'm okay."

And then Sam's face changed a bit. It wasn't quite disapproving, but it was a look that said he saw she was lying and he didn't like it. "Rachael, we both know that is not true." The words were soft and understanding and they hit her like bullets.

"Sam." Rachael shook her head, unable to say anything else past the lump in her throat.

"Come sit down, Rachael." He gently put a hand on her shoulder and directed her to the couch, where he had her sit. He sat down near her, but not so close that she felt crowded. "I am here because I am worried about you."

And she just couldn't take it anymore. She jumped up and hit her shin on the coffee table; the pain shooting through her and triggering even more rage. "Damn it, Sam! I don't want you to be worried about me! Everyone is worried about me! EVERYONE NEEDS TO STOP BEING WORRIED ABOUT ME!" She had spun around and was yelling at him, her hands clenched at her sides, her breath coming in gasps. And he was just sitting there looking at her calmly with just as much love as before, and she just couldn't stand it.

"But we do worry about you and nothing you do is going to stop that from happening." His voice was so calm. Why wasn't he yelling? If he started yelling, at least she would know how to handle that. Her dad always yelled. He would yell and insult and belittle and then the storm would pass until the next time. He wasn't following the script.

"I am going to work and cleaning my house and eating food! I AM OKAY!" She was yelling again, and she didn't know how to stop.

"We both know that is not true, Rachael." His dark blue eyes were so sad and his voice was so calm.

Rachael stared at him, seething. How DARE he sit there and so calmly call her on her shit? "What do you *want* from me, Sam?"

"Why are you so angry, Rachael?" Sam asked. "Why are you

angry at me?"

Rachael spun and started pacing and Sam let her, giving her space and time to dig through her thoughts. Why *was* she so angry at Sam and not at Diana or Ember when they had also confessed their worry and love to her? "I told Drake that my dad would never approve of me, and I do think that's true." She clenched her jaw and breathed heavily through her nose. "When I was first accused, he left me. Just turned around and abandoned me to my fate once he learned that I really did have magic."

For the first time, Sam's face betrayed his emotion and rage crossed it before he controlled his features carefully into neutrality. Rachael nodded. "In front of everyone I knew, the one man I was supposed to count on the most just left. The pastor, the one who was supposed to be the most moral man in the town, was pressing his erection against my back and promising me that the more I struggled the more he would like it." Sam's face was granite, he was clenching his jaw so hard. "I found death preferable to whatever he had in mind, so I let down my shields and cemented my guilt, and my dad walked away without a word." Sam stood up, and Rachael raised a hand. "Wait, there's more."

"*More*? Jesus, Rachael." Sam scrubbed a hand over his face, but remained silent.

"They locked me in an outbuilding to await my execution. I could see the stake they would tie me to. My mom and sisters each came to say goodbye, full of tears. But not my dad. He didn't come to say goodbye." Rachael stopped pacing and looked Sam in the eye. "No. My dad helped me escape."

Sam let out a breath. "Um."

Rachael nodded. "My dad snuck out, and while my guard was

asleep, let me out. He looked at me with the most disappointed look I have ever seen, and told me to leave and never come back." She took a deep breath. "He tossed that bag of clothes at me and a handful of money and then turned away without a backward glance. No one saw him and I would bet money he hasn't told a soul what he did." She was starting to breathe heavier and her hands were fisted at her sides. Sam didn't move, sensing she wasn't finished, but his face held the rage she felt.

"He could get them all out if he wanted." Rachael spat. "He could leave that poisonous place and take them somewhere, *anywhere* else. But he won't. He keeps them there, subservient and scared, because that's how women are supposed to be. He helped a convicted magic user escape. He *broke the rules,* the fucking hypocrite, but no one knows, no one is punishing *him. He* is still an upstanding citizen. But my mom and sisters are paying for my 'crime' because that's how it works there. And he is just letting it happen. They are taking the hits for him. Again. And he is just letting this go on!" The betrayal and anger rose again, filling her chest until she couldn't believe it wasn't visible.

"My mom is desperate enough to bring me back *to my death* to appease those assholes, but Dad doesn't seem to realize how serious it is. Or maybe he doesn't care. He is supposed to love his family. Why did he let me go only to condemn them?!" Guilt vied with rage now, and tears were making hot tracks down her face. "*He should have just let me die there*!" She screamed the last sentence and Sam was there trying to comfort her, but she was hitting his chest and yelling and crying and he was letting her take out all of her rage on him, his shifter strength making it so she barely hurt him.

Rachael didn't know how long she raged and tore at Sam, but eventually her voice gave out and she grew too tired to continue. She realized they were on the floor and she was leaning against him. He was rocking her and stroking her hair; his voice was a soothing waterfall of sound that she finally recognized as a lullaby.

"I'm sorry." She whispered. Her voice cracked and her throat hurt. "I'm so sorry. I think . . . I think that not seeing you since I came back —"

The singing stopped, but not the rocking or the hair stroking.

Rachael continued, "I think that not seeing you since I came back made me feel like you, maybe, didn't like me anymore."

Sam's arms tightened a little. "I'm sorry, too, then. I had only intended to give you space. We thought men might make you nervous or scared."

Rachael gave a soft laugh. "I think it's safe to say that, in this case, the emotion was a bit stronger than that."

"If I ever meet your dad, he and I are going to have words."

Rachael gave a small laugh. "I think you might have to get in line."

"Well, you tell me when you're feeling good enough to stand. While we wait, I have something to tell you."

Rachael nodded against his chest. "Okay."

"You're coming back to the farm. Today. This living by yourself isn't good for you." Rachael nodded again. Sam continued. "And you will talk to Drake." She tensed and he sighed. "I know there is pain there, but you cannot leave him like this, Rachael. I'm not asking you to date him, just to talk to him."

Rachael knew he was right, but she didn't have to like it, and she said so.

Sam laughed. "There's my girl." He began singing again, and she sighed, letting him comfort her for a bit longer.

Rachael sat in the car and looked at the farm for a while. Long enough that Sam finally told her that she couldn't sleep in the car and if she didn't get out he was going to send Diana to get her.

"Now that's just mean," she groused, but opened the car door, anyway. "They are going to make me feel bad for not being here." Rachael muttered as she stood next to Sam and tried to muster her courage to go in.

He put an arm around her shoulders. "They are going to be happy you're back. Just like I am."

Her eyes teared up, but she nodded. "Okay."

"Okay then, come on." Sam hefted her bag and walked in, letting her set her own pace behind him. Pixie started barking in greeting and Rachael found herself grinning.

"Sam? Is that you?" Diana's voice called out. He called back and then the door flew open and Diana was there, running towards her and Rachael was running towards her too.

"Oh, sweetheart, you're back," Diana's arms were tight and Rachael felt herself crying again.

"I'm so sorry, Diana. I don't know why—"

"It doesn't matter. You're home. Come on." She walked with Rachael, an arm around her waist, no recriminations or questions, just a smile, and Rachael felt a weight lift from her chest. "Your room is ready for you and—"

Before she could say another word, the screen door banged open and Pixie came barreling out, barking insanely.

"No! Pixie! It's nice to see you too! But NO JUMPING!" Rachael's words were useless as a wall of Rottweiler crashed into her, and down she went, laughing hysterically as Pixie greeted her with licks and nose bumps. All the while, Diana and Sam were pulling on him, trying in vain to get all 150 pounds of him off of Rachael, while also laughing and yelling.

With a final lick, Pixie sat down, panting, and Rachael sat up on her elbows, covered in dirt and dog spit, her hair completely chaotic, and she took in Diana and Sam. Both were breathing hard, Diana with her hands on her knees, Sam still upright due to his Shifter physiology, and Rachael just felt so at home and happy.

"What the hell is all the ruckus?" All feelings of contentment fled at the sound of Drake's voice. She'd known she would see him, but ever hopeful, she had hoped it would be later rather than sooner. "Rachael? Are you okay? What happened?" The concern in his voice made her feel guilty and that, in turn, made her feel angry.

"I'm fine." She got to her feet, ignoring his hand and also ignoring the look she saw pass between Diana and Sam. Rachael pressed her lips together and took a deep breath, trying to get a grip on her emotions. He didn't deserve her snapping at him.

Using brushing herself off as an excuse not to look at him for a little longer, she tried again. "I'm fine. Pixie just got excited welcoming me back."

"Welcoming you back." Drake repeated.

"You don't seem excited." Sam and Diana had made a hasty retreat and Pixie, no fool, had hightailed it with them. Rachael glared after them and then went to work, trying to corral her hair.

"Rachael, you can't even look at me." Drake said it matter-of-factly, but Rachael froze.

Slowly, she turned. Damn it, he was just as fucking handsome as she remembered, and those damn blue eyes saw way too much. "Stop looking at me like I am going to break into a million pieces," she snapped. "I'm not fragile."

Drake frowned at her and then cocked his head in a way that had her backing up a step. "I know you're not," he said.

"Then stop looking at me like I am!" she said.

Drake took a deep breath. "So, everyone else is allowed to worry about you, but I'm not?"

His words hit her heart sharply, and she clenched her hands at her sides. That's not what she wanted. She didn't know what she wanted. She turned around and stopped sharply when he made a growling sound of frustration.

"No, I've let you walk away from me too many times." His hand landed on her shoulder and he whirled her around to face him, his other hand grasping her chin to bring her face up to meet his eyes. "What is your safe word, Rachael?"

They had never officially established one. Not for sex. That he was asking for one now told her just how much he understood about her emotional turmoil. She knew they were going to talk, but if it got to be too much, he was giving her a way to stop. An emotional safe word.

"God, why do you have to be so fucking perfect?" she said loudly, angry at him for not giving her excuses to stay mad at him.

"Did you just call my brother *perfect*?!" Ember's incredulous exclamation was accompanied by gagging noises. Drake's face morphed into a mix of exasperation and humor even as Diana's voice rose from the bowels of the house in admonishment.

"Ember! Leave them alone! I raised you better than this! Eavesdropping on them, I cannot believe you! Get away from that window this instant, young lady!"

"I just want to make sure he doesn't mess it up! He's such a goober!" Ember was cut off in an indignant yowl as Sam wrapped an arm around her and pulled her away from the second-story window she was leaning out of. His other arm closed the window and waved.

Despite herself, Rachael felt herself grinning broadly and then giggling. Drake's face softened as he looked down at her, his own smile reflecting hers.

"There you are," he said softly, cupping her face.

Her laughter fizzled out, and her breath stuttered, but she didn't try to run. "Drake, I—"

"Give me a safe word, Rachael." He said it softly, but with determination. "We are going to talk, but I am not going to hurt you. If you need to leave, I'll let you go back to the Big House."

There was only one word she could choose that made her feel safe; it rose unbidden, and she spoke without hesitation. "Archer."

This family had taken her in and welcomed her. Drake had loved her. They were more of a family to her than her own had ever been. Yes, their name was her safety.

Drake's smile was dazzling and his hand on her face so gentle. "Come on then. I'm going to bring your bag, but you are under no obligation to stay at my house, okay?"

Rachael nodded and followed Drake silently to his small house, her stomach knotted with nerves. Once inside, Drake merely handed her bag to her, gently turned her toward the stairs, and said, "go on and freshen up. I'll be down here when you're ready."

She grasped her bag in both hands and watched him walk to the kitchen. Space. He was giving her space and time to collect her thoughts and calm down. She had expected to get into things immediately because that's how her family had always done it, but she should have known better. Or should she have? How could she have known better? "Different family, Rachael," she told herself as she climbed the stairs. "Of course it's not going to be the same dysfunctional shit."

She took a quick shower to wash out the dirt and dog spit and dressed in clean clothes. Downstairs, Drake had made tea and put together a spread of cookies and sweets, which he placed on the coffee table. He sat at apparent ease on the sofa, reading. He looked up at the sound of her entrance and waved her over. "Come on and have some tea and something to eat."

"You're treating me like a feral cat," she commented. "Make no sudden moves and feed me and maybe I won't bite you and bolt."

He flashed a grin at her. "It's not a bad strategy. Besides, food always helps. It certainly can't hurt."

She shook her head as she sat and picked up the mug of tea he had placed there for her. It was a strong black tea with no milk or sugar, just as she liked it. He had remembered how she liked her tea.

The silence stretched. Rachael was afraid to speak first for fear of bursting into tears or angry yelling, so she waited for him to give a sign of how he wanted this to go.

After several long minutes, he sighed. "Oh, Rachael, I am so sorry." The words were soft, and she looked at him sharply, trying to deduce what he was apologizing for.

He was looking back at her, his blue eyes sad. "I fucked up. I should have told you about the mating possibility before we ever had sex." He reached for her, thought better of it and dropped his hand. "I—" He frowned and thought for a minute. "It has never even been in the realm of possibility for a mating bond to form with anyone before this. Ever." His face was honest and open now, and Rachael felt her heart lurch. "Ember told me to tell you, but I thought I would have more time with you before it happened." He looked down into his tea. "I didn't want to scare you away."

Rachael closed her eyes against the pain that statement caused her, her hands gripping her mug of tea like a lifeline.

Drake's voice continued. "And then . . . and then it happened, and it was worse. I broke your trust by entangling you in something you weren't ready for with no warning. And with a magic there is no known way to undo. It was an unforgivable betrayal, Rachael. I am so sorry."

Tears were leaking out of her closed eyelids now, her breath shuddering in her chest. All this time she had been so angry at him, but she had forgotten that he was human, too. She had been selfish with her pain and forgotten that everyone makes mistakes. Gathering her courage, she opened her eyes and looked at him. He was stone still, as if it was all he could do not to move, as he watched her cry. "It takes three bonds to complete a mating, right?"

He nodded.

"And right now, we only have one." This time, it was a statement and not a question.

He nodded again.

She nodded her understanding and took a deep breath. "I understand, Drake," she said, her voice cracking. She gave a shaky laugh. "I really am like a feral cat."

Drake's face was filling with hope, but he remained silent. Rachael thought for a long time. "It was a huge breach of trust," she said finally.

"I know," was his soft response, regret filling each word. The hope in his face had dimmed.

"It's going to take a lot to build that trust back up," she closed her eyes against the pain on his face, turning back to face the table. "If you had told me in the first place, I might have paused things. I might have slowed things down, but—" she stopped talking and thought about it some more and then shook her head, staring at the food on the table. "I really don't think I would have run. And maybe you are telling the truth—" she raised her hand at his indrawn breath, "no, breach of trust remember? I *want* to believe you, but that doesn't mean I *can*." Tears were falling again because she really, really wanted to run to him. She wanted to fall into his arms and have him hold her and tell her everything would be alright and that she was safe. She wanted it more than she wanted air.

He closed his mouth, his hands gripping his own tea mug, and he nodded.

She began again. "Maybe you are telling the truth about not expecting a bond to form that first time, but it *feels* like you wanted the sex." She gave a sob, and he set his mug down and reached for her. "No!" She slashed her hand through the air, refusing his touch. If he touched her now, she would cave and it would be over for her. She needed to be strong here. He needed to know that she needed honesty.

He froze, his face stricken. "No, Rachael, I swear, that was *not* the reason,"

She took a deep breath, trying to stop crying. She was always fucking *crying*. "Trust is a bitch to get back once you break it." She shook her head with a wry smile. "It's the one true thing my dad ever said." Drake made a growling sound at the mention of her dad, but didn't comment. "After I left that day. . .Drake, you let me *leave*." Now she turned flaming green eyes at him, shimmering with unshed tears. "You broke my trust; I found out from your *family*, and then you let me go! The next thing I knew, I was kidnapped and I might never see you again." She knew it was unfair; she had asked for space and he had given it to her, but in her mind, letting her go only compounded everything.

Agony. The emotion that moved across Drake's face was agony. It darkened his skin and his eyes reddened, filling with tears. The pain on his face finally cracked the ice encasing Rachael's heart, and she cried out, dropping her mug in a spray of lukewarm tea. "Oh god, I'm sorry, I didn't mean it. It wasn't your fault. It wasn't." She threw herself into his arms, crawling into his lap, trying to press herself into him as closely as possible, constantly saying that it wasn't his fault, over and over again.

His arms closed around her like steel cables and his head lowered to rest on hers; tears fell like hot brands on her face as she stroked his chest, his neck, his cheeks. "When we couldn't find you, Rachael, I didn't know what I was going to do. I had come to talk to you, to apologize, and *you weren't there*." A sob rocked his chest and an echoing one rocked hers. "I thought you had gone, that I had chased you off for good. And then it was so much worse because I thought I might lose you without ever getting to say I love you."

"Oh god, Drake," Rachael whispered, pressing her face into his chest.

"And then you came back. They found you and you were whole and mostly uninjured, and I was so fucking happy about it."

"And I couldn't even look at you," she whispered.

"You couldn't look at me," he said into her hair, his arms never loosening an iota. "I never want to be the person who puts that fear on your face ever again, Rachael."

She sobbed into him. "It wasn't. It was never you."

He shook his head. "But it was, Rachael. By breaking your trust, I hurt you and I hurt you enough that you put me in the same category as Zakaria. And *I understand*."

She was sobbing uncontrollably now because he understood and because he wasn't angry at her.

"I will earn back what I broke. We will go slowly. Fuck, we'll move at a glacial pace if that's what you need. All I know is that I cannot work right without you." He was nuzzling her hair, inhaling her scent. "Nothing can ever hurt me more than how I hurt you."

"I was so afraid that I was going to die without ever seeing you again," she whispered into his chest. "That the last time we saw each other was full of anger and pain. And then I thought that we'd never have the chance to fix it. And I was just so *angry* about it." She took a deep breath. "I didn't want to think about it, so I just ignored it and shoved it back because I had to deal with Zakaria. When I saw you again, it just all erupted."

Drake let out a shuddering sigh, rubbing his cheek on her head. "You had every right to be angry."

"Drake?"

"Hmmm?"

"I love you, too."

A BEGINNING

Rachael had fallen asleep on Drake's lap not long after that. She had a vague memory of being carried upstairs and the covers lifted over her, but after that she knew nothing until she awoke the next morning. The sun was streaming in the windows and she blinked, disoriented for a moment, unsure of where she was.

"Oh, shit," she groaned, remembering. Drake's bed. She lifted the comforter and saw that she was still wearing all of her clothes except for shoes; glancing over she could see that the other side of the bed had not been slept in. He had carried her up here and then slept somewhere else. Padding downstairs, she saw he had been busy and made pancakes and bacon.

"Good morning," he said, passing her a plate. "You slept all afternoon and then all night."

Rachael, still unused to the luxury that was syrup, poured it sparingly, but also added peanut butter to her pancakes, a quirk her mother had introduced to her. "I haven't been sleeping all that well. I must have needed it."

Drake nodded. "Nightmares. I could hear you down here on the couch. I had to go up a couple times, but you just fell back asleep."

Rachael felt herself redden, but shoved pancakes into her mouth instead of talking. Her diet of coffee and cereal paled as the sweetness burst over her tongue, coupled with the saltiness of the peanut butter and the fluffy pancakes. "Oh my god," she moaned in ecstasy.

"I knew you hadn't been eating." Drake's eyes scanned her. "You've lost more than a little weight."

Rachael frowned, looking down at herself.

"Yes, you have. You hadn't had a proper shower in a while before yesterday, either. Don't worry, we'll get you back to fighting weight in no time."

Staring at him, she mouthed the words 'fighting weight' and he put a piece of bacon in her mouth while she gaped at him, which she ate. "Here, have some coffee. Cream and sugar. And then everyone else would like to see you too." He grinned at her.

Blinking, slightly shocked, she took a sip of coffee. Somehow she had gone from alone and un-slept to surrounded by friends and well-rested. Her brain was suffering whip-lash.

"I will take your bag back to the Big House, for now," he said, washing dishes as she ate. "We can talk later about all that. Maybe go on more dates. I'll walk you home and sleep here." He grinned at her, tossing her a wink as well. Rachael shook her head, amazed at what a difference eighteen hours and an emotional conversation made.

"I think that sounds great," she agreed, dragging her bacon through some syrup. "But I also think I need to find a place to live that's not with your family. It's just a little weird."

He eyed her while he dried a pan. "Tell you what. We don't date while you rest up and heal. When you're ready, we'll find you a place to live with a secure door. How does that sound?" He leaned on his arms, waiting for her answer.

Fears she didn't say crowded her mind. What if she was never ready to date him again? What if she found someone else instead? What if she just wanted to remain single forever? But he was willing to do this for her, so she nodded. "Okay, no dating for now."

Back at the Big House, Sam and Diana were cleaning up a big breakfast as well, and Rachael was happy to see Fernanda seated at the kitchen table sipping black coffee.

Dark eyes rose to greet her when Rachael entered the kitchen and then Fernanda stood, rounded the table, and embraced a startled Rachael in an encompassing and singularly amazing hug. "Welcome back, Sunshine," she said.

"Oh," Rachael hugged Fernanda back, just soaking in the glory that was that hug. "Thank you, Fernanda."

Pulling back, Fernanda gazed down at her and appeared to approve of whatever she saw because she nodded, gave her a smile, and then went back to sit down, leaving Rachael feeling somewhat shell-shocked. Ember reached over and took Fernanda's hand, lifting it to give it a kiss, and Rachael beamed at the pair. Fernanda scowled at her and all was returned to normal.

Pixie was next, coming over for greeting pets, which Rachael gave enthusiastically. Drake, who had passed through with her bag while she was lost in Fernanda's hug, returned to the kitchen and Rachael stood there, looking over her friends and loved ones, feeling, finally, like she wasn't alone. The jagged pieces that had broken were slowly gluing themselves back together; the fear and anger that had kept them from joining abated by the love and support of this adoptive family of hers. She knew that the fear and anger would rise again, but she also knew she trusted these people to help catch her when it did. It seemed unreal that she had a safe place to fall; part of her waited for the other shoe to drop even as she laughed and hugged and talked with everyone.

"Just remember something for me," Diana said, once she had Rachael to herself for a moment. They were gathering glasses for celebratory drinks, and Rachael had volunteered to help, hoping to escape the chatter and small talk around the table.

"Huh?" Rachael looked up, surprised. "Oh, what's that?"

Diana smiled, her eyes kind. "Just remember that even if something else happens, we're still going to be here."

Rachael frowned. "I'm sorry, what?"

Diana's smile didn't slip an inch. "I know it feels like you're balancing on a soap bubble; like we're all a pretend family, in a way." Sam came up behind her and put a hand on Diana's shoulder, smiling at Rachael as well. "When we say we love you, we mean it. I had hoped to have you as a daughter-in-law in the future, but if that doesn't pan out, I'll still love you. You will always be welcome here."

Rachael looked at Sam, who nodded. "You're ours," he said. "No escaping now."

Home is where the heart is, they say. Rachael was learning that home was where *acceptance* was. For the first time, she was where people saw her, really saw her, and accepted her for what she was. More than that, they loved her for it, jagged edges and all.

The End

ACKNOWLEDGMENTS

Thank you to my family, all of whom have supported me during the last year and a half while I researched and wrote and designed and ignored them so I could publish this book. I could never have done this without your love and encouragement. Thank my editor, Megan. She courageously found and eradicated all my colons and semi-colons and replaced them with em-dashes. Thank you to my beta readers, without whom my book would have a plot hole I had to fill in. I cannot express my gratitude to Ruthie and Emeric, my sensitivity readers, who helped me learn and grow and give you a novel that reflects the world we live in. And Jalen, thank you for helping to clarify my content warnings to help mitigate any possible harm my book could cause.

ABOUT AUTHOR

Evelyne has spent the last ten years being a mom and a homemaker. Prior to that, she was an English teacher with a Masters degree. Before *that,* she worked with animals in both rescues and animal hospitals. Kids and animals, those are pretty much the two core elements of her skill set. But deep down? When she looks back at her 42 years and wonders, what would she have done if she did everything over? She would have taken that tractor driving course at UC Davis, for one, and she would have started writing professionally a hell of a lot earlier. So here she is, starting over again, embracing the new, and embarking on the independent publishing journey. Thank you for coming with her.

9 798987 830307